Mel
Hope you find
ed a fun read
Lary W

Damey
&
Grandpa Tutor
By
Larry Webb

Also by Larry Webb

The following books can be found at Amazon.com and Barnes &
Noble.com
Really Short Shorts—A book of short, short stories
Sometimes Home Ain't "Home Sweet Home"
As Life Goes On – Book one
As Life Moves On – Book two
Taming Little Ike

Coming Soon
As Life Continues – Book three

Acknowledgements

A number of people committed a lot of time and effort into making this book a reality. First and foremost are the members of two particular writing groups: The *Skaaldic Society,* with a special tip of the hat to Linda Peckham; and the Delta Writers' Roundtable where I would like to express gratitude to Bill Koons, Jim Raushert, Jim Moses, and Jonathon Stars.

Sandbridge Beach, VA author of ten books at last count, Lee Carey, whose inspiration, knowledge, and encouragement during two special days at the beach where we "Talked shop." Just to let you know, Lee, I'm still smilin' and hope you're doing the same.

Also, special thanks to Judy Hazelo who took the time and effort to do a cover to cover edit of the entire book. So, if you see any typos, they're her fault.

The cover design was made by Tirzah Goodwin.

CHAPTER 1

I circle the block twice not wanting to arrive too early. Don't want people to think I'm eager about this whole thing, because I'm not. I climb out of my car and shuffle into the building with the sign on the wall announcing the offices of LAMBERT, LAMBERT, AND HOTCHKISS, ATTORNEYS AT LAW. I look at my watch—right on time, but probably late according to their standards.

"Good morning. How may I help you?" asks the receptionist.

"I'm Damarian Williams. I have an appointment with Mr. Lambert.

"Oh, yes. Everyone's been here for awhile. Follow me, please." No smile and I swear she lifts her nose when she stands. Come on, sweetheart, I think to myself. I *did* shower.

She struts back to Mr. Robert Lambert Senior's office, introduces me, and closes the door. Mr. Lambert looks to be about the same age as my adoptive grandpa, Bill Berkley.

After hugs with my white great-uncles, we all sit down and wait to go over Grandpa Tutor's will. Grandpa has left me something, and I have no clue what it might be. I know grandpa inherited a sack full of money from his own parents, but that has nothing to do with me. The only thing that even makes sense to me as to why I'm here, is Grandpa might have left me his watch. In the early days, every time I'd ask how much longer we had to work on reading, math, or whatever he was drumming into my head, he'd look at his watch and say, "Until we finish."

It's hard to believe that was fourteen years ago. I was only eleven years old when Grandpa came into my life and became my tutor, mentor, father-figure, and grandfather within a matter of a few months.

After shuffling papers for a while, Mr. Lambert looks up. "First off, I am giving each of you a copy of Mr. William Berkley's last will and testament signed two years ago on the fifteenth of March. I'll be reading from the original."

The attorney slides four envelopes across the desk towards us. My eyes flit back and forth among my three adoptive uncles. I wait to pick up my copy last, place it on the desk in front of me, and leave it. I have to place my hands on my thighs to hide the tremors. I know if I pick the thing up, I'll be visibly shaking. Don't want anyone to notice my sudden anxiety attack if I can help it.

With our copies in front of us, Lambert begins "To start with, I would like to ask you all to leave your copies in the envelopes until I finish what I have to say. Then you can take them out and read the entire text on your own. The first section deals with legal language that accompanies all documents like this. The important information starts on page three.

"The first bequeathal relates to Damarian. I'm not comfortable with how this part of today's proceedings has to be done, but it's what Mr. Berkley insisted upon. I have to read this first paragraph verbatim."

He stalls for a moment, pulls a tissue out of the box on his desk, and manages to drop the thing on the floor. While he blows his nose, I pick up the container without a word and set it back on his desk. Lambert reddens a bit and then continues. I try to make eye-contact with him to let him know if the paragraph is about me, whatever it says, it's okay. He doesn't look my way.

He stares at the document and doesn't look at anyone else either. Even more red-faced than before, he reads the part making him so fidgety. "Damarian, since you, '…ain't nothin' but a dumb little black kid,' you've turned out pretty darned well. The first thing

7

I've asked the attorney to do is to give you my copy of the laminated card you signed back on June 20, 2014, and then I want you to read it aloud."

He slides the card across his desk, expecting me to pick it up.

I laugh. For some reason or the other, hearing those words calm me down. Even my hands steady themselves and quit shaking. "I don't have to read that card *or* mine," I fish through my wallet, dig out my own copy, and place it on the desk beside Mr. Berkley's. "I memorized it years ago."

Standing up and positioning myself so I can see all three of my uncles and the attorney, I recite it from memory. *"I, Damarian Wayne Martin, am a very bright, mocha-cream- complexioned, African American Male. I can do or be anything I want with my life. I can be a doctor, scientist, lawyer, engineer, banker, accountant, entrepreneur, or anything else. I can become a politician and run for Congress, the governor's seat, or even the Presidency of the United States. The one thing I cannot ever do again is disrespect myself or anyone else."*

Proud of myself for being able to do it after all those years, I scoop both cards off the desk, slip them into my wallet, and sit down again.

The looks that pass between my uncles, along with the shuffling of feet, indicate to me they've never seen nor heard of those two identical cards. No surprise.

Those words had been strictly between me and Grandpa Tutor.

The attorney clears his throat and says, "Now, if you would all take your copies of the will out of the envelopes. I'll give you a few minutes to read them."

I pick up my copy, remove it, and stare at it somewhat amazed they still make printed copies of these things. Today everything is digital. After all, this is 2028—not the Stone Age.

. . .

. . .

As he sat there, Damey's mind drifted back fourteen years. Some of the history he remembered personally, some of the details of the story had been told to him. That first year with Grandpa had to be the most memorable period of time in his life.

William "Bill" Berkley, had been retired several years after having taught thirty-five years of secondary school English and history. In those days, he didn't have a whole lot to do except to mow the lawn and tend his garden. He'd considered checking with a nearby middle or high school to see if they had any kids who needed additional help a few hours a week, but figured he was too old. He knew darned well the kids would think so.

The day Damey and his mom, Shaundra Martin, moved into the home two houses down and across the street, Bill looked out the window and saw them. He didn't know it at the time, but Shaundra had been given the house by the Habitat for Humanity. Damey, he learned, had no idea what that even meant, except they had their own house and he was excited. They were moving out of the Project, a series of wall-to-wall apartments for low income families. New siding, new roof, carpeting, freshly painted walls, and new appliances—the place was absolutely beautiful. Damey even had a window in his bedroom that faced out into the backyard.

Bill watched, wondering what they were like and what the neighborhood was getting itself into. Nothing like that had ever happened in their middle-class neighborhood that he was aware of. Would they keep up the house? Mow the lawn? Control their dandelions?

Damey, who had no idea someone stood in the window across the street watching, was on a dead run most of the time. he wanted to help the movers by hustling boxes into the house and piling them wherever his mom said.

His mom worried the boy might be a little on the loud side so she kept shushing him. He was excited, and didn't care if he did bother the neighbors.

Bill smiled as he watched, thinking, he sure is a rambunctious little guy. They're going to be exhausted and starved when this day is over. I think I'll make up a pot of ham and bean soup along with some hot rolls to take over after the movers leave and things settle down.

Shaundra told the drivers which furniture and boxes went in various rooms. Then it was up to her and Damey to arrange everything after they left. Surprisingly, that was not his number-one priority.

"Damey, where are you? I need your help."

"Mom, everything's fine right where they put it. I wanna check out my room and put my stuff away."

"Honey, that can wait. Let's get the furniture first." She sighed slightly frowning and shaking her head back and forth.

"Mom!" Damey groaned. Under his breath, he mumbled something about leaving him alone, but she didn't hear that. Good thing.

"Damarian, get your butt in here, *now*!"

Damey had enough sense not to push her too far. She hadn't used the belt on him in over a year, because he'd learned to tell when her stress level approached the breaking point. Then it was time to straighten up his act. Very rarely did she raise her voice or say anything around him except for dinner-table-style conversation. Foul language was forbidden. Right then, she'd done both. He moved it.

"What, Mom?" he asked, trying to sound helpful.

"Grab the other end of the sofa. I want it centered under the window."

By seven that evening, the house looked presentable. With the furniture in place, the boxes emptied, clothes hung in the closet, even the beds were made. Both of them plopped down on opposite ends of the sofa, exhausted.

"Mom, we ain't had nothin' to eat since breakfast. I'm starved."

"Don't say 'ain't.' I know, honey, I'm hungry too. But, I'm not cooking. Grab my purse off the dresser. I want to see how much cash I have. We're going to have to go the fast-food route tonight."

Right then the doorbell rang. Shaundra and Damey looked at each other with that, "Oh, crap, we don't need company" look on their faces. Damey beat his mom to the door. She could barely drag herself off the sofa, but managed to get up and follow him.

"Hi, little man. I'm Bill Berkley from across the street in that brick tri-level. Brought you some homemade ham and bean soup, hot rolls, and a gallon of milk. I know you've been busting your tails all day and thought you might be hungry. If you've already eaten, throw it in the fridge and have it some other time. There should be enough there to last a couple of days, anyway."

"Oh, Mr. Berkley, you're a life saver. Thank you so much. I'm Shaundra Martin, and this is my son Damarian, or Damey on those rare occasions when he's good. Won't you please come in?"

"*Mom*," Damey growled softly as he elbowed her hip. She looked down and laughed at him.

"No, no. The last thing you need right now is company. I'll come over in a couple of days, and we'll get acquainted. How's that?"

"I don't have class Monday night," Shaundra said. "If you're going to be available, why don't Damarian and I come over to your house in the evening after dinner and return your pot. By then we'll have caught our breath and have the time to sit down and get acquainted."

"Sounds great. I eat at six and watch the news so anytime after sevem works."

"Damey, take the soup from Mr. Berkley and carry it into the kitchen, would you please? Don't drop it, and don't burn yourself. Oh, my, it smells so good."

"I hope I didn't put in too much garlic and onion. It does kind of wrinkle the nose if you take a good whiff of it."

"Not possible. And, thank you again so much. We haven't eaten since breakfast, and Damey was whining about his growling belly."

Mr. Berkley had no idea how good the ham and bean soup smelled and tasted to them. Both were starved and really didn't want to go out. It's a good thing he made an abundant supply because Damey ate two large bowls of the stuff before lifting his head and taking a deep breath.

• • •

The rest of the weekend sped by and Monday arrived quickly. During the day, Bill drove downtown and picked up a fresh apple pie with a crumbly crust from the bakery and a half-gallon of frozen vanilla yogurt. He told them later if it were only for him, he'd have bought blueberry, his favorite, but not everyone liked that. He thought everybody loved hot apple pie with what they think is ice-cream plopped on top. Bill figured Damey would never know the difference, and yogurt is healthier.

When Shaundra and Damey arrived with the empty kettle, Bill asked them in, and they all sat down in the living room. To break the ice, he gave them a little of his personal history. He talked about his career, his wife who had passed the year before, his three kids, and two grandkids and six great-grand children all close to Damey's age. His family didn't live that far away, but all of them had demanding jobs, school, and sports activities, so he didn't see them as much as he'd like. Their daily lives were as hectic as he imagined Shaundra and Damey's were.

"I'm curious about how Damey normally spends his time when you're at work," Bill said. Then with a twinkle in his eye, he proclaimed, "I've been spying on him all day. Around noon I looked out the window and saw him sitting on the door step stuffing potato chips into his mouth and drinking a cola. Later he shot baskets. Looked like he made a *lot* of them. An hour or so after that, I saw him riding his bike up and down the street. I thought maybe he'd gone around the block, checking out his new neighborhood, but wasn't sure. I did notice he didn't wear a helmet."

"That's just about what I do every day," Damey told him not commenting on the helmet.

"So, how old are you, Damey?"

"I'm eleven, almost twelve. My birthday's in September."

"Ah, one more year before you're a teenybopper."

"What's that?"

"That's what I used to tell my kids and middle school students. I told them they couldn't claim official teen status until they were sixteen. From thirteen through fifteen, they were teenyboppers. They hated that."

"I don't blame them," Damey answered with his lips curled up into a shy smile.

"So, Shaundra, what can you tell me about your family? From the looks of things, it's pretty much just the two of you.

"For the most part, it's just Damey and me. I work full-time and go to nursing school in the evenings. I hate it, because he's awfully young to be home and on his own so much of the time. I worry. Like all eleven-year-olds, he's just learning and experiencing a lot of things for the first time. Sometimes, his best ideas don't turn out that well. I wish I could provide more guidance.

"At least in the Project, the stay-at-home moms made it a point to keep track of all the unattended kids. That's just what everybody did. My parents are close by, but they and Damey have always clashed, so I keep him away from them as much as possible."

"They hate me," Damey said staring at his shoes.

"Oh, honey, they don't hate you."

"Yes they do. Last year when you made me stay with them a week while you were at that stupid internship thingie where you were sticking each other with needles, your father told me I should never have been born."

"What? You never told me that." Shaundra said as a tear slowly leaked out of her right eye and down her cheek. She wiped it off with the back of her hand.

"I figured you already knew how he felt. I told you they didn't even talk to me except to boss me around." He looked up noticing he'd made his mom cry. "I'm sorry, Mom. This was supposed to be a fun evening.

"I think it's time for some hot apple pie with ice cream," Bill said trying to diffuse the tension in the room.

The discussion about the grandparents ended as quickly as it started. The three of them made their way to the kitchen. Pie and ice cream sounded great to Damey. While Bill got the pie and frozen yogurt out of the refrigerator, Shaudra found the bowls and spoons after Bill told her where to look.

"Oh, the pieces are too big. I can't eat that much," Shaundra said.

"Don't worry, Mom. I'll help you with whatever you can't eat. You know me and apple pie."

"I can't believe this piglet's appetite. Fortunately, he did let me have a small bowl of the bean soup Saturday and Sunday night, but he inhaled the rest of it, except for the one bowl that's left. You have to give me your recipe."

"Um, easier said than done. I can give you the basic ingredients, but then it's one of these deals where I don't measure anything. I start throwing the stuff together with a handful of this, a bunch of that, and a cup-full of something else. Then, I pause, taste, scratch my head, and decide it needs another shot of something."

"Sounds about the way I cook," Shaundra laughed. "It never tastes exactly the same, but it's always good."

"I've got my recipe on the computer; I'll print you a copy."

Bill opened up the laptop on the kitchen counter, found the recipe, and sent it to the printer.

"Damey, would you run down to the family room and grab the printout for your mom? The light switch is on the wall. It's going to the wireless printer over by the window."

"Sure" Damey found his way down to the computer. "Wow! This is quite a layout," he said to himself not even thinking about anyone could hear him or not. "Would you look at the size of that screen? It's a TV screen used as a monitor. Not only does the old guy have two computers, but he's got two printers. One's a color ink jet, and the other's a laser. I could handle this."

While Damey inspected Bill's office with awe, Mr. Berkley and Shaundra rinsed the bowls and spoons and put them in the dishwasher. "You know, I'd like to tell you the rest of our story if you're willing to listen," Shaundra said. "I guess I'm still thinking about the remark Damey'd made about his grandfather. That bothers me."

Bill thought it was obvious she needed to talk. There didn't appear to be that many adults in her life outside of work and school.

By that time, Damey had returned with the printed recipe and stood in the doorway listening. Bill told the boy, "I've got a couple of games on the computer downstairs. Do you want to try them out, or do you want to listen to the old-folks talk?"

"If I'm quiet and don't interrupt, can I stay?"

"It's okay with me, if your mom doesn't mind."

"What I'd like to tell you is nothing he doesn't already know, so it's fine with me."

After Bill and Shaundra settled in on the leather sofa and love seat, Damey grabbed the huge lounger chair. That thing had enough room to fit three Dameys. He kind of bounced up and down. "Whoa! Is this thing ever soft. I could curl up in one of these all evening."

"If you push that button down on the side, the legs go up," Bill told him as he raised his own leg-rest on the sofa.

Shaundra sighed, frowned a little at Damey, and started her story. "My parents own their own *very* successful business and have always been professional in their dress, morals, language, and actions. In slang terms, they've always been uptight and extremely straight-laced. Therefore, from as far back as I can remember, I had to speak properly, act 'like a lady,' and 'be seen and not heard' at all times.

"I'm not sure if it was rebellion or what, but at fourteen I fell madly in love with this young guy at our school. At sixteen, I got pregnant. As soon as the test showed positive, my eighteen-year-old boyfriend disappeared. Somebody told me he'd gone to Oklahoma to work in the oil fields. I have neither seen nor heard from him since. When I tried to get some financial support for Damey, his parents told the courts they had no idea where he'd gone. I'm sure they lied.

"Damey, quit playing with the button on the chair. Leave it in one spot before you break something."

Bill smiled. His own great-grandkids loved playing with the buttons on the chair and sofa just like this kid. They were always getting yelled at too—unless it was just one of them and him in the room, and he didn't care. Never nagged them about it.

Shaundra continued with her story. "As soon as we found out, my parents insisted on an abortion. I refused. Then they demanded we adopt him out. They claimed that as long as I lived at home, they could dictate what I could or could not do. So, I moved out, went into a foster care group home, and kept Damey when he was born. It hasn't been easy, but if I had a chance to do it all over again, nothing would change. I love my baby.

"After walking out of the house, my parents cut off all financial help. From then on, I was on my own. Anyway, I still graduated from high school on time and with excellent grades without their help. Then I found an office job with an insurance company making barely over minimum wage before starting community college. It's a data-entry job—eight hours a day, and five days a week. It has to be the most boring thing in the world, but it puts food on the table.

"We lived in a low-income housing development up until the house across the street became available."

Shaundra didn't provide any detail about the circumstances of how and why the home happened to be given to them, and Bill didn't ask. He didn't feel it was any of his business. That's the type of man he was.

Damey's mom continued with her story, "If nothing unforeseen happens, at the rate I'm going, I should be able to graduate from school and get my RN in three more years. My biggest worry is Damarian. By the time

I get dinner around, it's already late. Sometimes when I have class, he gets lazy and won't fix himself anything to eat. I won't send him to bed hungry, so I'm getting him dinner at ten o'clock at night. I sometimes think it's his sneaky way of staying up beyond his bedtime."

"That is a little late for an eleven-year-old to be up—especially on a school night. Seems like somebody his age should be in bed by nine or so," Bill smiled pretending to scowl at Damey.

Damey laughed at Bill's expression but didn't say a word.

"I know. I agree completely, and he is on the nights I'm home. I just can't excuse myself in the middle of class and call him and tell him to get something to eat or turn off the TV and go to bed.

"Now that summer vacation has started, he's going to be home all day by himself. Damey's a good boy, but he's only eleven. It scares me leaving him by himself, but I can't afford day care so we're stuck." Shaundra paused for a minute.

It looked like to Bill that she was pondering about how much more she should say.

"So, how's he doing in school?" Bill asked squinting his eyes and looking concerned.

"Because of everything, his grades suffered this year big time. I believe all of them were donation D's. What hurts is that he really is a bright boy." The pained expression on her face showed especially in her eyes.

"He's very bright, but all he gets is donation D's?" Bill asked. He wanted more information.

As she looked over at Damey who was sitting motionless instead of rocking, she continued, "Every teacher he's ever had has told me how intelligent he is, but he just doesn't apply himself. Simply put, I think he has a poor self-concept. With him, it's easier to do nothing knowing he'll fail, than to try and make a mistake."

Bill thought for a minute before saying anything. He formulated a plan in his mind, and it sounded like fun. "Shaundra, tomorrow's your long day, isn't it? You've got work and school and don't get home until around 9:30 so Damey will be by himself all day?"

"Yes. Like I said, there's still one more bowl of that soup in the fridge. That and a peanut butter sandwich can be his dinner. He should be fine. He'll sleep in tomorrow and then have cereal and toast for brunch. Then he usually spends his day shooting hoops or riding his bike. If the weather's bad, he rots in front of the TV eating nothing but junk food all day. At least he's not out roaming around getting into trouble like so many kids these days. We've had some *discussions* in the past about that topic which involved the seat of his pants, but he's been pretty reliable for the past year or so."

Bill's mind had been racing while she talked. He didn't know if he really wanted to take on a project like Damey, but thought he'd toss the proposal out there.

"Shaundra, I've got an idea and am curious how you and Damey might feel about it. What would you think of rousting him out of bed when you get up? Then, before you leave for work, send him over here. I think it might be good for both of us.

"I miss the kids after teaching all those years, and it sounds like he could use a crash course catching up on some of the skills he's missed. Would you be willing to try it for a week and see how it works? If, at the end of that time, we feel like strangling each other, we can always go back to the way it is now."

"Wow! If that would help getting him back on track with his education, I'd love it. There are just so many issues."

Second guessing what might be going through Shaundra's mind, Bill also added, "After thirty-five years in the classroom and raising three boys of my own, I'll guarantee you, I'm not a pedophile. Let me say in front of Damey and you, if either of you ever feel uncomfortable for any reason, he's free to walk out the door any time."

• • •

Damey didn't know what he meant, but understood the concept that he could walk out any time if he felt uncomfortable around Mr. Berkeley. He'd ask his mom about the pedophile thing when they got home. He couldn't help wondering why some complete stranger would be interested in helping someone his age. He did mention a bunch of great-grandkids. Maybe he was just a nice old man who liked helping people? That'd be cool. Time would tell.

"It sounds great, but I can't let you do that. In the first place, I can't afford to pay you. Money's just too tight."

"I'll make you a deal. When he graduates from college and gets rich and famous, he can support both of us in our old age," Bill said smiling.

She liked that idea. "What about you, Damey? You haven't had any input on this conversation."

"That's because you told me if I was going to sit here and listen, I had to be quiet."

"No, *you* said that,"

"Whatever!"

"Are you willing to give it a try for a week?"

"Sure. Like Mr. Berkley said, we can't do any more than end up wanting to kill each other. Besides, I get bored being home all by myself. And, to be honest, I'm not very proud of my grades this year either. It's almost like I was afraid of school. I don't know why."

Damey got to thinking. Maybe his problems in school started after he spent that week with his grandparents. He wasn't sure.

That settled it. Before they went home, Bill took one of the three remaining pieces of pie and put it in the refrigerator. He sent the other two, along with the left-over yogurt, with them.

When they got home, Shaundra even let Damey have another half piece before he went to bed. What lay ahead sounded interesting and fun for both.

When she left for work at 7:30 the next morning, Bill and Damey started the next chapter in their lives.

CHAPTER 2

At seven-thirty, Damey looked up and saw Mr. Berkley watching him walk across the street. He wondered what the day would bring.

Bill opened the door and smiled. "Good morning, Damey. Did you sleep well in your new house last night, or did it seem kind of spooky and different?"

"Nah, I was tired and nodding off a little, so Mom made me go brush my teeth and take my shower at nine—even if it is summer vacation," he said raising his voice and eyebrows a little at the end as he threw his arms out to his sides, palms up as he looked at Bill like

26

it was his fault. He hadn't missed Mr. Berkley's comment the night before that eleven-year-olds should be in bed by nine. "I guess it was okay, though, because I fell right to sleep when I crawled into bed and then didn't want to get up this morning."

"Did you eat breakfast?"

"Didn't have time. I kept falling back to sleep until Mom came in and pulled the covers off, grabbed my foot and started to drag me out of bed. I woke up fast then, but it was too late to eat."

"That's okay. I haven't eaten either. Let's go out into the kitchen and grab a bite."

After a little discussion about Bill not having Fruit Loops, Captain Crunch, or anything good, and how his cereal looked like berries, straw, and nuts, Damey ate his breakfast. Not only did he manage to eat his cereal without adding sugar, but he also had a banana, toast slathered with cinnamon and honey, and some fruit juice. He wouldn't admit liking it, but ate every bite and even asked for a second slice of toast.

When they finished, Bill got up from the table and took his bowl and utensils to the sink. Damey sat there not quite knowing what to do. His mom usually cleaned up after him at home. It's just something she'd always done. "Grab your stuff and do what I do," Bill told him with a slight smile.

Damey got the message, the old guy'd be darned if he would wait on some kid. They rinsed everything and put it all in the dishwasher.

27

Damey noticed the fact that Mr. Berkley seemed to smile awfully easily. He'd been so friendly the night before, and today didn't seem to be any different. Mr. Berkley seemed to like him, and he barely knew him— nothing like his own grandfather who never smiled at him.

"You put the cereal and milk away, and I'll wipe off the table," Bill said.

After everything had been tidied up, they walked into the living room and sat down. Bill grabbed his chair by the window, picked up the paper, and asked, "What section do you want first—the front, the local, or the sports?"

"I don't never read the paper. We don't get it."

"You do now. Not only that, but we're going to talk about it. That's going to be a part of your 'Summer School.' You need to know what's going on in the world and where. It's a big old place out there, and everybody is different."

Two hours later they discussed Syria, O'BamaCare, and the Detroit Tigers. Mr. Berkley showed Damey how to Google a map of Syria and the neighboring countries, especially Afghanistan and Iraq.

Damey had fun doing that. He didn't know about Google Maps, so he was really impressed when they ended up printing one of the entire Middle East as well as one of their neighborhood. In the not too distant future, Damey would have that application used again for him for a more serious and personal reason.

Bill explained some of the difficulties those countries were having He also mentioned how and why the United States should or should not be involved.

Damey soon discovered that Bill never told him what he should think about any issue. They'd look at both sides, talk about them, and then he'd let him make up his own mind—topics like abortion, women's rights, immigration, war, and isolationism, just to name a few.

After discussing Assad, the concept of civil war, and poison gassing civilians, Bill swung the discussion to the American Civil War in the mid-1800s. "I don't want to overwhelm you on the first day, Damey, so I'll keep it brief and only made a few points of similarities and differences.

"Okay, time to get up and stretch. We're going to go out and change the water in the hummingbird feeders. I've had the sugar and water solution cooling on the stove since before you got here this morning so it should be okay. You need to go to the bathroom or anything first?"

"Uh, yeah."

"I'm going to grab the stepladder out of the garage. Meet me in the back yard when you're done. Don't forget to wash your hands."

"Duh!" Damey said with his mouth curled upwards in an impish grin, and then they both laughed.

Bill normally did this little solution-changing chore all by himself every week, but apparently decided to teach Damey something new. Besides, it got both of them off their butts for a few minutes. By the time Bill had situated the ladder under the feeder, Damey had finished in the bathroom and stood beside him.

"First thing we have to do is make sure the ladder is solid on the ground. If it isn't, it could tip and *somebody* could get hurt. Guess who's going to be climbing the ladder, and who that somebody is that would get hurt if it fell?" Mr. Berkley asked looking at Damey and raising his eyebrows.

"Gee, I wouldn't want you to get hurt, Mr. Berkley," Damey said holding his head straight but looking up at Bill with that same smirk on his face.

Bill looked at Damey's smile and twinkle in his eyes and said, "Yeah, right. Climb up there and unhook the feeder and hand it to me. I'll hold the ladder to keep it steady.

After rinsing, washing, and re-filling both the front and back feeders, the boy put them back in place and even carried the ladder back into the garage. After 'recess,' it was time to get back to summer school.

• • •

Bill reached into the lamp table drawer beside his chair and pulled out his old, original Kindle. "You ever use one of these?" he asked.

"No. Some of the kids at school have them. A couple of people even have iPads that have the Kindle app on it, but I've never used one."

"Okay, come over here and sit down beside me. Time for you to see what this thing will do. It's old, but it works."

Bill taught him how to turn it on, look at the various folders where he had books stored, and open up, *Taming Little Ike.*

"Look at the print. Can you read it okay, or do we need to make the letters bigger?" He wondered about the kid's eyesight, since he'd probably never had an eye exam. When families are struggling to put groceries on the table and pay their bills, that's not always high on the priority list. He knew that from experience after thirty-five years in the classroom.

"The print's fine," Damey answered. "I can read it."

"Good. While I open up my iPad and get to the same place, you go over and climb up on the sofa. Turn the light on, settle in, and raise your feet up if you want to get more comfortable."

He did as Bill watched Damey out of the corner of his eye while opening his own device to page one of the same book. While he situated himself, Damey started reading the book on his own. Bill could tell it fascinated the kid. Expensive, personal electronics were probably pretty scarce across the street.

"Okay," Bill said after they both appeared to be settled in, "this is what we're going to do. This book is about a nine-year old neglected and abused kid. You're going to read it out loud to me, and then we're going to talk about it."

"We are?"

"Yep. Start reading."

"Okay.

"Andy grunted as he tried to hoist the root ball of the flowering crabapple tree over the mound of dirt and into the freshly dug hole. Jen stood beside him grinning and holding the shovel.

'Come on, Andy, heave! Use some muscle. Do I have to show you how this is done?'

'Aargh!' Andy screamed as he dragged the damned tree over the pile of dirt and let it slide down into the hole. 'There, that's done! Now you get to do the easy part, filling in the hole. Hop to it, Jenny.'"

"What's 'hoist' mean?" Bill asked.

"I dunno."

"Try to picture in your mind what's going on. Don't just read the words, try to visualize the scene. What's he trying to do?"

"He's trying to drag a new tree over a pile of dirt so he can plant it."

After working on several vocabulary words with Damey trying to figure out their meaning in context, Bill showed him the dictionary feature. By the end of chapter three, Damey started to visibly slow down. Bill decided that was enough actual reading for then.

"Before we break for lunch, tell me what's happened. We know that the boy's mom sent little Ike from Florida to Lansing, but what else is happening?"

"He showed up looking goofy in purple hair and an earring with a skull and crossbones dangling off the thing. His dad didn't even know about him. His mom threw him away and sent him to his dad. His new mom didn't want him either, but by the end of the first couple of chapters she does."

"Why did the kid show up looking so 'goofy'?"

"He's pissed off at the world." Damey said scowling and squirming in his seat visibly upset.

"Ok, now, let's try this again in English that *I* can understand. I'm old and crotchety and don't like to hear eleven-year-olds use off-color language. Besides, you're the one sounding angry. Tell me about it."

"He's mad, scared, and has no clue to what's going to happen to him."

"What about you? Why did you suddenly get angry? Are you seeing yourself in this kind of situation some day?"

"No. My mom would *never* even think of throwing me away because of some guy. I guess I just got mad at his mother, that's all."

"Okay, I understand."

Bill and Damey spent the next half hour talking about what the boy thought might be going on behind the scene in contrast to what was actually said or done in print.

After lunch, Bill told him they were going for a bike ride. The old man needed to get a little fresh air and exercise. At least, that's what he said.

"Where's your helmet?"

"I don't wear those sissy things."

"You think I'm a sissy for wearing one?"

"No, I didn't mean it that way. I've never worn one and neither do any other kids my age. Besides, Mom can't afford one." His eyes fell and his voice got softer.

"Hey, just because those middle school girls think you're cuter than I am, doesn't mean I'm not wiser. I'd like to see you keep that handsome face and noggin all in one piece in case you wiped out on gravel and bounced your head off a curb, tree or some other such thing. The one I keep for my grand-brats is hanging on the back wall in the garage. Grab it."

"But—"

"Damarian," his voice rose.

"Ok, but I don't wanna look like a dork."

"You won't."

Bill and Damey rode approximately six miles which took a little over a half hour.   After they returned home, Bill showed him the various math games he had on his computer for his own great-grandkids and made him work on them for a couple of hours.

• • •

Damey didn't solely work on math games during that couple of hours in front of the computer. His mind battled with some of the issues in his life. He thought about similarities between his own life and the one in the book Mr. Berkley was making him read. His mom struggled putting a roof over their heads and food on the table, yet his so-called grandparents were rich. He didn't think that was very fair the way they made her suffer just because of him.

Why couldn't they help her out? Couldn't they forgive her for not getting rid of him? He didn't care if they didn't like him, but how could they throw away their own daughter? Would they punish her forever? Would they help her out if he killed himself? He wouldn't do that, but would they? Suppose he got hit by a car and died? Would that make a difference?

There were so many likenesses between his mom's situation and that of Ike in *Taming Little Ike,* he found it intriguing. He knew that's why Mr. Berkely made him read that book first. Will this old man end up as Mom's savior just like Ike's dad and stepmom seem to be in the book?

Bill timed dinner so they could eat and watch the news at the same time. After the news and during their second bike ride of the day, they talked about what they'd seen on TV. When they got back, it was down time. Damey went over to his house to shoot baskets in the driveway as Bill dug out his iPad. He wanted to make sure the kid got some outdoor play time. When it started to get dark, Damey came back.

"Is it okay if I keep reading that *Taming Little Ike* book while I wait for Mom?"

"Of course. Curl up and get comfortable."

When his mom dropped in about 9:30 to pick him up, Damey was sound asleep. Before waking him up, she told Bill, laughing, "He griped last night about the fact you said he should be in bed by nine, so what'd he do? He fell asleep at 8:30, and I had to wake him up to get him in the shower and bed."

Bill smiled and told her, "He crashed about then tonight, too. He did have a busy day, though."

CHAPTER 3

O n Wednesday, about five-thirty, Shaundra pulled into the drive. Dripping sweat, Damey grabbed his bike, smiled, yelled "Bye," to Bill, waved, and pedaled home. They'd played catch with a football in the front yard while waiting for her. Mostly, the game consisted of Damey running out for passes with Bill throwing the ball.

Later that evening, Damey watched the Tigers on TV before heading off to bed.

Bill called. "What's Damey think about his first couple days of summer school?"

Shaundra repeated as much of the conversation as she could for Damey's benefit. She laughed. "What'd he think of his first day? Damey said you're going to drive him crazy. Every sentence starts with either 'why' or 'what.' 'What really happened there?' or 'Why did he just do so-and-so?' 'How would you have done it?' He claimed his brain hurt because you made him think too much."

She listened to Bill's response and said, "That's what I told him too. Then I suggested instead of just reading the words, he should think about what's going on and try to figure things out. I told him I always try to guess what's going to happen next in a story. When I told him that, he grinned and said, 'Yeah, yeah. That's what Mr. Berkley said.' He liked his day, Bill. Said you were great."

As she talked, she smiled and nodded, and kept looking over at Damey. So far, she liked this arrangement. Meeting Mr. Bill Berkley had the potential to be one of the best things that ever happened to Damey. Oh, how he needed some kind of male role-model.

Shaundra listened for another minute, and then spoke. "I totally agree, but I hate to have you spend money on him. I just can't afford to buy one right now." She felt saddened and guilty by the admission. "Of course, if you do, I'll enforce it from this end."

Damey, focused on the conversation while staring at the TV screen. When Shanundra ended her call, Damey said, "I know darned well what you were talking about.

Mr. Berkley wants to buy me my own bike helmet. Mom, I don't want one. Do I have to?"

"Yes. It's for your own protection, and we aren't going to argue about it."

• • •

The next day, Mr. Berkley and Damey read and discussed the book for an hour and a half before Bill stopped. "Okay, that went well so we're going to do something a little different today. I want you to sit down in front of the computer in the family room and write a one-page summary of the story so far. Write in complete sentences using proper grammar, spelling, sentence, and paragraph structure. It's going to be like a mini book report. When you're done, print it off, and show it to me. If you need help, say so. I'll be over here on the sofa checking up on the wonderful world of Facebook on my iPad."

Bill kept his eyes on him most of the time as the boy struggled typing with his two index fingers. Watching him frown, wrinkle up his face, and sigh was a lot more fun than the political rants streaming on Facebook. He always thought that people should actually read the garbage they post and forward before they hit the 'send' button.

"Mr. Berkley, how do I print this thing?" Damey asked looking perplexed as his shoulders sagged.

"Ctrl, P, Enter—and then bring it over here for me to take a look. While you're at it, grab one of those red pens out of the pencil box on the desk."

Once a teacher, always a teacher. After explaining every mark he made on the paper, he handed it back. "I think you left out one fairly important thing, Damey."

"What? I thought I covered everything."

"You didn't mention Jen, Ike's new mother, buying him a gold stud earring. What was that all about? She and his dad, Andy, both had a fit about the gold-hooped earring with the dangling skull and crossbones he wore when he showed up at the airport."

"Oh, yeah, I forgot about that. Since she didn't want him at first, maybe she's letting him know everything's gonna be okay?"

"That works for me. Go ahead and type it again making all the corrections while I start lunch. Let's see, maybe I'll fix you an apple, an orange, a cup of steamed broccoli, and a banana. How's that sound?"

"How about a bag of chips, cheese dip, and a Coke?" Damey asked with a sheepish grin.

"Hummm, I'll figure out a compromise of some kind."

When Damey finished his rewriting his story, he brought the corrected paper up to the kitchen. After looking it over, Bill said, "That looks better. I've got a three-ring binder in the cupboard behind the computer that we can put your papers in for comparison later in the summer."

They went back to the family room and pulled out the folder which already had Damey's name stenciled on the cover. Damey wondered when Mr. Berkley had done that. He hadn't seen it previously. They used the 3-hole punch on the paper, put the sheet in the book, and stashed everything back in its place. Lunch awaited them on the table.

After a couple of grilled cheese sandwiches, tomato soup, and a glass of milk, they cleaned up their mess. Damey figured they'd head out on their bikes. Bill had other plans. "Get in the car, young un, we've got to go to a couple of places."

"Where we goin'?" Damey asked. He had a sneaking suspicion where, but tried to play dumb.

"We're going to the bike shop and get you a helmet, and then to Best Buy to see if we can find a typing program suitable for you."

"Oh, no, please. I really don't want one. Nobody wears them. I'll look like a freak."

"I've already talked to your mom about it last night. She agrees. It's a done deal. We're going to get you a helmet, and you will wear it each and every time you get on your bike, or you won't be riding it."

Figuring he should probably keep his mouth shut, Damey got in the car without another word and rode down to the little out-of-the-way bike shop near the old City Market. They parked beside the building and walked in.

A man walked across the floor to greet them. "Hey, Bill. How's it going? Who's your little buddy?"

"Hi, John. This is Damey. Damey, this is the owner of this place, John."

"He thinks helmets are for sissies. You still have that picture around of the kid who tried to do a wheelie out in the street in front of his friends?"

"Yeah, I do, Bill. Hi, Damey. Good to meet you," John said as they shook hands. "C'mon over here and look over the kid's helmets while I check my stash of pictures."

While John was gone, Damey looked at several of the head gear and even tried a couple of them while inspecting the thing in the mirror. He modeled the teal and purple model with the zigzagged lines twice. The helmets ranged from cheap, practical, cool, to super-cool. He took the zigzagged one off the rack and looked at it a third time. He considered the design super-cool.

• • •

John came out of the back room with the picture in hand. He motioned to Bill with his head to come over to where he stood. "Are you sure it's okay for him to look at this?"

"I know what you're getting at, but I want to make a point."

"Okay, but I still think he might be a little young. Oh, another thing. Teach him how to shake hands like a man. He limp-wristed me."

"He did?" Bill asked. "I've never noticed. In fact, I don't believe we've ever shaken hands. We'll work on it".

They continued to talk for a minute or two while Damey ignored them. Something else had caught his eye.

When they walked back, he had slipped over to a demo-bike they had on a stand. He pedaled it with his right hand while watching the flashing reflector on the back. The faster he spun the sprocket, the faster the light flashed. "Mr. Berkley, have you ever seen one of these? How cool is this?"

"A lot of people have those, Damey, especially those riding road bikes," Bill said.

"Damey, Mr. Berkley wants me to show you a picture. It's pretty gross. Why don't you sit down over here by the door beside the john and let me tell you a little about it first."

After Damey sat, John described an incident where a sixteen-year-old boy, who thought he was a stud trick-biker, did himself in. He liked freestyle—Jumping, Slides, Bunnyhops, Wheelies, and Stoppies. He *didn't* like helmets, knee and elbow pads, or anything else that might "hinder" him. John also mentioned that when one rides at a skate park, all of that stuff is required.

Unfortunately, anywhere else, a person can get away without it.

All sounded perfectly normal to Damey. He figured John would show him a picture of some kid with a bunch of scrapes and bruises sitting on the side of the road bawling.

John continued, "One day, when the kid in the picture decided to show off for his friends, he did a Wheelie out in the street in front of his house. Balanced precariously on its back wheel, the bike rolled over an unseen wide crack in the asphalt. The boy lost control and dove head first into the curb crushing his skull and killing himself instantly."

Damey shuddered thinking about it.

Then John handed Damey the picture. The extremely graphic photo showed a close-up of the dead boy's staring eyes as his face lay in a puddle of blood, crushed bone, and brain.

Damey's stomach reacted immediately. "Where's your bathroom? I'm gonna puke!"

"Right behind you. Run!" John said.

They stood outside the door listening to him heave his guts. After he finished and flushed the toilet, Bill walked in to make sure everything was okay. He grabbed some paper towels, soaked them in cold water, and wiped Damey's, mouth, cheeks, and forehead.

It took a few minutes before he felt brave enough to leave the restroom. With Damey's knees still wobbling,

Mr. Berkley put an arm around his back and walked him out.

"I've never seen anything like that. I don't ever want to again." Damey said offering no more arguments against a helmet.

John gave him a bottle of water to sip while he sat in the showroom until he felt better. A few minutes later, Damey stood up, hesitated, and then walked over to the helmets again.

Not long after that, Mr. Berkley and Damey left the store with the teal and purple zigzagged helmet personally fitted to his head by John, along with a flashing reflector for the back of his bike.

• • •

Their second stop for the day, finding a typing program at Best Buy, went on hold. They had more important things to do. Bill parked the car in the driveway allowing them some room to work. He pulled his toolbox off the shelf and set it on the garage floor beside the bike. He told Damey what he wanted, and then Damey's had to find the right tool and hand it to him.

The installation would have gone faster if Bill had grabbed the tools himself, but he wanted Damey to learn something new. He had to point at, describe, and try to stay calm since Damey had no clue about three-quarter inch sockets, Phillips screwdrivers, and wrenches. Bill shook his head in disbelief. How could an eleven year-old not even know the difference between a regular screw driver and a Phillips?

After installing the reflector, they attached the bikes to the rack on the back of Bill's car and headed to a place Damey didn't even know existed. Damey found the flashing reflector much more intriguing than the helmet, and he wanted to try it out. The queasy stomach had been long forgotten, but not the lesson.

• • •

That night, when Shaundra stopped at Bill's to pick Damey up, she found her boy curled up on the sofa sound asleep again. He had the new helmet cradled in his right arm as he dozed. Stretching and yawning, he made his way out to the car. By the time Shaundra backed out of Bill's drive, drove two houses down, and pulled into their own garage, he'd become alert enough to show her his new gear and tell her about their two-hour ride on the river trail they took instead of working on math or learning how to type in the afternoon.

"I think Mr. Berkley's spoiling you. I hope you don't let him down." Shaundra said with a concerned expression on her face.

"I won't," Damey said. He loved being spoiled by that old man. No way would he screw it up.

CHAPTER 4

Damey and Mr. Berkley worked about two hours on book five of the series of ten Damey read that summer from the author of "Taming Little Ike" and Lee Carey, an author Bill knew from Virginia Beach. Lee wrote mysteries, books about the beach, talking dogs, teenagers, and other topics. Damey loved reading the stories, but analyzing the "Whys?" and the "What would happen if he'd done it another way?" part frustrated him.

That was the day Damey got all flustered and slapped his hand down on the desk hard enough to tip over Bill's coffee mug. Fortunately, it was empty. "I feel like my brain is an acorn squash that's been cut in half and the seeds scooped out for butter and brown sugar. So what do you do? You try to cram a whole watermelon in that little hole. Thinking too much makes my brain hurt."

"Okay," Bill said rolling his eyes and supressing a grin. "Let's look at it another way."

"No! I can't learn all this crap. You keep forgetting that I ain't nothin' but a dumb little black kid."

Bill stopped, sat back in his chair and gazed at him for a minute without saying anything.

Damey couldn't look at him. He dropped his head and stared at the floor with tears running down his cheeks.

"Do you know what you just said?" Bill asked."

"Yes,"

"How did it make you feel?"

"Like shit," Damey whispered, still unable to look up as he wiped his cheeks with his arm.

"Keep it civil. Now, how would you feel if I said that to you?"

"Bad," he said slowly shaking his head back and forth. "Really bad."

Bill pulled a tissue out of the Kleenex box on his desk and handed it to him. Damey blew his nose and wiped his cheeks again with his sleeve.

"Has anyone ever said that to you?"

"Yes."

"How would I feel if you said, 'You ain't nothin' but a dumb ole white man?'"

"Terrible."

48

Letting the message sink in for a few seconds, Bill responded, "So you know how it feels. Let me tell you something, Damarian. It's not true. It doesn't matter if you're black, brown, white, yellow, or purple polka-dotted. *You* are what is important, not the color of your skin."

Silence filled the room for maybe a minute before Damey looked up. "Do you really mean that, Mr. Berkley?"

"Little man, you have no idea how bright you are. I wish all the students I had for all those years picked up things as quickly as you do. You've grasped more in the past month than some of my students did in a whole semester."

Bill continued on with his rant until Damey dropped his head again staring at the floor. Realizing that maybe the boy suddenly thought he was being scolded, Bill stopped in mid-sentence, took a breath, and said, "Get in the car. We're going for a ride."

Damey had no idea where they were going and didn't dare ask. His eleven-year-old imagination went wild. He's taking me to the juvenile center. He's taking me to Mom's job and dropping me off telling her I'm a hopeless case. He's taking me out of town someplace and gonna throw me out and make me find my own way home.

Bill drove straight to the local paint store about a half-mile away. Once inside, he led Damey to the color chart, took the boy's arm in his hand and flicked through the brown tones until he found one that matched. The chart indicated his skin color was Mocha-Cream.

"See? You're an eleven-year-old, Mocha-Cream-colored, African American male. You are not, 'nothin but a dumb little ole black kid.' You're a human being, and I happen to like you just the way you are. So there!"

Bill wrapped his arm around Damey's shoulder and walked him back to the car. That's when the boy got an even bigger jolt. They drove down the street to the Quality Dairy where Bill bought two giant Death by Chocolate ice-cream cones, threatening his life and well-being if he let it spoil his dinner.

"Fat chance of that happening," Damey said sporting a smile for the first time.

Normal after summer school snacks at Bill's house consisted of bananas, oranges, apples, or whatever else happened to be in the fruit bowl. He never let Damey eat junk food. The ice cream was an extra special treat for both of them.

The next morning when Damey rode his bike over for his lessons, they had breakfast and chatted like nothing had happened. When they went down to the office, there were two printed cards sitting on the desk. Bill slid them across to Damey and told him to read one of them out loud.

Picking them up, he scanned both to see they were identical. Then he read, *"I Damarian Wayne Martin am a very bright, mocha-cream-complexioned, African American male. I can do or be anything I want with my life. I can be a doctor, scientist, lawyer, engineer, banker, accountant, entrepreneur or anything else. I can become a politician and run for Congress, the governor's seat, or even the Presidency of the United States. The one thing I cannot ever do again is disrespect myself or anyone else."*

"Do you understand what you just read?"

"Yes."

"Deep down in your heart and soul, Damey, I want you to know and believe it."

"I do, too."

"Okay, that's a beginning. Now, before we get back to work on what we were doing yesterday prior to the meltdown, I want you to sign both copies, and then let's run up to Office Max and get them laminated. One goes in my wallet, and you memorize and keep the other."

"Can we ride? That's a long way to run," Damey asked grinning from ear-to-ear.

"Smart alec. Get in the car."

When they returned, it was back to reading, analyzing, and writing. After lunch, they took their six-mile bike ride, and then it was math. Bill relied mostly on computer math programs and games for that part. He led Damey to believe that when it came to that side of the brain, he'd been born numerically illiterate. He told him he even had a calculator attached to his check book.

51

About three o'clock, Bill declared, "Enough, Damey. This stuff gives me a headache. I don't even know what you're doing."

"Oh, these are just fractions. They're easy. Percentages and fractions are alike only different."

"Well, from now on, you have to start taking a percentage or fraction of each day for some good, old-fashioned, outdoor playtime. Can you believe the summer's half over, and you haven't had any time for just you? All you've done is hang with me. You've got to get some normal kid-type exercise."

"We haven't just sat around and done nothing but school. You've taken me swimming at the city pool every week, we've gone to several museums and walked around, and we take two half hour bike rides every day. You took me to a Tigers' game. Not only that, but we've mowed the grass and weeded the garden every week. I'm not gonna grow roots."

"Get on your bike and go ride around the neighborhood and see if you can find some other kids. There's gotta be somebody your age around here, someplace. If you don't find anyone, come back and shoot baskets at your house for a while. You can practice your slam-dunks."

"Slam-dunks? The rim's ten feet high."

"So? You'll only have to jump six-feet straight in the air—either that or grow a couple dozen inches. Whatever. You've got a goal to shoot for. Now, get out of here and go find somebody to play with and be back by six for dinner."

Damey looked back and noticed Bill watching as he rode up the street. He smiled and waved. The old guy really did care about him.

• • •

Damey never returned during the afternoon to shoot baskets. Bill wondered and half worried about what he was up to. He wanted him to find someone his own age to spend some time with—a nice kid who would be a good influence and friend to him, not some little hood. School wouldn't start for another four or five weeks, and he needed to find a friend way before then.

His great-grandkids all came over at various times with their parents, but that'd only be for a couple of hours. Other than that, it was normally just the two of them.

• • •

About five to six, Damey burst through the front door slamming it against the wall as he raced into the house shouting, "Grandpa! Grandpa! Guess what?"

"What?"

By the time he reached the kitchen, he'd slowed down to a snail's pace. Feeling sick with embarrassment and shame, he hung his head, and said, "I'm sorry. I didn't mean to do that. Mom warned me."

"What are you talking about?" Bill asked lifting Damey's chin so he'd look at him. He took his clean handkerchief out of his pocket and wiped the tears leaking out of kid's eyes. "What's going on? You charge in here all excited and then crash. What's up?"

"I called you Grandpa instead of Mr. Berkley. Mom told me that would be rude. I always call you Grandpa Tutor at home."

"One thing at a time. First off, I want to know what was so exciting when you first burst through the door?"

"I've got a friend," Damey said smiling through his teary eyes. "He lives right down the street about a block. He told me he's the only other kid on our whole street. We shot baskets at his house for a while. Then we rode our bikes down to the river where he showed me his secret fishing spot. He's gonna come down here at seven and ride with us if it's okay with you. If it's not, when he gets here, I'll tell him we'll do it another time."

"Of course it's okay. So, what's your friend's name?"

"Alex, it's Alex Veras. Actually, his real name is Alejandro, but everybody calls him Alex. We're just alike that way. When we're good, or around friends,

54

we're Damey and Alex. When we're getting yelled at, we're Damarian and Alejandro."

"Well, good." Bill laughed at the analogy. "I can't wait to meet him. In the meantime, let's get back to the 'Grandpa' thing. For me, 'Mr. Berkley' is too formal, 'Bill' is too informal because of our age differences, but 'Grandpa' works perfectly. I'd be proud to have you call me Grandpa. That way you can be another one of my great-grandsons."

Damey wiped his face with his sleeve again as Bill grabbed him, pulling him into his chest for a hug.

Then he took Damey's cheeks in both hands and lifted his head again. "Heaven help me! Do I have to suffer through another boy going through puberty? I'm too old for this. I think we'd better eat."

CHAPTER 5

About the time Grandpa and Damey finished cleaning the dishes after dinner, the doorbell rang. Damey raced to the door and let Alex in. After he introduced them, Bill shook his hand. "You've got a good firm grip, Alex. Shake hands with Damey, I want to show you both something."

They both stuck out their hands feeling like a couple of dorks. Bill watched as Damey held out his hand a little limp-wristed again.

"Okay, you're both doing pretty good, but I want to show you how men shake hands. Put a little energy in it when you stick your hand out, like it means something.

Grab the other guy's hand and squeeze, not a bone crusher, but tight enough so the other guy knows you have a hold of him."

He showed both the boys individually, and then had them shake hands with each other again. Finally satisfied, he asked, "You guys ready for our ride?"

As Bill and Damey got their bikes out of the garage, Alex wheeled his off the sidewalk and met them in the driveway.

"Where's your helmet?" Grandpa asked.

"At home," Alex answered. "I don't always wear mine even if my parents do nag me about it."

"You do when you're riding with us. Damey, show him where the spare is in the garage and Alex can wear that one tonight."

After their ride, Alex and Damey decided to shoot baskets across the street with Grandpa's reminder to be home by dusk ringing in their ears.

As summer raced along, Alex ended up coming for some of the morning reading and writing and all the afternoon math tutoring sessions. Bill managed to drive both of them crazy, because since he claimed he knew absolutely nothing about math, they had to teach him. He would make them explain everything two or three different ways to get it through his thick skull.

Little did the boys realize at the time, but by the first of September, they'd mastered the entire scope of sixth grade English and math and most of the seventh. Between the games and math programs Grandpa picked out, Alex and Damey stood well ahead of where they would normally be.

From three to six, they were on their own. They rode their bikes over to a park on the edge of town almost on a daily basis. It was maybe three miles from home if they rode the more direct, heavily traveled routes. Taking Grandpa's suggestion, they took side streets and lesser traveled roads to get there. It was a little longer, but not that much. A number of boys that Alex knew from school met there every day to play pickup games of baseball. Not only were they getting in some good, healthy outdoor play time, but Damey met a bunch of new kids whom he would be going to school with in the fall. Starting his brand new school would be a little easier than he'd originally feared.

The park was multi-faceted. There were swings, slides, monkey bars, ball fields, a disc-golf course, walking trails, and a large wooded area owned by the state situated off the end of the trails that nobody used.

Summer passed by quickly, and on the last Friday afternoon before vacation ended, Bill happened to be looking out the window about the time they were due back. He watched as the boys rode up the street, stopped for a moment by the curb several doors down, and strapped on their helmets. So, the little dudes are trying to pull a fast one? We'll see about that.

He didn't say a word about it that night, but the next day, as soon as they left and were out of sight, he grabbed his camera, and jumped into the car. He took the main roads to the park so they wouldn't accidentally see him, pulled in about fifty yards from the ball diamond, and waited.

When the kids returned home at six, he met them at the door. "Alex, before you go home to dinner, I want you to come in for a minute."

They walked in wondering what the heck was going on. "What's up?" Damey asked.

"Both of you sit down beside each other on the loveseat. I want to show you something, and then we'll discuss it."

They sat down sneaking peeks at each other knowing something was wrong from the tone of his voice. They had no clue what they'd done, and weren't all that sure they wanted to. Grandpa handed them a picture.

"What's this?" he asked.

"It's Alex and me riding into the park."

"What else can you tell me about the picture?"

"You must've taken it today 'cause we're both dressed like we are right now," Alex said.

"Take a close look at the picture, boys. What's wrong?"

Both of them stared at the photo having no idea what he was talking about but feeling more and more anxious. "I give up. I don't know what the problem is, but you're mad at us." Damey answered.

"Take a look at your heads."

"Helmets!" Alex blurted.

Both boys blanched and squirmed in their seats. They knew the rules. And they weren't just Grandpa's rules, their parents enforced them now as well.

"Damarian and Alejandro, pay very close attention," Bill snarled, not sounding like his normal self at all. "I talked to both of your mothers this afternoon after I took this picture. This is the way it's going to be. I will be keeping closer tabs on you in the future when you're out on your own. My handy little camera with the powerful zoom lens and I will show up at the most unexpected times and places. You won't see us."

Slightly shaking and afraid to even look at each other, they listened wondering what was in store. Punishment time had to be coming next. What would he do?

"This time you both get off with a warning. Next time will be different. Damarian, if your mother or I catch you riding again without your helmet, your bike will be locked up in my garage for one week, and you will be grounded for the same length of time. Alex will be off limits, and playing outdoors with your friends will not be allowed. Any outside activity will be restricted to mowing, weeding, or working. I may want the sidewalk edged, and possibly the garage floor washed and painted that week. Not sure. Locking your bike up probably won't make a whole lot of difference to you anyway, because you probably won't be able to sit on that hard, stiff, bike seat for a couple of days. Do I make myself clear?"

"Yes, sir," Damey answered with his voice quavering as he stared at his knees.

"Alejandro, if this does happen again, I will be notifying your parents as well. Your mom told me this afternoon that the three of you would discuss it at dinner tonight. So, you'd better get home. See you after seven for our bike ride?"

"I hope so," Alex mumbled. His voice also sounded shakey.

As soon as he was out the door, Damey spoke up. "Grandpa, I'm sorry. It won't happen again. I remember that picture at the bike shop. I was stupid. I know. I promise."

"Okay, I'll take your word for it. Let's not talk anymore about it tonight. Let's eat in peace."

After dinner, they waited around until seven-fifteen for Alex, and he didn't show.

"Should I call him to see if he's coming?" Damey asked.

"No, that might not be a good idea. He's always here before now when he comes. Apparently tonight's out for him. Let's get our ride in. I'm sure you'll find out what happened tomorrow."

When they returned, Damey picked up his Kindle, curled up on the sofa, and started to read. Unable to concentrate, after fifteen minutes or so, he set the device down. "I hope Alex is okay. He told me his dad is kind of strict."

"I'm sure he is. His mom was angry with him, but I doubt he'll get much more than a warning—this time."

The next afternoon after lunch when it was time for their afternoon bike ride, Alex rolled up on his bike—helmet securely in place.

"Mr. Berkley, I'm sorry. I know better. It won't happen again. I won't let it. Have you ever heard of an old saying that goes, 'What's good for the goose is good for the gander?'" With his lips curled slightly downward, there was no sign of Alex's normally happy demeanor.

"Yes, I know what it means," Grandpa answered smiling.

"I don't," Damey said baffled.

Alex looked at him, "I didn't either, until Dad explained it. It means, if we get caught without our helmets again, whatever happens to you, happens to me, and I want no part of that."

"I don't either," Damey said. "I won't get on my bike without my helmet again."

"Me either. By the way, the reason I didn't come down last night was because my dad took me down to the bike shop and asked the owner to show me the picture he showed you. Mr. Berkley told Mom all about it."

"What'd you do when you saw it?"

"I puked my guts out all over the floor as I ran into the bathroom. I didn't make it in time."

"Oh, yuck! How gross was that! At least I made it to the john before *I* heaved."

"Time to ride, boys," Bill said smiling.

CHAPTER 6

Not too long into the second chapter of their lives, Shaundra and Bill decided that Damey would spend Tuesday and Thursday nights at Grandpa's. Those nights, Shaundra never got home until at least nine-thirty. Then she found him asleep on the loveseat or sofa, so it meant waking him up, going home, and shooing him off to bed. They figured it would be better to keep Damey the on a schedule and get him to bed on time especially with school almost ready to start. Besides, that gave her a chance to go out for coffee with her classmates without having to worry about her son.

"Okay, pick out a toothbrush. There's a whole bunch of them there at the back of the drawer."

"How come you gots so many?" Damey asked.

"Every time I go to the dentist for my six-month check up, the hygienist gives me a new toothbrush. I ask for the skinniest one she has, but the handle is always too fat to fit in the holder, so I go to the drug store and buy one that fits. Then I toss the other one in there. So, you see, you've got quite a choice."

Damey looked at the pile of brushes and thought the old guy must have been going to the dentist for a long time. There had to be a dozen tucked away in the back of the drawer.

"Lay your brush on a paper towel to dry when you finish." He folded one and put it inside the drawer against the side. "The mouthwash is down there." He opened the door under the sink and pointed at it.

"Now, I don't know what you do at home, but you should floss, brush, and rinse with the mouthwash every morning and every night before or after your shower. The towels are in this cabinet, and behind this door is the laundry chute," he said opening it and pointing out the device. "Throw your dirty clothes down the hole to the basket below and hang your towel over the side here until it dries, then down it goes."

"I don't never floss. That's dumb. Mom tries to make me all the time, but I don't unless she's in the bathroom when I'm brushing. What's the big deal?"

"There's a sign hanging on my dentist's wall right in front of the examination chair. You can't miss it. It says, 'You don't have to floss all your teeth, just the ones you want to keep.' Anytime I'm in a hurry and want to skip that step, I think of that sign. The purpose of it is to stimulate your gums to keep blood flowing in there close to your teeth. If you don't, you can get what is called periodontal disease, and your teeth fall out. Not fun."

Damey thought about that a minute. He'd seen old people with no teeth. It looked gross. He decided he'd floss.

• • •

About three weeks after school started in September, Grandpa rolled Damey out of bed on a Friday morning at seven-thirty, fed him breakfast, and sent him off to school—just like every Wednesday and Friday. That afternoon, the boys rode home, dropped off their backpacks, grabbed a snack, and headed for the park like normal. When they got there, none of their friends were around.

"I'll bet they all went to that big pep rally at the high school. I think it's dumb 'cause we can't go to the game tonight anyway because it gets out so late, so why bother? Besides, that's a high school thing. That's not us." Damey said.

"So what're we gonna do?" Alex asked. "It's just you and me."

"Let's walk the disc-golf course. We've talked about it enough times. We've just never done it, and there's nobody playing so we won't bother anybody."

"Okay, let's lock our bikes up at the rack where the first hole starts and go from there," Alex said. "You ever think you'd wanna play?"

They locked up their bikes to the post, took off their helmets and slipped them over their handlebars, and looked across the green, grassy field to the first cage. Looked to be almost the length of a football field away.

"I dunno. It looks like it would be fun, but all we've ever seen is guys playing from here to the first cage at the edge of the woods. I don't even know where the course goes from there."

"Let's find out," Alex said.

They started walking pretending they were hurling discs as they went, watching them soar, shaking one out of a small tree, and laughing all the way. The dirt paths between the next baskets were narrow and lined with trees on both sides—easy place to lose a disc. Half way to hole number two, Damey asked, "What's with this Liam dude we have in first hour? What's his problem? All he does is snarl and act stupid."

"He's a bully. He's as dumb as a box of rocks. He's in the eighth grade and likes to pick on younger and smaller kids like us. He calls everybody faggots, me a greasy spick, you the N-word and on and on it goes."

"I don't like that. How come he gets away with it?"

"His dad is the superintendent of schools."

"What's that mean?"

"He's the boss of all the schools in town. He's the principal's boss, so naturally the principal lets the fat turd get away with anything he wants. Last year, I saw the jerk bounce a kid off a locker on purpose, and the principal saw him do it. So, what'd Mr. Rogers do? He put his arm around Liam's shoulder and told him, 'Be careful where you're walking, Liam. You might accidentally hurt somebody.' Does that suck, or does that suck?"

They talked a little more about Liam and then changed the subject. He wasn't worth their time, and besides, there were more important things to do, like fetching their pretend shots on the course.

About hole eleven, Damey grabbed Alex's arm and stopped him. "Shhh, look over there."

"What? What're you lookin at?"

" It's a pure white deer, standing to the left and behind that big pine tree."

"Oh, okay. I see it. What's it doing?"

"Looks like he's eating. Don't see any others around."

"Let's see if we can sneak up and get closer," Alex said. "I've never seen a white one before. Dinky horns—fuzzy. Let's plan Indian and stalk the thing."

"Oh, yeah," Damey said laughing softly as he covered his mouth. Then he whispered, "You're brown, I'm black, we're playing red, and stalking white. How cool is that? I've never seen a deer up this close except at the zoo. If we stay back a ways and don't scare it, maybe we can follow it until it gets back with its litter or pack or whatever they call their families. I wonder if they're all white?"

"I dunno, but we gots to be quiet. By the way, I think it's called a herd," Alex said putting his finger to his lips.

They followed the deer as quietly as they could for at least a half hour into the woods until the stag lifted his head, sniffed the air in their direction, and bolted.

"That was fun," Alex said, "but I think we'd better head back—that is, after I pee on this tree that's lying on the ground. Wonder how that happened? Looks like it just fell over 'cause it was top-heavy or something."

"Beats me."

Alex showered one side of the root ball, and Damey did the other. Then they headed back to the course figuring it would take a little while because they had followed the deer so long. Over an hour later, after another rest and potty break, Damey stopped dead in his tracks. "I think we're in trouble."

"Why?"

"Isn't that the same tree we peed on earlier?" he asked.

"I don't know. Let's go look and see if the dirt's still wet."

They walked up to the root ball, and sure enough, there were two damp spots. They had walked in a circle.

"Damn!" Damey said. "Now what're we gonna do? Seems like we've been walking for hours."

"I donno. I'm hot and sweaty. Feet hurt. Hungry. Tired. Starting to get dark. Can't see where I'm going. Gonna sit down and lean against this tree for a couple of minutes. Gotta get off my feet."

"Maybe we should just stay here. We're already late for dinner. Mom's gonna have a hissy-fit. You know what's gonna happen, don't you? Mom'll call Grandpa, he'll call your house, and then they'll come and find us. Then we're gonna be in all kinds of trouble. Probably get grounded forever. As if that ain't bad enough, my butt itches."

"Wondered why you were all-of-a-sudden scratching it. You started it soon after you pooped a while back. Thought maybe you didn't wipe."

"Yeah, I did with a bunch of leaves, but it itches bad."

As night descended upon them, the temperature chilled so they huddled together trying to keep warm. Eventually, they fell fitfully asleep. One of them would squirm or shift positions, and the movement would wake the other. It was going to be a long night. Unusual for him, Damey was the squirmier of the two. He couldn't get comfortable. He scratched some more.

• • •

Shaundra called Bill about seven-thirty, "Are Damey and Alex over there by any chance? I haven't seen either one of them since I got home from work. Damey's backpack is here, so I know he came home after school, but there's no other sign of him. Dinner's cold, and I'm worried."

"No, I haven't seen him since he left this morning. Everything was fine then. He ate breakfast, talked non-stop, and off he went. Did you check with the Veras's?"

"No, I called you first."

"Let me call Pablo and see if he knows anything. I'll call you back."

"I've got no idea where they are," Pablo said. "They're late. I thought they were probably with you. I was just getting ready to call you when the phone rang."

Bill thought Pablo sounded a little grouchy.

"Margarita's getting herself all uptight, because it's not like Alex not to be home on time for dinner. He likes to eat too much. Why don't we take a ride over to the park, break up the football game, and drag them home?" Pablo said.

After they ended their conversation, Bill called Shaundra who sounded like she was on the verge of tears.

"I want to go too," Shaundra said.

71

"Okay, I'll pick you up on the way down to Veras's."

When they arrived at the park, the ranger was in the process of locking the chain gate for the night. Bill pulled up right in back of his vehicle, blocking it in. All three of them got out of the car and walked up to him.

"We're closed for the night, folks. I lock the gates at sundown," he said.

"We have two missing boys and are pretty sure they came here after school. They do almost every day," Pablo said gruffly. No park ranger would be keeping him out.

Seeing the strained looks on everyone's face, the ranger smiled and tried to ease their fears. "There are two bikes chained to the bike rack down at the beginning of the disc-golf course. I figured that whoever they belong to hadn't finished their game yet. They can easily get out by just riding around the posts here at the gate. Happens all the time."

"We need to look at those bikes and see if they belong to our boys," Shaundra told him.

"Okay, how old are these kids anyway?" the ranger asked unlocking the chain gate. His wife had just called, and his dinner was getting cold as well.

"Mine turned twelve last week," Shaundra said. "When's Alex's birthday, Pablo?"

"He turns twelve next month."

"Hum, they are young, aren't they? Follow me."

He jumped back into his vehicle and led the group down to the bike rack. Sure enough, the bikes were Damey and Alex's.

"They've gotta be in here someplace," Bill said. "It's dark. How do we find them?"

"I can drive this vehicle on the golf trails and the hiking paths. Get in, and we'll see if we can find them."

The ranger drove every available trail and path in the park. His lips curled downwards knowing his wife's lack of patience when it came to him being late for dinner. He felt thankful the other three couldn't see his face. By the time they finished, it was nine o'clock and pitch black. Without headlights, it'd be impossible to see anything on the trails.

"I guess I'd better call the police and see if they'll bring over one of the search and rescue dogs," the ranger sighed. He'd hoped they'd find the kids so he could close up and go home. He took his phone off his belt and made the call. When he ended, he said, "They'll be here shortly."

Then he talked to his wife for the third time, moving away from the group as he tried to explain to her his predicament.

Fighting back tears, Shaudra said, "I *know* something direful has happened to the boys. They are either hurt or someone abducted them."

Bill and Pablo tried to calm her, but found it difficult when they had the same suspicions.

When the police car pulled in and stopped, the cop got out of the vehicle and then opened the back door. "Come, Max."

Out jumped a beautiful eighty-five pound male German Shepherd who immediately went into the "Heel" position and walked with Officer Jackson to the group and sat down without being told.

After explaining the situation, and letting him know that, no, the kids had never run away or pulled a stunt like that before, the officer looked down at Max, and said, "Time to go to work, boy."

Shaundra, Bill, and Pablo stood nervously behind looking back and forth at each other as the officer had the dog sniff the bike seats and helmets. Max didn't have to be told what to do. He started walking towards the first hole.

He veered back and forth apparently following the path of one boy or the other as they played their imaginary game. The going was slow because the humans were trying to follow without stepping into a rut or walking into a tree. Jackson and the park ranger each had flashlights so luckily the three worried relatives were able to hang together and follow along behind them without too much trouble. Max didn't need a light.

Roughly a half-hour later, Max veered off the disc-golf course in the vicinity of the eleventh hole. "This is strange," Bill said. "Wonder why they left the path?"

"Because they're two kids who use their heads as storage units for their baseball caps instead of thinking about what they're doing for a change," Pablo said.

Another half-hour went by, and Max suddenly sat beside a large tree. Officer Jackson walked up to see what Max had found. "Feces. Somebody went to the bathroom. Come on, Max. Find the boys."

"Wait a second," Bill said.

"What? You wanna look?" Jackson asked.

"No, what's that green vine wrapped around the base of the tree?"

Officer Jackson told Max to sit while he went over to check things out with his flashlight. The other four followed. "Oh, no," the park ranger said. "That's a huge batch of poison ivy, and look," He shined his light to the right of the bush closest to the excrement. "There are a bunch of the leaves missing, and sure enough, there they are beside the pile."

"Oh, no!" Shaundra gasped. "We've got to find them fast."

Ten minutes later Max picked up his speed and disappeared from sight. Out of the pitch-black night came a blood-curdling scream. All five of the searchers laughed. The kids were alive and loud. Max had done his job.

By the time the adults caught up to the dog, Max was sitting and both boys were on their knees petting, nuzzling, and loving him. After the hugs and kisses from the parents, came the questions. "Who screamed and why?" Pablo asked smiling with his arm securely wrapped around his boy in a loving hug.

"Me," Alex answered sheepishly. "I guess I'd fallen asleep and dreamed that a giant wolf was tasting me trying to decide whether he wanted to eat me or not. Then I woke up with Max licking my cheeks. I freaked."

"You'll have to excuse him," Officer Jackson said. "He loves salty tears, wet or dry. You must have had some on your cheeks, and he wanted to lick them clean. He doesn't eat kids. He loves them.

"But I do have a question, and we need to have a straight answer—no hedging. One of you had a bowel movement right next to a large tree and cleaned yourself with the green leaves at the base of the tree. Which one of you was it?"

"Me," Damey said. "I couldn't help it. I couldn't hold it any longer. I'll come out tomorrow with a shovel and take care of it, but right now I itch really bad. I've got to take a shower or something."

"No, burying it's not the problem. You wiped with poison ivy. Either your mom or grandpa will have to take you to a Redi-Care tonight and get your little problem taken care of before it gets any worse. Good luck.

CHAPTER 7

Modesty in a medical facility is like using a four letter expletive in church—verboten. Shaundra told the lady at the desk what happened as Bill talked to Damey, trying to keep his mind off the problem. Fortunately, the place had no other patients, so a nurse took the three of them back to a room immediately.

"Strip completely and put on this sexy hospital gown. Then sit down right up here," the nurse said patting the center of the hospital-style examining table that she'd covered with a roll of paper.

As he squirmed, crinkling the paper on the table, Damey complained, "Mom, it's cold in here. Can't you at least tie up the back? What if someone comes in?"

"It's a waste of time, Honey. Besides, nobody will come in unless they're a doctor or nurse. When the doctor does comes in, he or she is going to want that side of you wide open anyway. And you should probably try to quit wiggling. You can't be doing yourself any good."

"But it itches so bad." Damey braced himself with both hands on the bed and scooched back and forth trying to scratch it.

"Damey, nine times eight—quickly," Bill barked trying to distract hm.

They worked on multiplication tables and other math games for fifteen minutes or so until another lady walked in. For all Damey knew, it could be the janitor. He tried to wrap the gown around his backside.

"Hi, honey. I'm Dr. Sarah Perkins. I understand you've got a little problem. Want to tell me about it?"

"My buddy and I got lost in the woods, and I had to go to the bathroom. I didn't have any toilet paper, so I used leaves. I guess they were poison ivy 'cause they itch and sting like crazy. My right hand and hind end are driving me nuts."

"Okay, I need you to roll over on your belly and try to center yourself right in the middle of the bed where that crease is."

He lined himself up the best he could. As he settled, she told him to hold on to the sides of the bed while she arranged things. Then she pushed a button, and the middle of the thing started to rise turning his body into an upside down V. Then she lowered the examining table so his raised butt was below eye level. "Snap" went the latex gloves as she slipped them on making him jump.

Mortified almost to tears, Damey originally thought she'd just listen to his story, give him some pills or anti-itch cream, and send him home. He had no idea this would happen. Frowning, he grit his teeth and scratched his hand on the side of the bed.

"Mom, Grandpa, come take a look at this. We've got one heck of a mess," she said as she spread his cheeks apart for the whole world to see.

Mom and Grandpa had sat down at the head of the bed facing him, so they wouldn't embarrass him any more than necessary. They knew what was coming. Following the doctor's dictates, they stood up, walked over, and took a look. The entire infected area was already blistered and raw. Shaundra gasped, and Bill winced and shuddered a bit. Looking at the damage made them both feel half nauseous.

"Damey, you stay right there and don't move. I've got to get a couple of things and will be right back," the doctor said as she pulled off her gloves, tossed them in the trash, and sped out the door without another word leaving him completely uncovered with his bottom aimed at the ceiling.

He lay there in all his glory hoping and praying nobody else would come along and look at him. Mostly he feared one of his classmates would walk into the room with a broken finger or something and occupy the bed next to his on the other side of the curtain. He'd die of mortification. *What if it was a girl?*

Five minutes later Dr. Perkins returned with several boxes and a nurse. "Which one of you is going to be medicating him at home?"

"Probably both of us," Bill answered.

She slipped on another pair of latex gloves and said, "At his age I don't want to give him oral antibiotics if I don't have to. If this gets infected, that's another story. However, he's going to need three treatments a day for a week, and then you can cut down to two until the blistering and discomfort are gone—probably another two weeks. So, watch what I do and repeat it morning, noon, and night. In about one week he needs to visit your family doctor to see how he's healing. If he can't get you in, come back here"

As the nurse put on her gloves, and they arranged their supplies, Dr. Perkins explained what they were going to have to do and why. "I know it's embarrassing, but at home you need to get yourself in this position. Strip from the waist down and prop yourself on your hands and knees, drop your head down and leave your bottom up with your legs spread apart.

"Another way," she said winking at Shaundra and Bill where Damey couldn't see her, "is for Mom or Grandpa to sit down in a chair and have you lie down over their knees with your bottom sticking straight up.

You've probably been in that position often enough so it might feel more natural to you."

Damey turned his head to the side and down as he peered up at her out of the corner of his eye with a scowl. She laughed out loud along with his mom and grandpa. In no mood for jokes, he didn't think her option of his getting into a little boy spanking position was one bit funny.

Then the nurse spread him apart even wider, as the doctor demonstrated the procedure. She started by washing the entire area with a special soapy like substance that was a bit gritty. Then she rinsed, patted dry, and applied an antibiotic anti-itch cream. Then she had Damey get up, stand in front of the sink, as she showed him how to wash and treat his own hands. They'd have to be done three times a day as well, but, at least, he could take care of them.

Before they left, she supplied them with enough medications to last a day or two until they could get to the drugstore. She also gave Damey an extra tube of the anti-itch cream to keep in his pocket so he could apply it to himself after each bowel movement. She also gave him a written doctor's excuse to miss school for the next week.

On the way home, Bill swung through a drive-through restaurant, but it was a waste of time. Damey fell asleep before he finished his burger and fries.

Saturday and Sunday, Shaundra had a nursing internship requiring her to be at the hospital for twelve hours each day. The plan had originally been for Damey to go over to Grandpa's after breakfast on Saturday morning and spend the weekend with him. Instead, he dropped Shaundra off, and took Damey to his house and put him right to bed. He could get his shower in the morning.

At seven-thirty, Grandpa woke him up. "Go take your shower, young un. Wash *everything* real good with soap and water and be sure to rinse completely. The better you do, the less I'll have to. When you get out and are all dried off, don't get dressed, but put on this robe, tie it up in front, and call me."

Grandpa arranged the latex gloves and all the medications on the dresser so they'd be ready before going back downstairs to the living room. When Damey called, Grandpa had him get in the position the nurse had suggested sideways on the bed. Then, he lifted the robe, cleaned and medicated the affected area, dropped the robe, patted him on the shoulder a couple of times, and told him get up.

"Wash and medicate your hands before you get dressed." Then he walked out of the room. Bill did everything possible to protect the boy's privacy and dignity.

Alex showed up around ten wanting to hear all the gory details. He and Damey went down to the family room while Damey told him everything, pacing the floor as he talked. He couldn't sit except for short periods of time. They still managed to laugh, carry on, and make a lot of noise. Bill smiled. It sounded good that maybe he was able to get his mind off his troubles. Alex could do that.

After lunch, Grandpa said, "Alex, why don't you go down to the office and play some computer games while I treat Damey's blisters?"

"You mean I can't watch?"

"No!" Damey yelled. "Quit laughing. It's not funny. Grandpa, he's sick. Haven't you got a baby thermometer around here so you can take his temperature?"

"Okay you two, knock it off. Alejandro, down. Damarian, up!" Grandpa ordered smiling broadly. Both headed to their designated areas laughing.

The rest of the weekend crawled by very slowly. Alex spent the time between breakfast and dinner with Damey. They watched a lot of movies and sports and acted silly. Damey spent the majority of his time lying on his belly on the sofa or pacing. If the itching and burning didn't drive him nuts, nothing ever would.

The next week Grandpa home-schooled Damey to the best of his ability. Obviously, Damey missed out on all the lectures, labs, and class work. However, Alex brought his homework assignments to the house every afternoon, and that gave Grandpa something to work with.

In his spare time, Damey even finished the book they were working on in English class, so he started

"Flash the Humble Hero" by Lee Carey, a story that had a couple of talking dogs. Lots of fun.

As usual, Grandpa made Alex and Damey teach him as well as each other the pre-algebra assignments. He thoroughly frustrated both of them with his inability to comprehend until they'd explained everything at least three different ways.

• • •

After returning to the redi-care on Friday, a doctor cleared Damey to return to school. He looked forward to Monday with fear and relief. The discomfort had eased quite a bit, and he could sit for at least an hour at a time, but he knew he'd be the butt of a whole lot of jokes.

Right on cue, Liam, the dude repeating seventh-grade math, started hassling as the tardy bell rang. "Hey, Damey! Aren't you supposed to be in the girl's gym classes every hour today demonstrating the proper care and treatment of poison ivy?"

Nervous laughter broke out here and there around the room, but most everyone looked at Damey to see how he'd react. He didn't disappoint them.

With a flushed face, he fired back, "Listen up, asshole," as he tapped the palm of his left hand with the middle finger of his right. "Can you hear it, or should I turn it up?" Then he did with extra emphasis.

"Hold it right there!" Mr. Allen yelled at them as he walked into the room. There will be zero bullying in this class. Is that understood, Liam? And, you, Damarian, do not retaliate by swearing. Do you understand? Ignore people when they're making fools out of themselves."

Damey nodded his head, yes, and Liam tried to defend himself. "I wasn't bullying him. He's my friend. I was just joking. I didn't mean anything by it."

"You're not *my* friend," Damey mumbled under his breath hoping Mr. Allen didn't hear him, but he did.

Mr. Allen raised his voice for the first time all year. "When someone is hurting or in pain, you don't make jokes," he snarled. "Don't you think Damey's embarrassed enough knowing the whole school is aware of what happened to him? That's bullying, and it's unacceptable."

His anger startled the class into complete silence. Then Liam broke it as he turned to face Damey, "I'm sorry. I was trying to be funny, not hurt your feelings."

Damey nodded. Staring at Liam, he could see the slight smirk on his face. Mr. Allen started class.

After the dismissal bell, Damey walked up to his teacher as Alex waited by the door. "I'm sorry. I shouldn't have sworn at him."

"That's over and done with. Now, I want to know how you're doing. Glad you were able to sit all hour. I hoped that'd be the case. If you had to get up and stand in the back, it would have called more attention to your problem."

"Me too. I was scared I wouldn't be able to make it, but I got interested in what you were doing and kind of forgot about it."

"Now, about all your classwork from last week. Between Alex and your grandpa, they must have gotten the concepts across. All of your assignments were perfect—just like always."

Alex, hearing his name mentioned, joined them. "Trying to get it through Damey's grandpa's thick skull is horrible. I don't know how you teachers do it with the dumb kids like Liam."

Mr. Allen smiled and looked over at Damey, "I thought your grandpa was a teacher."

"He was. He taught English and history, but when it comes to math, he's very slow. We have to explain everything to him two or three times and in different ways in order to get it to sink in. He drives us nuts."

Laughing, Mr. Allen looked at the clock. They'd be late to their next class, so he wrote them a pass and shooed them out the door.

CHAPTER 8

As usual, weekends ended up as family days. Grandpa stayed home, and a slew of his kids, grandkids, and great-grandkids almost always showed up at various times to visit. The scenario seldom changed.

"Where's Damey?" Sean asked the moment he walked in the door.

"Doesn't your *favorite* great-grandfather at least get a hug before you run off to play?"

"Yes, but that's 'cause, you're my only great-grandpa. So there!" Sean laughed. After dutifully hugging Grandpa, he asked again. "So where is Damey? Why isn't he here? Is he with Alex someplace?"

"I really don't know if he's home or not. Why don't you call over to his house and find out?"

"What's his cell phone number? I'll text him."

"He doesn't have his own cell phone. He's not thirteen yet—the official age for cell phone ownership."

"*Grandpa!*"

"Don't *Grandpa* me in that tone of voice. Just 'cause you're a spoiled brat and talked your parents into buying you one doesn't mean everyone has." He laughed and messed up Sean's hair.

"*Grandpa!*"

"Just call his house. If his mom answers, believe it or not, she doesn't bite. Speaking of biting, he'll be here at six for dinner even if you don't find him. His mom's got a date tonight so I'm babysitting him. And, make sure you tell him what I said when you find him. He hates it when I use that 'babysitting' word."

"Oh, yeah. Bet he really loves that. Anyway, that's three hours away—way too long to wait. I'll call and find out where he is."

Sean walked into the kitchen to call so the adults wouldn't disturb him. Nothing like a bunch of yakking going on in the background when you're trying to concentrate on an important phone call. After hanging up, he moseyed back into the living room.

"He and Alex are over to the park. Can I ride your bike over? All you gots to do is tell me how to get there."

"No, you'd probably get lost. I'd better take you. We'll have to put the bike on the rack and throw the helmet in the trunk so you can get home—unless, of course, you want to run alongside them while they ride their bikes."

"Is it the same park we always went to?" Andy, Bill's grandson, asked. "Wouldn't it be easier to throw it in the back of my Suburban than to hook it up on the back of your dinky little ATS—especially since I've got you blocked in and would have to move it anyway?"

So they did. When the three of them arrived at the park, eleven boys were scrambling furiously on the wet and muddy grass trying to recover a fumbled football. It had rained all of the previous night, and more was on the way. After locking up the bike, Bill and Andy watched for a minute to see how things would play out. There were five on one team, six on the other. Damey saw them and waved.

"You're on Alex's team, Sean. That'll even up the sides."

On the first play from scrimmage, Alex wobbled a pass to Sean who at first bobbled and then secured it, before running into the end zone. They played on about a forty-yard field. After watching a couple of minutes, Grandpa and Andy decided they could go back home and leave the kids to themselves.

At six o'clock, the boys rode up the street, right on time. Alex continued towards home for dinner, as Sean and Damey walked into the kitchen through the garage door.

"Stop where you are!" Marge, Sean's mother, barked. "Don't move. Take off your shoes. You're both filthy and sweaty. Dinner's ready, but neither of you is eating until you've had a shower and changed clothes. Now move it."

They probably set a record showering and changing out of their wet, grubby, grass-stained clothes. Sean put on some of Damey's clothes promising they'd be returned soon. Not totally happy about it, the adults held up dinner for a couple of extra minutes so the kids could join them.

As everyone cleaned up the table after dinner, lightning flashed and cracked close enough to make all of them jump. Then they heard the wailing of the tornado warning.

Grandpa grabbed the remote. "Better turn on the TV and see what's going on,"

Sure enough, the whole area had been declared a tornado watch until ten o'clock that evening. As they read the 'watch' bulletin, the local forecaster broke in with the news that one had been sighted on the ground about ten miles to the south headed east.

"Whoa," Andy said. If the kids hadn't held up dinner fifteen minutes, we'd be right where that tornado is passing now." He took a deep breath and looked out the window.

Their original plans had them leaving right after dinner. They lived about forty minutes to the south.

"Why don't you just stay here tonight? I've plenty of room. You and Marge can have the guest room and the boys can either sleep together in Damey's bed, or one can sleep on the sofa downstairs."

"I like that idea," Marge said. "I'm scared to death of thunder storms, and tornadoes take my panic level to a whole new level. If this thing doesn't ease up, I'm sleeping in the crawl space under the house."

As evening progressed, the storm abated. However, the watch continued until ten as originally forecast even though the warning had expired earlier.

The evening turned out to be fun for all. Alex called after dinner to see if he could come down. Naturally, they told him yes, so his dad drove him. Freshly showered and changed himself, he didn't want to get drenched riding his bike. As soon as he got there, the three boys disappeared down the steps to the Wii game connected to the television in the family room as the adults talked and gossiped about the rest of the relatives on the main floor. During the course of the evening, the older generations might have set a new family record. They only yelled at the kids three times to keep their volume down—which was somewhat ignored anyway. The boys still whooped it up and laughed rather obnoxiously when one bested the other.

Right on cue at 8:45, Mr. Veras pulled into the driveway and waited. Grandpa yelled at Alex to let him know. He trotted up the steps, slipped on his poncho, yelled his goodbyes to everyone, and raced out the door on a dead run. The heavy rain hadn't let up, but at least the lightning had.

"Ok, boys," Grandpa said. "What's it going to be? Do you want to sleep together in Damey's bed, or would one of you prefer to sleep on the sofa downstairs? It's getting to be that time."

"Why can't we both sleep in the bed?" Sean asked. "That sofa wouldn't be very comfortable. There's that big dip between the cushions."

"Grandpa, there's all kinds of room. It's plenty big enough for both of us," Damey added.

The two of them looked at each other with that, "Duh!" expression and shrugged their shoulders. Adults could be so stupid at times. Why wouldn't they sleep together?

"Damey, show Sean the stash of extra tooth brushes, and…"

"I know," he interrupted. "Floss, brush, and rinse." He turned his head and rolled his eyes. Sean snorted trying to keep from laughing.

"Grab Sean your extra pair of pajamas while you're at it, Damey. Sean, throw them down the laundry chute after you get dressed tomorrow morning."

After going through their pre-bed routine, they crawled in. Neither one felt the least bit sleepy. They'd been having too much fun and were still excited.

"I saw you've got "Call of Duty: Black Ops" on the Wii. You ever play that one?" Sean asked. "My dad won't let me have it."

"I can't either. Grandpa says it's just for adults. None of the great-grandkids can play it. He claims there's too much bad language and violence. I tried to convince him that it probably doesn't have one word on there that I haven't heard before."

"Or used," Sean laughed.

"Yeah, that too, but I didn't mention it. I did tell him that shooting people and blowing them up was all make-believe and didn't mean anything. Just 'cause I wanna play the game isn't going to turn me into some deranged killer."

"What'd he say to that?"

"He said I was deranged enough without it. The game's still a 'No.'"

"Quiet down up there and go to sleep. It's getting late," Andy yelled from the living room.

"Let's pull the covers over our heads so we can talk. Then they can't hear us," Sean said. "I really want to try that game, but I don't think we're gonna get a chance to sneak it in. Going home right after breakfast."

Damey thought for a minute, "We could wait until they're all asleep, slip down, and check it out. No lights, no volume, they'll never know."

The more they talked about it, the more excited they got. Before long, they tossed the covers back because it

93

started getting hot and stuffy under there, but that didn't dampen their spirits.

At ten, Andy walked over to the steps and yelled again. "If I have to tell you two to be quiet and go to sleep and quit giggling like a couple of little girls one more time, I'm coming up there."

Like flipping the switch on the riding mower, the upstairs turned instantaneously quiet. "Shhh. We don't want that," Sean whispered. "Dad takes no prisoners when he's mad. We've got to keep quiet."

"How we gonna stay awake if we can't talk?" Damey whispered.

"We'll just keep each other awake. If you doze off, I'll jab you in the ribs. If I do, you do the same. This is gonna be our only chance. We gots to do this."

And that's what they did. Using their pillows to muffle any sounds, they managed to keep each other awake by jabbing, poking, and prodding.

After the news at 11:30, the old folks decided it might be time for them to follow suit. "Quick," Damey said. "They just turned off the TV. Roll over on your side and pretend you're asleep. They'll never know the difference."

With the hall light on, Grandpa and Marge sneaked in and checked on them. Both were lying on their sides, seemingly sound asleep.

"Aren't they precious?" Marge commented. "Almost cherubic."

Grandpa watched Damey's breathing pattern before answering. "Precious I'll go along with, but cherubic? Not so sure about that."

After all the adults finished their own nightly duties of flossing, brushing, and rinsing, etc., they dispersed to their own rooms, closed the doors, and went to bed. Grandpa lay on his back and listened. He knew Damey wasn't asleep. Wondered what they were up to. Almost ready to doze off himself, he heard the bed squeak across the hall. He waited. Maybe one of them had to use the bathroom. He'd listen to see if the toilet flushed or the bed squeaked again as someone crawled back in.

Fifteen minutes later Grandpa eased out of bed, slipped open his door as quietly as possible, and walked softly to the stairs. No lights anywhere except for the flashing of the TV down in the family room. Moving as stealthily as he could, the kids never saw him until he stood in front of the screen, arms folded and staring at them.

"Grandpa, Grandpa," they both exclaimed simultaneously before spouting every excuse they could come up with in the five seconds he gave them.

"Shut-your-mouths-now!" Grandpa snapped. "Not only were you faking sleep, but you sneaked out of bed and came down here to play the Wii in the middle of the night. To make things worse, you're playing the game that you both know is off limits. That game is for your parents, not you. You have your own games. You have exactly five minutes to get into bed and be sound

95

asleep. If I hear *one* word out of either of you, I guarantee, *both* of you will sleep on your bellies tonight. Go!"

The next morning Sean and his parents headed out after breakfast without a word being mentioned about the previous night.

Damey couldn't stand the suspense any longer. "Grandpa, how did you know? We never made a sound when we sneaked out of bed and went downstairs. We even had the volume turned off on the TV. You couldn't have heard it, and neither one of us said a thing out loud—I don't think."

"When you're asleep, you breathe slowly and deeply almost purring like a kitten. When Marge and I checked in on you, you were breathing like you do when you're nervous or in trouble, like right now. I knew you were faking, so I lay awake and waited to see what you two were up to. I guess I found out."

"Grandpa, I'm sorry. It'll never happen again," he stammered, worried about what his punishment would be.

"Promise?"

"Yes."

"Well, then. I guess you'd better go check up on Alex and see what he's up to this morning. Looks like it's a beautiful day out there."

CHAPTER 9

D amey felt nervous about parent-teacher conferences. He knew his grades would be okay, but had no clue what his teachers might say when sitting across the table from his mom and grandpa. He didn't want to go, but Grandpa thought he should. Mom really didn't care one way or the other, so she let him choose. Damey stayed home where he could sweat it out in peace.

He tried to concentrate on homework, but couldn't get anything done. All he could think about were all the negative things that had happened since school started? Would Mr. Allen rat on him for swearing in math class? His brain wouldn't turn off. Will Mom and Grandpa yell at him because he doesn't have all As? Grandpa kept telling him that with his brains and ability to learn, anything below an A was unacceptable. Did Grandpa realize how hard he had to work? Just because school was easier than it's ever been in his life, doesn't mean anything. Grandpa's was a lot harder on him than his mom or teachers. Bullshit! He had to quit worrying about it. His brain hurt.

The custodians had set up tables in the gymnasium with ample spacing so teachers and parents could converse without their discussions being overheard by others. Bill and Shaundra walked into the gym and looked around. They were early. A handful of kids accompanied their families, but most of the parents showed up by themselves.

At the entranceway into the gym, they spotted a table set up so participants could get printed copies of each student's report card. They walked over and picked up Damey's. People could check their kid's grades on quizzes, tests, homework, etc. on line, but it was good to get personalized feedback from the teacher as well. According to Grandpa, kids act differently at home than they do at school. Also, the online version didn't show citizenship grades. Those ranged from 1, meaning excellent to 3, meaning needs improvement.

Shaundra didn't have a computer with Internet at home. She knew she had the ability to check on the computer at work, but hadn't. She'd pretty much turned over that faction of Damey's life to Grandpa. He checked every day, and knew exactly what grades to expect. The printed copy agreed. Damey had three A's and three B's along with three 1's and three 2's.

While looking at the printout, Shaundra choked up a little. "Bill, you're a miracle worker." she wiped her eyes. "I've never seen anything that resembles this on one of Damey's report cards. Teachers have always told me he is smart and capable, but never applies himself. I never expected anything like this. In fact, I hoped for C's."

"Shaundra, he's very bright, and he gets all the credit. He worked his tail off all summer catching up, and has continued during this first semester. Believe it or not, he's actually beginning to enjoy learning, thinking, problem-solving, and looking at things in different ways.

"Why don't we start with first hour and move through his day? His math teacher, is number one on the agenda," Bill said.

They looked around until they spotted Mr. Allen's table. He had one set of parents talking to him already, but nobody waiting in line. They sat in a couple of chairs behind the tape on the floor and waited.

When their turn arrived, they walked up and introduced themselves. "Mr. Allen, I'm Shaundra Martin, Damey's mom, and this is our neighbor, Mr. Bill Berkley."

"Glad to meet you, but I'm a little surprised. I half expected Grandpa Tutor to be with you. Please sit down."

Bill and Shaundra both laughed.

"Guilty as charged," Bill said with a smirk on his face. "Damey calls me Grandpa to my face, but refers to me as Grandpa Tutor to everyone else. He calls me that because I've been tutoring him since last June."

"You're not his biological grandfather then?"

"Nope, it's more psychological than biological. I'm his grandpa, he's my grandson, and we let it go at that."

"You've got to tell me your system. He's made amazing progress. You're a retired English teacher, right?"

"Sure am. Fought the good fight for thirty-five years. I've been lucky. Damey's very smart and has caught on because he's willing to work hard. That's the system."

Shaundra wouldn't let Bill brush off the credit for Damey's newly found success. "First off, he absolutely loves Bill to pieces. But, I don't know how he's done it either, because this marking period's results shocked me. Have you seen last year's grades?"

"Yes, Ms. Martin. We check all transfer student's records. Last year he received a D- in math, and right now he's almost 100 percent. He missed a couple of problems on quizzes at the beginning, but since then he's been perfect."

Mr. Allen got this big smile on his face. "I hate to rat out on Damey, especially since he's not here to defend himself, but I will. All I hear out of him and Alex, who also does very well, is, 'When it comes to math, Grandpa is so *slow*.' Then I have to watch the eye-rolls before they whine and complain that they have to teach and explain each and every problem at least three different ways before you figure it out."

Mr. Allen laughed again. "Then I hear about how Grandpa claims a person's never too old to learn, so he's bound and determined that they're going to teach him this pre-algebra they're studying. Now, believe me. I *know* there's more to this story than what I'm hearing."

Shaundra listened with a huge grin on her face. "You have no idea how many times he's come home after a session whining that his brain hurts. Grandpa makes him think too much."

"Has Damey ever told you that I have him go to the board and explain certain problems the other kids are having trouble with? I tell him to do it like he would to Grandpa Tutor, and the kids all understand it. He uses all these different analogies I'd never think of, and the other kids get the point. One day he used the flashing light on his bike reflector to explain one problem. It had to do with ratios and how fast he had to pedal to get a prescribed number of flashes. I use him a lot," he laughed again, reddening a bit.

"I didn't know about that. Did you, Shaundra?" Bill asked somewhat puzzled.

"No, but I'm not really surprised. He rarely brags about anything he does—good or bad. How did that start?"

"One day when I struggled getting across a point to the majority of the class, Alex piped up and said, 'Have Damey explain it like he would to Grandpa Tutor.' So I did and have been using him ever since."

Bill smiled. "If I tell the two of you a secret, will you keep it from Damey?"

Both nodded in agreement sharing a furtive smile.

"Back in prehistoric days, if one had a degree and a teaching certificate from the State of Michigan, he or she could teach anything in middle school. I earned my BA in math. I taught pre-algebra my first two or three years. Then, one day the principal asked if I would be willing to teach an English class the next year. I said sure. I loved it, loved the challenge. Within three years they had me teaching all English. By the time I transferred to the high school, they had changed the law saying you had to have a degree in whatever you taught. The law grandfathered me in, because I'd been teaching it so many years."

"No kidding!" Mr. Allen exclaimed. "You were a math major in college, and you're making these kids *teach* you the pre-algebra you actually taught? That's a riot. I love it."

"Yeah, but don't tell them," Bill said as he motioned to zip his lips. "They'd crucify me. But, you know how it works. One learns something much more thoroughly when he teaches it. That's why they both know it so well."

Teaching Grandpa math had been a scam. The three of them had a great laugh.

"Oh, we won't tell him," Shaundra said. "You know the old cliché, *what you don't know can't hurt you.*"

Then she looked at Bill, "I hope you don't think I'm too nosey for asking, but why did you transfer from middle school to high school? You connect so well with that age group—at least you do with Damey and Alex."

"It was a combination of things. Part of it was mid-life crisis, and I wanted a change. The other piece happened to be a new principal at the high school. He wanted to bring in hard-core grouches like me who would make the kids toe the line and still teach them something in the process."

The rest of the conferences went just about the same. Each one brought out new information, and secrets were traded. They had been almost the first to arrive that night and practically the last to leave. Bill had to explain his techniques to every one of Damey's teachers who had looked at last year's grades as well.

Damey only received one comment that could be considered negative. When they got to his science teacher, Mr. Kerley, Bill asked. "I'm okay with the B, but why a 2 in citizenship?"

"Not sure exactly how to explain this, but sometimes Damey pushes things too far. He would be much happier if it were just he and I in the class. When we're having a question and answer period, he raises his hand each and every time. I can only call on him so many times during the course of the hour. He gets frustrated, and then I get the big sigh, the pout, and the mumbling under the breath."

"I understand exactly what you're saying. I get that same thing between him and Alex and they're the only ones there." Bill said.

Kerley spoke up. "How many times have I heard, 'Not fair. It's *my* science class too. I gots to know this stuff for high school and college. You ignore me most of the time.' I told him one time he was going to trip over his bottom lip. Everyone in the class thought it was funny except him. He pouted the rest of the hour."

"That sounds like my Damey," Shaundra laughed. "He loves positive attention and hates the negative."

Smiling, Mr. Kerley asked, "I've reminded him numerous times we have twenty-six kids in this class, and all have to get equal opportunities."

The last teacher they visited was Mr. Tyrone Williams, Damey's gym teacher. Shaundra introduced herself and Bill, Mr. Williams said, "Ah, my little Damey's mom. Man, I like that kid. He's gotta be the nicest little guy in this school."

Shaundra sat a little straighter and puffed out her chest. She loved hearing all the compliments about her son.

Walking out of the gym, Grandpa said, "I felt like excess baggage on that last conference. You and Williams make a date to meet for dinner over the weekend so you can tell him all about Damey's past, and I sit there twiddling my thumbs feeling like a snoop."

Shaundra laughed. "I didn't know Damey had a black gym teacher. He sure is a good looking dude."

"Damey's oblivious to race. Look at all his friends. I do know, however, Damey really likes this guy. He told me in gym class Williams was teaching them wrestling moves and has used him as one of his demonstrators. I found it a little interesting since Damey's never been on a wrestling mat in his life, but then, probably none of the other seventh graders have either."

"That's true. But it probably seems natural to Damey because his other teachers do it as well. Like Mr. Allen said, he makes Damey demonstrate math problems all the time."

Bill walked into the house with Shaundra. They planned to share the evening's report with Damey. However, they found him spread out on the sofa, sound asleep. His homework lay on the floor beside him untouched. That was okay, because he had study hall in the morning. Mom sat down beside him, waking him.

She lifted him up, pulling him into a hug. "I love you, baby, but it's late and you've got to get to bed. You've got school tomorrow."

He noticed Grandpa and Mom both smiling at him, Damey beamed. Their expressions told him conferences went well. He could quit worrying. Time for bed.

CHAPTER 10

That weekend, Shaundra and Tyrone met for dinner and drinks so they could re-hash Damey's life. It's a sound educational practice to get to know one's students as well as possible. They talked about Damey at least 20 minutes during their private three-hour parent-teacher conference.

Unbeknownst to Damey, Tyrone and Shaundra started meeting most Tuesday and Thursday nights after her class. At first, it was just for fun. Shaundra hadn't dated anyone in a long time and wanted to enjoy herself. She saw no reason to tell Damey. She didn't want to give him any wild ideas. He talked about *Mr. Williams* all the time. Breaking Damey's heart over a fun relationship, which she assumed would never go anywhere, would be the last thing she wanted.

After three weeks of regular dating, she had to talk to Bill. She called. "The kid's asleep. Any chance you can come over? I need to run something by you."

"What about? Anything I can wrap my mind around between my door and yours?"

"Tyrone."

"Surprise, surprise," Bill smiled. "I'll be right there." He knew they were dating, but didn't know how serious things were. Apparently he was about to find out. He slipped on his light jacket and walked out.

Shaundra waited by the door and opened it as he walked up the steps. "Hi, Bill. Glad you could come over. Coffee's almost done."

They went into the kitchen and Bill sat on one of the barstools at the counter while Shaundra grabbed the cups. Sound didn't carry from there to Damey's bedroom like it did from the living room.

"You haven't told him yet, have you?" said Bill.

"No, and I don't know when or if I should. That's why I wanted to talk. If he knew about our relationship, and then nothing came of it, it would crush him. He practically worships the guy. Every day I get a replay of gym class. You can only imagine how much I've always wanted to know about the differences between single-leg takedowns and arm-drags."

"I know. I get the same play-by-play. You realize, don't you, Damey will want to go out for wrestling when the season starts?"

"Oh, I suppose. Then I'll get to hear that much more about Mr. Williams this and Mr. Williams that."

"That's another reason. Before your relationship gets much more involved, don't you think Damey should know?" How would it go over if you two were out to dinner some place and one of his buddies like Alex spotted you? Would you want that to happen?"

"No, that's why I always drive downtown and park by the bank when we date. Tyrone cruises up, I jump in, and we head out of town. We never eat in Lansing."

"I still think you should tell him, even if it isn't totally serious at this point. How many times have you heard that we're the only two adults in the world he really trusts? I'd hate to jeopardize that."

"Okay, I'll tell him in the morning. Expect a visitor before noon."

"I'll be looking forward to it," Bill said as he stood up and walked to the sink to rinse out his cup. "I'll pretend to be totally ignorant about the two of you and then sit back and enjoy watching the pre-pubescent adrenalin ooze out of his pores."

• • •

"Grandpa, Grandpa, guess what!" Damey yelled as he charged through the front door about ten the next morning.

"I know. The leaves need raking again. How much ya gonna charge me this time?"

"What? I never charge you nothin'. You know that. 'Sides, that ain't why I'm here. Gotta tell ya somthin'"

"Don't say 'ain't,' and here I thought you were about to con me out of a whole pile of money just to rake my leaves. Thank goodness. So, what're you all wound up about this fine morning?"

"Mom and Mr. Williams are dating. Not serious, not going steady, just friends. Just having a good time. He's comin' over this afternoon and the three of us are going out to lunch. How cool is that?"

"Sounds like fun. Probably I should go along to make sure everybody behaves themselves. Wouldn't want them sneaking kisses in the restaurant or anything. That'd be embarrassing."

"Grandpa! They wouldn't do that."

"Oh, okay. I guess I'll have to leave you in charge then. You'll probably have to sit between them to make sure they behave."

Damey laughed. "Yeah, right. I can just see myself as the enforcer—keeping mom and Mr. Williams from making fools out of themselves."

110

• • •

That afternoon, right at one p.m., Tyrone pulled into the driveway. Damey opened the front door for him with a wide, open mouthed grin exposing nearly every tooth in his head. "Hi, Mr. Williams. Come on in. Mom's almost ready."

Tyrone walked in, put his arm around Damey's shoulder, and gave him a little hug. "So, how are you doing, big guy?"

"Fine, Mr. Williams. Fine."

Shaundra walked in. She and Tyrone hugged and shared a quick peck on the lips.

"Before we leave, I want to discuss something with Damey," Tyrone said looking serious. "It'll just take a second. Damey, you know what my first name is, don't you?"

"Ah, yeah. Tyrone."

"Okay, let's cut a deal. When we're in school, you have to call me Mr. Williams. When we're out and about, like now, it's Tyrone or Ty. Sound fair?"

"Sure. Sounds good to me."

"You okay with that, Shaundra?

She nodded and smiled at the same time.

Later at lunch, Tyrone looked at Damey and said, "You know, wrestling starts the second week of

November. You're too darned short for basketball so you're going out for wrestling."

"I am?"

"Yep. What do you weigh? Do you know?"

"According to our scales, I'm about 72 pounds when I get out of the shower."

"Perfect. We have a 74 pound weight class in middle school, and that leaves you some growing room. The next weight down is 67 pounds, but I won't let you cut weight so that's perfect."

"What days are your meets on?" Shaundra asked.

"Tuesday and Thursdays, which makes it hard for you, but I'll be able to tell you all about them so you won't really miss much. I'll have someone video Damey's matches on a cell phone and send them to you."

That settled it. .

The rest of lunch consisted of mostly friendly banter. Tyrone liked to pick on Damey, and Damey loved the attention.

CHAPTER 11

A bout a week before Thanksgiving, Bill called Shaundra asking what they were doing for dinner on the big day.

She told him she planned to get one of those pre-cooked chickens and a pumpkin pie from super market and go from there. Since it'd be just the two of them and Tyrone, they didn't plan to make it a big deal or anything. They'd have a nice meal and watch the parade and football game on TV. That's about it.

Then Bill told her he'd like to have the three of them come over for dinner. His whole family would be there. It'd be as boisterous as it gets, but it always turned out to be a lot of fun—especially if the Lions happen to win their game for a change.

Damey sat across the room listening intently as he tried to decipher the conversation. "Oh, Bill, we can't crash your party like that," his mom said. "I haven't even met most of your family. I know most of your older great-grandsons because of Damey. Don't know many of the adults."

Bill told her that it was time she did. She'd fit right in. "Besides," he groaned, "can you imagine the guff I'd have to put up with from the 'greats' if the three of you didn't come? When they visit, I'm lucky to get a 'Hi, Grandpa' and a hug before they start asking for Damey. I think they forget the brat doesn't live here."

"Sometimes, it seems like he does." Shaundra laughed, and then asked, "What can I bring and what time?"

He paused for a minute, raising his eyebrows, trying to think of something they could actually use, and then said. "Grab a pound or two of that cranberry sauce from the deli and call it good. I cook the turkey and dressing, and then all the daughters-in-law and granddaughters-in-law insist on bringing everything else, each trying to out-do the others.

"There's always so much food around, you could feed half the town. Then, they insist on leaving me most of their leftovers, so I end up having Thanksgiving for a week. After a while, enough is enough." He hated to have to throw out food. This year, anything extra could be pawned off on Shaundra. Damey was a human garbage disposal. That kid would polish off the leftovers.

Bill then went on and explained that they usually plan on dinner around two, so everyone shows up between twelve-thirty and one to catch up on all the gossip before they eat. All the males of the clan end up in the living room screaming at the TV, and the women hide in the kitchen complaining about the racket. After the game, the kids disappear either downstairs or outdoors depending on the weather.

Also, he told her, she could almost set her watch by it. Two hours after dinner, the boys would all magically reappear wanting another piece of pie, while the women all groan because of their own bloated conditions.

"It sounds like fun. Are you sure it'll be okay?"

"Definitely. I want all three of you here."

• • •

"Mom, Ty, everybody's there. Let's go. Grandpa said twelve-thirty."

"He said twelve-thirty to one, and it's not even twelve-thirty yet."

"It's close enough. I've already seen Sean, Adam, and Marty. The others are probably almost here. Come on!"

"Okay, let me get the cranberries out of the fridge. I still think we should wait a little."

With Shaundra and Tyrone's nervousness showing on their faces and Damey's bouncing all over the place unable to contain his excitement, the trio made their way across the street. Damey wanted to carry the cranberries. Shaundra prayed he wouldn't drop them.

Watching the two of them made Ty smile. Walking up the sidewalk, he could feel her trembling body against his as he draped his arm around her waist. He didn't feel much better. He'd never met any of the family except for Bill.

Grandpa held the door for them as they entered. He shook Ty's hand and hugged Shaundra. He'd get his hug from Damey after he set down the bowl.

Damey carried the cranberries into the kitchen, set them down. One of the aunts threw her arm over his shoulder and squeezed. "It's about time you got here. Those monsters downstairs are driving us nuts. They came up about ten minutes ago bound and determined they were going over to get you. We almost had to hogtie them. Get down there and let them know you're here," she said patting him on the back. Then she shooed him towards the steps. He headed that way, but not before he and Grandpa got in their hug.

The ladies pulled Shaundra into their circle. Those who hadn't met her introduced themselves with genuine smiles making her feel welcome. She relaxed quickly.

The deafening din in the background helped. Everyone was enjoying themselves.

Same thing happened with Ty and the men of the family. Within minutes he'd plopped in front of the TV with the rest of them cheering on the annual lost cause.

"Notice how the noise level cranked up downstairs when favorite cousin showed up?" Sean's mom laughed.

Concerned that Damey might be causing problems for the adults, Shaundra said that she'd quiet him down. She apologized for him, saying he let himself get all excited over the day.

The aunt laughed, "No, no, no. It's not his fault. He appears, and the others get all wound up. They're the ones who get noisy, or should I say noisier. Damey's so soft spoken, you'll never hear him over the others. Besides, by now, they're probably busy comparing notes on the latest mischief they've gotten themselves into and didn't get caught at. Wouldn't want to interrupt that session. Sometimes I'd love to be a little mouse in the corner listening in on their conversations—or not."

Shaundra smiled as she listened to the racket downstairs. "Personally, I always thought 'boisterous' should have been spelled with a 'y' instead of an 'i.'"

The ladies nodded and laughed as they scurried around trying to get the table and dinner organized.

Following tradition, they served dinner right at the beginning of half-time. The intertwining odors of turkey, sage dressing, garlic, squash, hot rolls, and

117

everything else wafted through the air causing as many hunger pangs with the adults as it did the kids.

The "Are we ever going to eat?" comment echoed through the house more than once.

Shaundra refilled the crackers, cheese dip, and relish-tray appetizers. "Those boys are sneaky little devils. This stuff hasn't been on the counter twenty minutes."

One of the aunts spoke up, "Poor babies. Torturous stomach deprivation will be the end of them." Then she yelled at a couple of the kids. "Guys, save some of the pre-dinner snacks for the adults. You're going to spoil your appetites."

After eating, everyone helped with cleanup until the women kicked the males out so they'd have room to maneuver. The guys had already declared the football game a lost cause, and it was only the end of the third quarter. Still, they watched it to the bitter end. When the gridiron disaster of a 45-14 point loss finally ceased, the boys went out to the back yard and started their own game.

The ladies had no more that sat down after cleanup detail when the kids trooped back into the kitchen. Adam acted as group spokesman since he was the eldest at thirteen. "Mom, we got to talking about the pie, and all of us had really tiny pieces. That's not fair. Can we have some more, please?"

Before she could even formulate a reasoned response, Grandpa, their protector-in-chief, popped into the kitchen. "That sounds like a good idea. My piece seemed pretty puny too. I think I want some of that chocolate mousse this time."

With the women literally rolling their eyes, Grandpa, sons, grandsons, great-grandsons, and Tyrone all circled the table like a flock of vultures demolishing the leftover pies.

With that agenda item finished, the boys returned to their game as the 'old folks' continued with their news and gossip sessions spread throughout the house.

With daylight fading, everyone pretty much decided to call it a day and get on the road before dark. Marty's mom yelled out the door. "Boys, come in and get washed. Everyone's getting ready to leave."

As soon as she shut the door, Sean yelled out, "One more kick."

"Not towards the house!" Damey yelled waving his arms.

Too late. The best punt of the day toppled end-over-end right at the kitchen window.

"Oh, shit!" said Damey under his breath as he raced towards the house trying to catch it. He leaped as high as he could and the middle finger of his left hand deflected the ball upwards and out of harm's way. However, his shoulders slammed into the window sill causing his head to whiplash into the glass. The collision left a circular shattered indentation.

Damey landed in a heap crushing two late blooming mum plants. He lay on the ground gasping to get his breath back. By the time he'd staggered to his feet and breathed semi-normally again, the back door crashed opened, and the yard filled with Ty and snarling male relatives.

"Grandpa! I did it. My fault. I'll pay for it and help you take it out tomorrow. I'm sorry," Damey cried out talking as fast as he could while rubbing the back of his head, still catching his breath.

None of the other boys said a word.

Grandpa walked over to him and pulled his blood covered hand away from his head. "Turn around and let me take a look at that."

"Grandpa, I'm really sorry. I didn't mean to. I'll fix it."

"Oh, be quiet and stand still so I can look. You're bleeding. We've got to get a cold compress on this and stop the flow. Fortunately, it's not gushing like most head cuts so I doubt if you're going to need stitches."

Tyrone, as a wrestling coach and physical education teacher had basic emergency medical training and took Damey by the arm and led him to the sink. He made the boy lean over it while he used lukewarm tap water to wash out the blood and gore so he could check him over. After patting his hair, face, and neck dry with paper towels, he turned him around and held up his finger. "Hold your head still and look straight ahead. Okay, pupils are fine. Now, as I move my finger, you follow it with just your eyes."

Satisfied that all he suffered was a bump and scratch with no signs of a concussion, he turned him loose.

"Grandpa, I'm sorry. I didn't—"

Using his infamous, stern, tone of voice, he interrupted the apology. "Damarian Wayne Martin, it was an accident. Nobody did anything on purpose. It happened. End of discussion. We'll fix the window tomorrow. Your head is more important than the window. Understand?"

While speaking, he made eye-contact with Tyrone and each of his grandsons as well who had been suspiciously glaring at the other kids. Everyone understood there was more to this story, but nobody said a word. It could wait for the rides home.

CHAPTER 12

About eight-thirty, Grandpa walked across the street. Tyrone had left without quizzing Damey, and Shaundra was out in the kitchen cleaning up from their late evening snack. Damey let him in.

"Hi, brat. What are you doing still up? Figured you'd be asleep by now."

"Not nine o'clock yet. Don't go to bed 'til then."

"Oh, okay. So, how's my boy feeling?"

"Fine. Had a little headache so Mom gave me a Tylenol. That helped."

"Let me see," Grandpa said as he took Damey by the shoulders and turned him around.

Shaundra walked into the living room and said, "Hi, Bill. I've got decaf poured out in the kitchen. How do you want yours?"

"Black's fine," he said as he softly rubbed his fingers over the bump.

"Ow!" Damey winced.

"Still a little sore, isn't it?" Grandpa asked.

"Just when somebody touches it. Mom and Tyrone made me yelp too. Both of them poked at it just like you did."

Bill walked out into the kitchen, grabbed his coffee, and sat down on one of the bar-stools at the counter.

"Ty checked him over one more time before he left," Shaundra said. "When he felt the back of his head, he thought the bump had gone down about half way. Hopefully, it'll disappear overnight. He even tracked his eye movements again. Still no outward signs of a concussion. Ty told me the symptoms to look for—you know, dizziness, vomiting. So far, so good.

Bill listened satisfied that Damey had nothing more than a bad bump with a scratch on it. He turned to the boy and said, "The reason I came over is because Sean just called and admitted the whole thing had been his fault. I thought you ought to know before you headed off to bed and worried all night."

"He did?" Damey said as his eyes popped open and jaw dropped. "Is he okay?"

"Yes, but you're going to have to wait until you see him next time to find out all the details, 'cause I'm not

going to tell you what he said. You two can talk about it
when he comes. All I'm going to tell you tonight is that
everything is fine between Sean and his dad. He's not
afraid of him anymore."

"Good. You probably didn't know it, but Sean was
really scared of him," Damey said with a sigh. "I feel
better all ready."

"I know, and he'll let you in on all the details. In the
meantime, while we're here in the kitchen where the
light's bright, I want to see something else."

Shaundra and Damey both looked puzzled. Neither
had any idea what Grandpa had in mind.

"It's better to do it out here where nobody can see
you through the window when we make you strip."

"What?" Damey exclaimed with his eyes half
bugging out of their sockets.

"Just teasing you," Grandpa said. "But I do want
you to take off your sweatshirt. I want to look at your
back."

"Why? What'd Sean and his big mouth tell you?"

"According to him, you hit the window sill with
either the top of your back or shoulders and it knocked
the wind out of you for just a few seconds. He also said
he saw you rubbing it a while later. I want to check it
out."

Damey shrugged out of his sweatshirt and turned
around so they could see. A slightly swollen bruise ran
across the width of his back just below the shoulder
blades. It stung a little when Bill prodded it, but nothing

appeared broken including the skin. That satisfied Grandpa.

"Looks like you're gonna live," Grandpa said, "but we still need to talk. Are you awake enough to do it now, or do you want to wait until tomorrow morning?"

"Now. I won't be able to sleep if I have to worry about something. But, Grandpa, before you start yelling at me, I checked both savings accounts—my regular one and my retirement. There's fifty-two bucks in each. If that's not enough for the window, I've got more stashed in my drawer upstairs. Allowance money I haven't spent."

"Just being nosy, you started with a hundred in each account, how could they be down to only fifty-two?"

"There's a hundred and fifty-two in each account, but that first hundred is yours. You put it in to start 'um. That don't count. If I ain't got enough money, I'll work for it somehow. Ty said he'd come over and help me with the window tomorrow too."

"Number one, I'm not going to yell at you. I don't want you crying, because I want you to listen. Number two, I have a friend who owns a window company. I called him tonight before I came over, and he's coming between twelve and two to replace the glass. Number three, you are not paying for it. It was an accident. You can watch him if you want, but you can't quiz him about the bill. He works by the hour, and the more you yammer at him, the more it's going to cost me. We're lucky. He'd planned to take the day off tomorrow. Last, but not least, don't say 'ain't'"

"Not fair."

"Tough, that's the way it's going to be. Now, listen, we essentially went over this whole discussion earlier today, and we're not going to do it again. New subject—I understand now why you took the blame for the window. You wanted to protect Sean who thought his dad would whip him. That in itself is admirable. However, in the process, you lied. That's unacceptable. Talk to me."

Grandpa sat back in his chair and picked up his coffee cup, took a couple of sips, put the cup down, and looked at Damey, who stood there, shifting his weight from foot to foot. He wiped his eyes with his shirt sleeve as puberty kicked in again. He didn't know what to say as Grandpa and Mom waited.

With eyes glistening and a steady flow of tears running down his cheeks, he finally spoke. "Grandpa, I didn't mean to lie to you. I'm sorry. I really am. I didn't even think of it that way. Sean's dad scared him. He thought his dad was just looking for an excuse to whip him. I had to protect him. He's my cousin and my friend."

"Suppose I punished *you* for breaking the window. Would it be worth it then?"

"Yes."

"What if I decided to punish you somehow now for lying to me? Would that change anything?"

"No, I'd a still done it. It'd hurt my feelings, but I'd still do it. Don't think it'd make me feel any worse than I do now if you did."

During the entire discussion, Shaundra sat sipping her coffee and watched Damey's face as he reacted to Grandpa. Damey had never had a father-figure in his life. He needed the one-on-one.

"What a great pair you two make," she mumbled softly, thinking out loud more than talking to them. "Why can't my own parents accept Damey? They'll never know what they've missed."

Grandpa and Damey were so focused on each other, they hadn't heard or noticed.

"Well, I'm not going to punish you in any way for what happened," Grandpa said. "But, I do want you to think about something. Protecting someone from harm is noble. Lying not so, there's a fine line separating the choices we sometimes have to make. Let me throw a hypothetical at you. Do you know what that word means?"

"Got no clue," Damey sniffed.

"Go into the bathroom and blow your nose real quick, and wash your face while you're at it."

Shaundra poured coffee again while they waited without a word. They looked at each other and smiled.

When he came back, Grandpa continued. "Hypothetical means 'suppose,' or 'what if' something else happened. What I'm talking about here, is *suppose* that four years from now you're over to Sean's house, and his mom wants him to take the car and go to the store to get something, and you ride with him. What if, a block from the house, he stops the car, fills up his pot pipe, and takes a few tokes before continuing to the store.

"When you get back to the house, his dad suddenly remembers something else they need, jumps into the car, and races off to the store. What's going to happen?"

"He's gonna smell it and freak out when he gets home."

"Are you going to protect him and take the blame?"

"No way! If he does something like that, he's on his own. Even if they do legalize pot before then, it won't mean kids can use it. You think he'd really do that?"

"I have no idea what things are going to look like in four years. That's why it's a hypothetical question. My whole point is, sometimes we have to make choices about what is right or wrong. I think this time *maybe* you made the right choice. What do you think?"

Shortly after that, Grandpa went home leaving Damey to his thoughts. Damey and his mom watched out the door with the porch light on until Grandpa unlocked his door and went into his house. "He worries about you," his mom said.

"Weird, isn't it. He's got this whole flock of kids, grandkids, and great-grandkids, and he still worries about me. He's the only grandpa I have, and I worry about him."

"He loves you to pieces and wants the best for you. Why do you worry about him?"

"Just 'cause he's old, I guess. I don't want to ever lose him."

I don't think you have to worry about that right away. At least, I hope not."

They cleaned up the kitchen, and Shaundra poured another half-cup of coffee. As she shooed him off to bed, she picked up the paper to check out the local news. It mysteriously showed up on the porch one day, and Damey never thought a thing about it. He just read it because he knew that Grandpa would quiz him on it.

• • •

Two weeks later Sean popped in at Grandpa's unannounced. His dad had a friend in the hospital and wanted to visit, so he brought his son because Sean wanted to talk to Damey. He wanted to give him a full report on their ride home and their evening on Thanksgiving.

The boys went out and sat on the patio. He told Damey that as they rode, his mom and dad talked about dinner, the Lion's game, various tidbits of news and gossip they had picked up, but not one word about the window.

He said he spent most of the ride staring out the window, scared and nervous. "I only spoke when Mom or Dad asked me a direct question. I could feel my voice quaver every time I answered. I really felt stupid about it. I wondered if they could they hear it too. When we hit the city limits, I couldn't take it anymore, so I finally spoke up.

"I told Dad the broken window had been my fault, and that you'd taken the blame for me."

He said his dad looked at him in the mirror and said, "Really? Tell me about it."

"So I said when Marty's mom called us in, I wanted to get in one last kick, and you yelled at me waving your arms, telling me not to because I was facing the house. I didn't think it was any big deal 'cause I'd never kicked one that far. When I did, the ball tumbled over and over right at the window."

Damey sat rocking slowly on the patio chair listening, not saying a thing. He let Sean get it out of his system.

Sean described how he'd told his dad how Damey'd taken off on a dead run trying to stop it and ended up crashing into the window pane.

Sean looked at Damey and said, "I thought you had to've hurt your back, but you didn't say anything about it at the time. After Ty washed the blood out of your hair, I saw you kind of rubbing your back against the refrigerator. That's when I whispered to you and asked if you'd hurt anything else, and you shook your head no giving me that 'leave it' look. My parents wanted to go, so I didn't say anything more about it."

Sean continued. After telling his dad, he said his dad asked, "I don't understand. Why did you let Damey take the blame? Why didn't you speak up right then? That wasn't fair to him."

Embarrassed to admit it to Damey, he said he couldn't help it, but had stupid tears running down his cheeks and his head hanging when he finally answered his dad. He said, "I didn't want you to whip me in front of all my cousins. I wanted you to wait until we got home."

"Whip you? You mean, like, with a belt?" his dad asked.

"Yes."

He said, "Have I ever whipped you?"

"No."

"Then why did you think I would do it now?"

"Cause you said you were gonna," Sean told him.

Then Sean told Damey that his dad looked totally confused. He hadn't even swatted him since he was a toddler, much less spanked or whipped him. He had no idea where this came from.

He said, that's when his dad told him, "All I know is that for the past couple of months, you've acted half afraid of me, and it's time for us to get to the bottom of it."

Sean said that during all of the back and forth between him and his dad, his mom said absolutely nothing. She told him later that she and his dad had talked about the tension between the two of them and thought he was either going through a phase or something puberty related. That's why she decided to do nothing but listen for the time being and let them talk it out.

"Okay, I'm all ears. Go back to the beginning and tell me everything. Where and when did you ever get this idea?" Sean said his dad asked.

So he let him know, "One day I told you about my friend at school, Jacob, whose dad can be a mean drunk. I said that about once a month, Jake's dad beats him with a belt. Then he's all apologetic and spoils him rotten until the next time it happens. When I asked him why he didn't tell our counselor at school, he said. 'No way,' it was worth getting his butt beat every month or so just so his dad would bribe him with money and electronic goodies in between. He's got everything imaginable.

"After I told him," Sean said. "Dad said, 'Maybe that's why Jake is always so polite and well-mannered around our house?' Then he looked up and said, 'Hum! Maybe that's what I ought to start doing to you every time you screw up. It'd be a good way for me to get a little extra exercise, and you'd probably start behaving better.'"

"You took me seriously?" Sean said his Dad asked.

"Yes."

Then he said, "Sean, I meant it as a joke. I thought you knew that. I even messed up your hair and laughed at you when I said it. I would never *whip* you. Is that

132

why you've been avoiding me the past couple of
months? You were trying to stay away and out of sight
on purpose?"

"Yes," Sean said he answered.

Even while Sean told Damey the story, he teared up
and wiped his face with his sleeve remembering how
horrible he felt. "I told Dad I didn't think he liked me
anymore."

He went on to tell Damey that's when they pulled
into the garage. "When we got out of the car, Dad and I
looked at each other for a few seconds with tears
running out of both of our eyes. We grabbed each other
in a long hug. He almost broke my back he squeezed so
hard. Mom shook her head and smiled as she grabbed
some packages out of the car and walked towards the
house. Dad kissed the top of my head and held me for
the longest time."

Then Sean told Damey, later on that evening, with
their worlds back in order, his dad looked up wide eyed
from where he'd curled up on the sofa and spoke,
holding his index finger in the air. "Oh, I almost forgot,
there's one more thing we have to do tonight before you
go to bed, young man."

"What's that?" Sean said he asked.

His dad took his cell phone out of his pocket and
punched in one of his contacts. When the person
answered on the other end, his dad said, "Hey,
Grandpa, just wanted to call and thank you again for the
day. Everything was great. Everything except for the

Lions getting blown out as usual on their annual Thanksgiving catastrophe When are you gonna do something about that?"

Sean said his dad laughed listening to Grandpa's answer on the other end. After chatting back and forth for a minute or two, his dad paused, and then said, "Oh, before I forget, Sean wants to talk to you. He has something to tell you about the accident this afternoon."

Feeling his heart beating like crazy against his rib cage and his hands shaking, Sean said he took the phone his Dad held out to him. Dirty trick, he remembered thinking to himself. He hadn't known what his dad planned to do.

After Grandpa said, "Hi, big guy," with his normal cheerful tone of voice, he said he relaxed and told him the story. Grandpa didn't even yell at him. He thanked him for telling him the truth, and then they ended the call.

"Wow! That took guts." Damey said. "How do you feel now? Are you still scared of your dad?"

"No, not a bit. Just like today. We laughed and joked all the way over here."

"Great. Glad to hear it."

"You know what I think is strange, not one word has been mentioned since that night about any of it— just like it never happened. Yet, I remember that ride home and evening like it was some kind of computerized image burned into my brain."

"Wanna play some catch with the football?" Damey asked.

"Sure, but no kicking."

CHAPTER 13

Ambling from their lockers towards Mr. Allen's first hour pre-algebra class, Damey noticed Liam and a couple of his buddies headed towards them, against traffic, shoving kids out of their way as they cursed them.

"Pass them on the left, Alex," Damey said. "Liam's on the inside."

Alex looked at him with a strange expression wondering what was up, but sidled over as Damey nudged him that way with his shoulder.

"Oh, boy. Check out the two faggots headed our way, guys." Liam shouted as he and his buddies laughed. "It's that greasy little spick and his nigger butt-buddy."

The boys looked straight ahead. As they passed, Damey kept a blank expression on his face. At exactly the right spot, he twisted his body hard to the right, gritted his teeth, pursed his lips, and let fly a round-house doubled-up fist straight into Liam's solar plexus dropping him to his knees with a loud "Ooomph!"

Then Damey lost it. Before Liam hit the floor, he pounced on him screaming epithets and flailing lefts and rights pummeling the much larger boy on the face and head. Spatters of blood, snot, and saliva flew.

He didn't hear or feel Alex screaming and trying to pull him off.

Time stopped as a hall full of kids stood there gawking in shock as Damey got in at least twenty blows before Mr. Allen grabbed him in a bear-hug and hauled him off. "Whoa, big fella. Cool it. What's going on?"

"Lemme go," Damey shrieked. "I'm gonna kill that bastard."

Holding his still kicking, flailing body in the air, Mr. Allen shook Damey hard, yelling in his ear. "Stop it!—Stop it *now*!—Settle down—Easy boy—That's better. Can I let you down now?"

Damey, red-faced, sweaty, and still angry, nodded.

Mr. Allen put him down gently but continued to hold on to his wrist. By then crowd control had settled in. At least a half dozen other teachers were herding kids off to class while one tended to the dazed Liam who by then had managed to sit up. Even the principal showed up along with the school nurse. News traveled fast.

Mr. Rogers, the principal, took charge snarling. "Mr. Allen, would you walk Damey down to the outer office, please?" Then he turned his attention to Damey. "You take a seat by the windows across from the secretaries and wait for me. I'll get to you as soon as I can."

Damey, mad as he still was, almost smiled. He knew Rogers had a problem. How would he deal with this one? Liam's a bully and a bloody mess, and his dad's the boss of the school district.

• • •

The school's secretary called Shaundra and asked her to come and meet with the principal. However, they were short-handed at work, and she couldn't get away. She told the secretary she'd call Mr. Berkley to see if he could go over and take care of whatever needed to be done.

When she called, Bill was dozing in his lounge chair with his iPad balanced on his chest. He jumped, the iPad flew, but he fumbled around and finally answered. "Hello," he blurted a little louder than normal.

"Can you go over to the school and get Damey or at least deal with whatever's going on. The office just called, and I can't get away. We're short-handed because of the flu, and we're up to our ears in finalizing the month-end data."

"What's going on, Shaundra?" Much more alert than when he'd answered. Bill felt a knot in his stomach. He sensed trouble.

"The secretary said Damey got into a fight and beat up some kid. She wouldn't tell me anything else."

"Damey? Got into a fight? Our Damey? Are you sure they have the right kid?"

"Yes, she put him on the phone so I could talk to him. He's angry and upset. I could tell by his voice and the way he talked. Anyway, he wouldn't tell me anything except he wanted to kill the kid. I told the secretary that I'd try to get you to go, otherwise, I'd be there during my lunch break between twelve and one."

"I'll go. You know, I'll probably be bringing him back here. Most schools have zero-tolerance when it comes to fighting. The big question is whether he'll get kicked out temporarily or permanently."

Bill paced back and forth as he talked. His mind kicked into overdrive. Every thought reflected negative results.

"He sure doesn't need to start over in another new school right away. He's been doing so well. It'll probably depend on who started the fight and why.

Have you heard about him having problems with any kids at school?"

"Not a word."

"Me either. I'm on my way."

As Bill drove to the school, his mind swirled. He kept saying to himself, what the devil is going on? Damey's the softest spoken, mildest mannered, easygoing, loving boy I've ever seen. All the kids like him. His teachers love him. Something's terribly wrong. I hope Damey didn't get hurt. He's not a fighter. He's a brainy little runt.

When Bill got to the front door of the school, he found it locked. He pushed the button on the speaker beside the door.

Damey had been sitting there half in a daze replaying the incident over and over in his mind, wondering what was going to happen. The buzzer jarred him awake, and he could hear the conversation between the secretary and his grandpa. Before she would buzz him in, he had to identify himself and his purpose for being there.

Squirming nervously in his seat, Damey watched Grandpa walk in, pause, look at him, and head to the desk without speaking.

"Hi, I'm Bill Berkley. Damey Martin's mom called and asked if I'd come on her behalf to get him and find out what's going on."

"Hi, Mr. Berkley. We've been expecting you. I'll let the principal know you're here. Why don't you go sit with Damey while you wait? He's been looking so forlorn. I almost feel sorry for him. Almost, but not quite. I saw the damage he did to the other kid's face. He's a vicious little dude."

I'll bet the principal would love to hear one of his secretaries make that remark, Bill said under his breath as he walked over and sat beside Damey without a word.

Damey heard it too. He didn't consider himself vicious—just pissed. He didn't like people thinking that way about him.

Neither one spoke. Damey stared at the floor, and Grandpa ignored him except for an occasional glance. Damey could sense it when he did, but didn't say a word.

Shortly, the principal came out of a room down a hallway behind the main office, walked over and introduced himself. "Mr. Berkley," he said offering his hand. "I'm Mr. Rogers. Won't you and Damey come back to my office, please?"

Bill stood up and shook hands with him, while Damey sat there without stirring. Bill tapped Damey on the shoulder a couple of times with the back of his hand as he sat glued to the seat. "Let's go," he said using *that* tone of voice ordering him to stand without a word and follow.

Mr. Rogers sat behind his desk while Grandpa and Damey sat in front. "So, Mr. Berkley, my understanding of the situation so far is this. When all the kids were headed to their first hour class, Damey sucker-punched a boy, knocking the wind out of him, and then brutally pummeled the kid until Mr. Allen pulled him off. He was so angry, Mr. Allen literally had to pick him up off the floor until he settled down enough to set him back on his feet.

"According to the other boy, the assault was totally unprovoked. I have not heard Damey's side of the story but I want to now. I needed to wait for a parent or family representative to be present."

"He's a lying son-of-a-bitch," Damey flashed angrily and wide-eyed, finally showing some life.

"Damarian!"

"Grandpa, he lied! He's the biggest bully in school and thinks he can get away with anything just 'cause his dad is the superin-whatever-the-hell you call it."

"Damey, keep it civil. I want to hear your side of the story too, but you've got to calm yourself down. You know what's appropriate and what isn't."

"Damey, how about if you start at the beginning and tell us what happened as you see it. We're not in any big hurry. Tell us everything." Mr. Rogers sat back in his swivel rocker, folded his arms in across his chest, and rocked slowly, waiting.

Damey told his version. The bullying began back in September. Liam picked on a lot of younger and smaller kids. For some reason or the other, he thought Liam seemed to zero in on him and Alex for extra attention. Just because they were best friends, he called them fags with a heavy emphasis on the "S" word and the "N" word. People laughed at his bullying, trying to stay on his good side so he wouldn't pick on them. That made it even worse. It made Damey and Alex feel like the other people were okay with what Liam did.

He said Liam bounced them off of lockers, made fun of them, and made their lives miserable at school. When Liam screamed at them that morning before school loud enough for everyone in the hall to hear and laugh at them, he snapped.

By the time he'd finished his story, he'd calmed down, spoke very softly, and had apparently lost his rage. Damey looked right at the principal and told him he didn't know why he'd lost his cool, he just had.

When he finished, Mr. Rogers sat there for a minute thinking, still rocking with his arms folded across his chest. Finally, he stopped rocking, sat up, and spoke. "Damey, I believe what you've just told me. However, assaulting someone is never a good way to solve a problem. Why haven't you ever reported the bullying? If that's what he was doing, that's unacceptable as well."

"It wouldn't do any good. His dad's the boss around here. Other kids have reported him and nothing's happened. He just does what he wants."

"Yes, I admit, he has been reported for minor bullying, and I have talked to him. I've also talked to his father about the situation, and he's not happy either. However, that doesn't excuse your actions. I'm going to give you the minimum punishment for fighting, in accordance with the school code-of-conduct. You are to be suspended for three days. Today doesn't count because the day's almost half over. Return to school on Monday."

"Before I take him home," Grandpa said. "Is it permissible for him to go to his locker to get his backpack, helmet, and all of his books? He's going to need them for the next five days," Grandpa said.

"That'd be fine. Let me buzz the secretary."

She tapped on the door and opened it.

"Would you escort Damey down to his locker so he can get his supplies, and then bring him back here while I talk to his grandpa for a couple more minutes?"

The secretary nodded without speaking and looked at Damey.

Without another word, he stood and headed to his locker. Thankfully, he didn't see anybody in the hallway so he didn't have to stop and explain anything. The only person he really wanted to talk to was Alex.

While he was gone, Bill told Mr. Rogers he wanted to make sure he got all the homework, worksheets, and extra credit assignments he could get his hands on. They also decided that since Alex was in all his classes, he could take anything to Grandpa's house the teachers were willing to send on a daily basis.

Rogers pulled a school brochure out of his desk and handed it to Bill with the teacher's emails. He said he'd leave a note with Bill's email address in all Damey's teacher's mailboxes to reflect what they'd discussed.

Bill told him he didn't need the brochure. He was already connected to the school's website with a password because he kept track of Damey's grades. If he had any questions, he could find their emails on the school directory.

Damey walked back into the office loaded down with his backpack and helmet and stood there as Mr. Rogers explained how the superintendent had come over and picked Liam up and taken him to the Redi-Care downtown to make sure his nose wasn't broken or his brain concussed.

He also told Bill that the super was well aware and concerned about Liam's bullying, and wanted to hear Damey's version of the incident. They both knew there had to be more to the story. The superintendent planned to make an immediate point to Liam and get the kid into counseling.

Damey hated it when people talked around him like he wasn't there, and that's exactly what they did. He felt invisible.

When they got ready to go, Grandpa took the backpack and told Damey to get on his bike and head for his house. He'd meet him there, and they'd discuss this further before they got down to doing a little school work. As Damey headed for the bike rack, he could feel his body tremble. He'd be punished. How? The thought scared him. Grandpa had never punished him before.

Grandpa arrived first and Damey found him sitting in his chair finishing the paper when he walked in.

Damey stood in front of him squirming and shifting from foot to foot as he always did when feeling guilty and nervous. "What are you gonna do to me?"

"I'm not going to *do* anything. But, as far as your mom and I are concerned, you are one-hundred percent grounded until Monday morning. Alex can come for about five seconds a day to drop off assignments or handouts from your teachers along with any special instructions. That will take place here in the living room. He'll give you your assignments, pick up your completed homework, and leave—period.

"There'll be no friends, no phone calls, no TV except for the news, no playing football outdoors in the afternoon after school with your buddies, nothing that would resemble fun. You can do school work, rake leaves, pull weeds, any other chores your mom and I decide, and read. That's it. Incidentally, I did call your mom when I got home to make sure she and I are on the same page. We are. Any questions?"

"No, sir." Damey stood still stared at the floor. For the first time that day, he showed his normal emotions as the first tear dropped off his cheek. He watched it soak into the carpet.

"Here, get started on this while I go stir up some lunch," Bill said handing him the paper. "You know your mom's worried to death about you. All she really knows is that you got into a fight this morning, and the school called her wanting someone to come and get you. She didn't have time for me to explain everything when I got home. As if her job isn't stressful enough right now, you're causing her more headaches." Bill growled at him making sure Damey understood his actions caused problems for more people than himself. "Since I only gave her an abbreviated version over the phone, *you* are going to tell her the whole story tonight. I will check with her later after you've gone to bed to make sure you didn't leave any parts out."

CHAPTER 14

Monday morning Damey pulled into Alex's driveway on the way to school, jumped off his bike, and walked into the house. He found Alex in the kitchen rinsing out his cereal bowl when he walked in. Alex's mom greeted Damey like nothing had happened. She didn't pry. Alex would tell her everything.

Alex couldn't wait to get out of the house and on the way. As they were attaching their helmets, he exclaimed, "You're not gonna believe this one. Liam didn't get kicked out of school like you did. He came every day. In fact, his dad brought him back to school Tuesday afternoon with his face all black and blue, cotton tubes stuffed in his broken nose and taped over so he had to breathe out of his mouth. He had scratches, and cuts all over his face. He looked a mess. You done good, Bro."

They coasted down Alex's driveway and into the street. They were in no hurry. Both had a lot to tell. For the first time in almost a week, Damey felt free again.

"What? That's not fair. Here he is, dumber than a pile of cat turds in a sandbox, and could care less about school, and he gets to go. Then, there's me. I like school and get good grades and get kicked out. That totally sucks!"

Excited and grinning from ear-to-ear, Alex responded. "No, no, no! Think about it Damey, it was great. It made him the laughing stock of the school. A skinny little seventh grader who he towered over and outweighed by thirty pounds had kicked the crap out of him. Everybody laughed and poked fun at him. I'm sure that's why they made him come back just so he'd see how it felt.

"You know how he's always spouting off in class about stuff he knows absolutely nothing about? He hardly said a word in math the rest of the week. He sat there and pouted all hour every day. The only thing I remember him saying was on Thursday when Mr. Allen told him that he'd better get working on his missed assignments. He said, 'Why? Damey doesn't have to come to school and do any of this stuff. Why should I have to? That's not fair.'"

Laughing so hard, Damey almost lost control and wiped out on his bike. "Really? That idiot actually said that?"

"Yes, so Mr. Allen walked over to his desk and picked up your assignments I'd given him out in the hall before class, stuck them under Liam's nose and told him, 'Oh yeah? What do you call these? I have every one of Damey's homework assignments plus that extra credit I gave out Tuesday. I don't have any of yours.' Then Liam put his head down on his folded arms atop the desk and didn't lift it for the rest of the hour. Everybody laughed until Mr. Allen made us stop. Then he gave us another lecture. Said that by laughing at Liam, we were bullying him, and it wasn't right. Sure felt good though."

• • •

Damey looked a little forlorn as they neared the school. He brought up a problem to Alex that had been weighing on his mind. "I hope I didn't lose any of my friends over this. I'm really sorry I lost my cool. I've never done that before."

"Lose your friends? Damey, you're a freaking hero. Everybody loves what you did to Liam, and everybody thinks you got screwed over big time by being suspended when he didn't. It's a win-win for you. Hold your head up high when you walk into the school,

Dude. You don't have a mark on you, and Friday he was still scratched up and black and blue. He hadn't even taken the cotton tubes out of his nose yet. Looked like a dork."

The mob around Damey's locker got so big, a couple of the teachers including Mr. Allen, checked it out just to make sure nothing bad was going on. Unfortunately for Damey, something did. One of the cuter girls forced her way through the mob, threw her arms around his neck and kissed him on the cheek and said, "Thank you Damey from all of us."

Damey flashed crimson, much to the delight of all.

Laughing, Mr. Allen broke up the hysterical crowd sending everyone off to first hour class.

During the school day between classes and at lunch, Damey told Alex and their friends about his exciting week of school work, raking their lawns in twenty-degree temperatures, zero contact with friends except for the five minutes with Alex to trade assignments, and no television except the history and science channels plus the news. He even had to wash and wax the linoleum floor in their kitchen at home. In his spare time, he rode the stationary bike in Grandpa's family room and read his Kindle. Jail couldn't be any worse.

• • •

That afternoon after school, Damey stood at his locker digging out his helmet and homework for the night. Alex elbowed Damey and said, "Oh, oh. Guess who's walking right at us?"

As Damey looked over his shoulder to see who Alex was talking about, Liam spoke. "Damey, we need to talk."

"No. I've heard everything out of your mouth I want to hear. Don't ever say another word to me again unless you're asking for permission to kiss my ass."

"I think we should go out behind the school and have a fair fight just you and me."

"Liam, there ain't no such thing as a fair fight. You're three or four inches taller than I am, and you outweigh me by thirty or forty pounds of fat. How could we ever have a fair fight?"

"I want the chance to kick your ass without us getting caught. That's all."

"Not gonna happen, Dude. If you ever as much as lay a finger on me, Alex, or any of the Bows, I'll be forced to break my new promise of nonviolence and use my junior black belt in karate and kick-boxing. If I do, I promise, you won't get off the ground until the ambulance crew scrapes you up and plops you on the stretcher. *Double* promise."

"Bull! You ain't got no black belt in karate and kickboxing. You ain't tough enough."

Damey bristled. "You got no clue what I did at my old school or why. There's nobody here who knew me last year. You saw with your own squinty eyes, the ones still black and blue and half shut, how fast my hands can move. Are you so stupid you want to take a chance to see how fast my hand-foot combination is? Really?"

"Alex, is he bullshitting me? Does he have a black belt?"

Alex paused for a moment before answering. Then with a very serious, faraway look in his eyes, he responded. "Liam, we've never talked that much about his old school and what he did or didn't do. The only thing I know for sure is one day when Damey was looking for something and couldn't find it. All of a sudden, he remembered it might be in the guest bedroom's closet that's always locked. He went into his mom's room, grabbed the key, and opened it.

Since I was standing there with him, I looked inside. "In the back of the closet, I saw a trophy case full of medals leaning against the back wall. I asked Damey what it was, and he slammed the closet door shut and locked it. He told me to 'never mind' and 'forget it.' He didn't want to talk about it. I figured it was none of my business so I never mentioned it again. Fact is, 'til just now, I'd forgotten about it. You know as much about his black belt as I do, but maybe that's where all the medals came from? I don't know, but I sure don't wanna find out the hard way."

Liam visibly squirmed and tried to brush his discomfort off. Apparently, Alex's story validated the black belt question, and he seemed to change his mind about fighting Damey. He didn't look like he wanted to anyway. His face looked like it throbbed just thinking about getting battered again.

"Okay, Damey, one more question, and then I've got to get home. I'm still grounded. Probably will be forever. Who and what are these Bows you mentioned? If I have to avoid them, I might as well know who they are."

"The Rainbow Gang is the group of kids I work out with for two and a half hours every day after school. The gang is mostly minorities. We're working on our conditioning, strength, and athletic skills. As you know, the best athletes in the world are minorities."

"That's a bunch of bull and you know it."

"Really? Do you know why kids of African heritage are fast, quick, strong, and smart like me? That's because Africa is full of tigers. That's why you don't see many slow, dumb, fat kids like you in Africa. Just think! If you lived there, you'd have been one of those guy's afternoon snack long ago.

"Why do you think the best hitter in baseball is Hispanic? Hispania is full of flying bats. Kids at a very young age start carrying baseball bats to swat them with. They get very good and deadly with them. Which reminds me, two weeks ago Alex wanted to bring his bat to school—in October? I don't know why, but I talked him out of it. It was the day after you tried to trip him on the steps. Remember that day? Wonder why he wanted to bring his bat? Any ideas? Ever wonder why they call a baseball bat a bat? Think about it."

By this time a small group of kids had gathered around to watch and listen. Most were grinning, some were outright laughing. Damey was on a roll.

"Not only that, did you know that sumo wrestling originated in Japan, Asia, and the Orient. That's why they're so big, Asia is huge. How would you like to have a 650 pound sumo dude spatter you into the ground? I have a lot of friends from my old school who...

"But wait. Did you know that all the Olympic Nordic ski champions are from Nordia? It's all mountainous there and snows all year round. They don't have roads, busses, trains, or planes. They get everywhere by skis. The average Nordian boy has size 16 shoes by the time he's twelve. If they're just going a short ways, they use their feet as skis. How'd you like to have one of those guys use those size 16s and kick your ass, Liam? I can arrange it, if you'd like.

"And, did you know why all Olympic ice skaters are from Iceland? Iceland is a sheet of ice. Babies are fitted with ice skates as early as they are shoes here. They live on them. Inside the house they wear wool stockings, and outside they wear skates year around.

"Also, did you know there are more Spaniards in one of the European countries than any other place on earth?"

By that time an even larger crowd had gathered shaking their heads and laughing knowing that Liam was believing everything Damey told him. By the next day the entire school would be laughing at him. The news of this bull session would be all over by morning.

"Uh, okay, maybe. So who are these guys in your gang?" Liam asked. He looked completely confused about what he'd just been told.

"All I'm going to tell you is there is one Black, one African American, one Hispanic, one Mexican, one Oriental, one Asian, one whose grandparents were born in India, one Native American, one white, one Caucasian, and one who is racially mixed. Do you see why we're called the Rainbow Gang? We've got every color covered. Alex and I are two of the gang. You figure out the rest, and you'd better not make a mistake and bully the wrong person. Got it?"

Liam walked off with his head down as he stared at the floor with laughter ringing in his ears—nasty, sarcastic, hurting laughter. He wasn't used to being bullied, and he didn't like it.

With that, Damey closed his locker, and the boys walked away as the crowd dispersed still laughing and repeating the yarns among themselves. For the first time, Damey saw Mr. Allen and Mr. Williams leaning on the lockers across the hall together slowly shaking their heads with ear-to-ear grins. Damey nudged Alex to check out the other side. Both boys smiled and gave a quick wave.

"You think I convinced him?" Damey asked as they strapped on their helmets at the bike rack?

"I think so. That had to be the biggest line of bullshit I've ever heard in my life, and he ate it up. I've never heard anything so funny."

"Don't give me all the credit. We're two peas in a pod, buddy. You see the expression on his face when you described the secret trophy case and medals I supposedly have locked up in a closet? As swollen as they are, he still managed to pop those big ugly eyes wide open."

Laughing out loud with a double fist-bump, both boys sent rocks flying behind them as they spun their tires racing out the gravel driveway of the school. One-sixth of the Rainbow Gang would be late for their basketball game at the youth center. They had to hurry.

• • •

That night at dinner, Damey told his mom the whole story. She laughed. After they cleaned up the table, the two of them settled into their spots with their favorite past times for the evening. Shaundra had the television on low so it wouldn't bother Damey and his Kindle.

The longer he sat, the squirmier he got. Shaundra knew something was bothering him. Normally, when he got into his book, he'd talk out loud and make comments he didn't even realize he was making. How many times had she heard him say, "No, no! Don't do that," or something else that made you smile knowing he was totally engrossed. That night he wasn't doing it.

Shaundra looked at him. "What's the matter, Honey," she asked.

Damey put down his Kindle and stood up. "I've got to go talk to Grandpa."

"Why? It's getting kind of late isn't? You're going to be over there tomorrow night anyway. Can't it wait?"

"No. I have to go fess up about my huge lie today. He's gonna be mad at me, but at least he'll get it out of his system before tomorrow. Hopefully, I won't be long."

Damey walked across the street taking his time. He had to, but he didn't want to. As he walked up the sidewalk, he could see Grandpa on the sofa watching the television. Must be a Pistons game on or he'd be reading in his chair. Damey tried the door, and it was locked. He rang the bell and waited.

"Hi, brat. Come on in," Bill said swinging open the door. "Didn't expect to see you tonight. What's up?"

Damey walked in, hugged his grandpa, and told him they needed to talk. They both sat down, and Bill turned off the TV. He raised the leg rest on the sofa, stretched out, put his hands behind his head and waited.

Damey repeated the story again just like he'd done at home. He felt guilty because he'd told Liam an outrageous lie, yet felt it was okay. He told him the more ridiculous the story got, the more Liam swallowed it. With the kids all laughing at Liam in the background and making cruel comments to him, the adrenalin surged and he just kept piling it on. He knew he'd done wrong, but couldn't help himself. That's why he came over to tell Grandpa and take his punishment.

Bill put the leg rest down on the sofa, held up his hand and motioned with his index finger. "Come over here and stand right here," he said as he pointed beside his leg.

When Damey positioned himself where Grandpa had pointed, Bill took his arm and turned the shaking boy over his knee stretching his jeans tightly over his mounded buttocks. As Damey held his breath and tightened his cheeks, Bill swatted him one time on the bottom hard enough to make a faint slapping sound, but soft enough so the kid didn't really even feel it. Then he lifted him back up.

"There! Do you feel sufficiently punished for your horrible misdeed?" he asked with a twinkle in his eyes and upturned lips.

"You're not mad at me?" Damey asked with wide open eyed disbelief. He had that 'What the hell is going on?' look on his face. "You scared me."

"No, I'm not angry. In fact, I thought it was exceptionally funny and creative. See, that's what I meant about that 'fine line' thing we talked about. You knew you'd never win a fair fight with that kid. He's too big. So you protected yourself as well as how many other kids from his bullying by making up the story about your karate/kickboxing thing and Rainbow Gang. Not identifying the members was brilliant. If it works right, he won't bully anybody because he doesn't know for sure who might be in the gang and who isn't. So it's another win-win for you and all the other kids in school.

"Not only that, but he got a good taste of his own medicine. With all the other kids making fun of him and laughing at him, I'm sure he knows how bullying makes a person feel. I'm betting he doesn't like it either. Damey, as you prepubescent types say, 'Ya done good.'"

"Pre what? What'd you call me?"

"Google it. Now, give me a hug and get yourself home. It's darned near your bedtime so spend a little quality time with your mom. You won't see her tomorrow after breakfast."

"Okay, see you after school. Bye." The fluttering on his insides had disappeared, and he smiled for the first time since he'd left his house.

Bill returned his wave and smile. "Night, Damey. Sleep well. See you tomorrow—and, hey, don't forget to check your bottom in the mirror tonight when you take your shower. It's probably all red and bruised."

"*Grandpa!*"

CHAPTER 15

In November, wrestling season began. Damey hadn't learned much in gym class. Mr. Williams used him as a demonstration dummy several times, but he really had no clue. For the most part, he went through the motions.

He found keeping their growing relationship separate and secret more and more difficult. Obviously, Alex knew all about it, but nobody else did. In class and on the mat, Damey referred to him as either Coach or Mr. Williams. He never slipped and called him Ty. Damey noticed something else as the season progressed, Coach never refereed any of his wrestle-offs with other kids.

One night at dinner, Damey asked him point blank. "Ty, how come you never ref any of my matches? Is that on purpose? How come?"

"Think about it. You wrestle junior varsity because the starter is an eighth grader with a year's experience on you—actually two because he started in the sixth grade. Regardless, he still has to earn his spot every week by wrestling everyone in seventy-four pound weight class who challenges.

"Suppose you had a real close match one day and won on a questionable call while I reffed. You know I would never intentionally show favoritism on the mat, but would the other kids buy that? I know Alex knows all about us, and some of the other kids probably do. Can't you just hear the rumors? 'Damey won because Coach is dating his mom.'"

"Alex wouldn't say anything."

"No, he'd probably be cheering for you. Regardless, we can't take any chances. Besides, I'm not ignoring you. You are my favorite wrestling dummy. It gives me a chance to beat up on you a little and give you mat and whisker burns." Ty laughed and gave Damey a little fist bump on his shoulder.

"You never beat up on me." Damey scowled taking him seriously again.

"Just teasing. I'd never hurt you on purpose, and you know it."

• • •

Unhappily for Shaundra, the middle school matches all took place on Tuesday and Thursday evenings so she couldn't go. Grandpa didn't miss a one. Damey had a winning record wrestling on the JVs, but barely. He and Alex talked about it, and Damey decided if he could drop to a lower weight class, he'd wrestle varsity and would win. To do it, he had to lose seven pounds.

Shaundra noticed the difference in his eating habits and called Bill. This was a class night for her so he'd be feeding Damey. "Is the brat trying to lose weight?"

"I don't know. Why?"

"He's not eating like normal. He's picking at his food, and I half think he went into the bathroom after dinner last night and stuck his finger down his throat, but I didn't mention it."

"I'll keep an eye on him tonight at dinner. It's just the two of us so I'll watch what he eats and keep tabs on him afterwards. No meet tonight so everything should be normal. I'll let you know. Gotta be careful how I spy on him, 'cause after the wet-dream prevention lecture I gave him, I promised that anything he did in the bathroom would be personal and private."

When Shaundra got home from class, she called Bill knowing Damey would be in bed. "What happened?"

"He did it again. After eating nothing to speak of for dinner, he went to the bathroom. I sneaked over close to the door and could hear him retching."

Shaundra's voice dropped in pitch. "I won't let him do that. I don't know what he's up to, but he's not going to spiral into some kind of eating disorder. I'm sure it has something to do with wrestling. If it does, I'll make him quit."

"Instead of either one of us getting involved," Bill said, "let's call Tyrone. He'll know how to handle it. You want to call him, or do you want me to?"

"I will."

• • •

The next night after practice, Ty told Damey and Alex to hang around after they showered. He wanted to take them home. He'd already called their moms, and they were good with it.

While dressing in the locker room, the boys shared their concerns with each other under their breaths making sure none of the other kids heard them. Ty had never offered to take them home before. Were they in trouble? Had they done something wrong? Both of their stomachs were rumbling, especially Damey's. He hadn't eaten enough lately to prevent it from acting funny, nerves or not.

As Ty drove to the mall on the other side of town, most of the talk had to do with wrestling—which school was coming up next on the schedule, what Ty thought their chances were, and basically small talk. Sitting in the back seat, the boys made worried eye contact with, questioning expressions. They weren't going home. Where was he taking them? He hadn't said.

When they got to the mall, Tyrone led them directly to the food court. He walked up to the dessert store and ordered three large hot-fudge sundaes. With Damey and Alex looking at each other with that, "What—?" expression on their faces, Ty told them to grab one and come sit down.

Each picked up a bowl and followed Ty to a table. "Normally, I give this lecture earlier in the season to the whole group, so thought I'd just hassle you two with it today. I'll repeat it tomorrow before practice. You know, it's like doing a single-leg takedown. One has to practice it to make sure he has the thing down pat.

Ty raised his eyebrows a little as he slowed and softened his tone. "Anyway, what I wanted to run by you two is the fact that in middle school, cutting weight is strictly forbidden on my teams. If you're overweight and lose some naturally through training, that's one thing. Dieting? No. Since I plan on using you two for examples tomorrow, I wanted you to be prepared and not think I was mad at you or anything. At your age, you are growing. You flow in and out of growth spurts.

That's natural. That's why each weight class adds a total of three pounds throughout the season. By the time we have our final tournament, your weight class will be seventy-seven, Damey, and, Alex, yours will be eighty-five."

"I'm not dieting," Alex blurted out.

"I know. I'm just going to use the two of you and your weights as examples."

Damey didn't say a word. The warm, thick, and rich tasting fudge on the ice cream made his mouth water. The whipping cream melted. He grabbed a napkin and wiped edge of his lips and chin quickly trying to hide the oozing drool. He took small bites of his sundae at first before gobbling it down. He flicked his eyes back and forth between Ty and Alex hoping and praying that Alex didn't say anything about him. He felt a hint of moisture on his forehead.

"Anyway, Alex, that's why I would never let Damey wrestle at sixty-seven pounds or you at seventy-four. It's against the laws of nature. You are supposed to eat and gain weight. You are growing boys. Wrestling varsity or junior varsity at your age is irrelevant. The important thing is that you are learning a new skill, getting a ton of exercise, enjoying a team experience, and having fun.

"Damey, I noticed today at weigh-ins you'd dropped two pounds. I don't like that. You're too skinny as it is. Losing weight is not going to happen. Why? If you gained two pounds, you'd be stronger and healthier. You wrestle at seventy-four and Alex at eighty-two. That's the way it is. The only way it'll change is if you go into a growth spurt and gain weight. Do I make myself clear?"

Both nodded. They understood.

"One more thing before we leave. This hot-fudge sundae better not spoil your appetites for dinner. If it does, you're in big trouble. In fact, I think I'm gonna mooch dinner at your house tonight, Damey, so I can keep an eye on you." He looked at Damey and smiled at the 'big trouble' comment.

As they stood up, Ty smiled and winked at Alex and then popped Damey on the shoulder again before they threw away their licked-clean bowls.

Totally relaxed and feeling like a heavy burden had been lifted from his shoulders, Damey looked up at Ty and smiled. "You don't have to worry about it spoiling my dinner. I'm starved."

They got home a little before Shaundra arrived from work. The smell from the spaghetti sauce that had been brewing in the Crock Pot all day permeated the house. The garlicky blend of beef, tomatoes, strong, eye-watering onions, chili beans, and whatever else she'd put in there started the gastric juices flowing on Damey. His stomach rumbled. He couldn't wait to put something else in his stomach. He grabbed an apple out of the fruit bowl.

Ty lifted the lid on the Crock Pot, stirred the concoction, and said, "Set the table, little dude, and I'll start the noodles. Is your grandpa coming over tonight? Seems like your mom said something about it." He knew Bill would be. Shaundra told him the night before when she called him and told him of the situation and invited him to come as well.

"I dunno. Probably," said Damey. "He usually does when they're ganging up on me."

"Ganging up on you? What are you talking about?"

Damey tried to frown and look serious. "Ty, I know one of them ratted on me to you, and I don't care. I'm so hungry I could eat that whole pot all by myself. And you know what else?"

"No, what?" Ty said as he rubbed his finger across the counter wiping up some of the sauce that had dripped before sticking it in his mouth.

"You were right. I felt weaker out on the mat the past few days. No energy. Didn't feel like myself in class either."

Ty looked over at Damey and smiled. "This may come as a surprise to you and all your buds, but adults aren't totally stupid. Sometimes they really do know what's best for you."

Damey looked up and returned the smile. Life was good again.

CHAPTER 16

Damey's best Christmas ever came and disappeared much too quickly. They had a Christmas tree for the first time Damey could remember—maybe ever. Grandpa had an extra one in the crawl space under his house so had Damey get on his hands and knees, creep in, and haul it out. He also had tons of extra lights and bulbs because his wife used to change things up every year or so. Grandpa and Damey hauled it all across the street so the boy, his mom, and Ty could decorate it. Ty was spending a lot more time there, and it all seemed perfectly natural and good to Damey.

Since Ty planned to spend the holiday week with his parents in Chicago, Shaundra, Damey, and Tyrone had their Christmas together on Friday night before Winter Break started. Ty gave Damey a Wii set for their TV at home and Shaundra a necklace. He hadn't seen his parents since the previous summer, so he intended to stay until right after New Years.

Christmas for Damey typically consisted of socks, underwear, a new shirt and pair of pants, and maybe one or two inexpensive toys. That year Shaundra saved the best for last. Tucked behind the tree where Damey wouldn't spot it lay his new iPad that she and Bill had gone in together on. Nobody ever mentioned what percentage Grandpa paid and what percentage Shaundra managed, but Damey knew.

The iPad had the Kindle app installed when he opened it. Grandpa had installed his account on the device so Damey had access to the four or five-hundred books already purchased.

Grandpa told him later he could order any book or game he wanted as long as he read the book and, "Really, really wanted the game."

When Damey and Shaundra went over to Grandpa's for dinner, Damey had a couple more gifts to open—both games for his new Wii. Shaundra received a gift as well.

Damey sat on the floor in the living room leaning against the wall by the fireplace. He smiled as he watched everyone opening their gifts. I don't stand a chance. Mom, Grandpa, and Ty either plot and scheme against or for me continuously. How surprising! Ty gave me a Wii and Grandpa gave me the games I wanted. How did he know my two favorite games? Did he find out from Alex? That turd's as bad as they are. He won't tell me nothing either.

• • •

Nobody had any great plans for New Year's Eve. Ty was still in Chicago for a couple more days, so Damey and his mom planned to stay home. Bill stressed to Damey, "New Year's Eve is amateur night. All the once-a-year drunks get out there with the regulars, and it's a mess. The smartest thing to do is to stay home. It's fun to see if you can keep awake long enough to watch the celebrations going on around the world on TV as people greet the New Year."

So, that became the plan. Shaundra had jumped in the shower New Year's Eve afternoon when her cell phone rang. Damey answered it.

"Hello," Damey said not recognizing the number on the caller ID.

"Uh, I wonder if I reached the wrong number. I'm trying to get a hold of Shaundra Martin."

"You've got the right number. She's in the shower. Can I take a message?"

"So, uh. Who are you?" the caller asked.

"Damey Martin. Shaundra's my mom."

"Really? How old are you, Damey?"

"Twelve."

"What month were you born in?"

"September. Why?' Damey asked. "Why do you want to know all about that stuff? You don't even know me. I don't think I want to talk about me. You can ask my mom. If she thinks you should know, she'll tell you." Damey had been warned about strangers, child molesters, and other creeps. The way the guy talked made him suspicious.

"Just curious. Let's see, that means you were conceived in December thirteen years ago. Interesting." He said as his voice drifted off to the point where he was almost inaudible.

"I'm not gonna talk any more about me," Damey said raising his voice. "You want Mom to call you or what?"

"Hey! Don't get your shorts tied in a knot," the caller snarled. "I'm an old friend of your mom's. I'm just trying to be friendly and interested. That's all. "So, what do you look like, Damey? Like how tall are you, and how much do you weigh?"

"I'm gonna hang up," Damey practically yelled as he reached for the 'End' button.

"Hey, wait," the caller yelled back trying to stop him. "Didn't mean to spook you or anything. Got a pencil and paper so I can leave a note for your mom?

"Yeah, just a second," Damey said a little softer but still speaking with an edge.

With his mouth turned down into a scowl, Damey dug out a notebook and pen so he could take down the message thinking that the guy sure was a nosy piece of crap.

"Okay, go ahead," he said with a slight edge to his voice.

"Okay, write this down. My name is Xavier, spelled with an 'X,' and my phone number is 450-463-9721. Ask your mom to call me."

They hung up, and Damey went back to the game on his iPad, but he couldn't concentrate. He kept thinking about the phone call. There was something about that guy that irked him. He asked too many questions. Stupid!

Damey's mind continued to churn. Ty's never asked me personal questions like that, and he's a friend. More than that. At least I hope he might be someday. He and Mom have been dating about three months. Don't know how serious it is with them. Mom says they are friends, period. The only thing I know for sure is that Ty has never stayed the night. I know they go out every Tuesday and Thursday night after class when I'm at Grandpa's, but Mom never tells me nothin'.

Fifteen minutes later, Shaundra came out of the bathroom all fresh and clean wearing the new robe Damey had bought her for Christmas, with Grandpa's help, of course.

"Mom, you had a phone call. The guy kind of freaked me out. He asked all kinds of questions about me. I didn't like that. I quit answering them after a while. Told him he had to ask you."

"Like what, Honey?"

"Stuff like how old I am, my birthday, and when you got pregnant for me, how big I am, what I look like—crud like that. When I asked him why he wanted to know, he said he was just being curious and making conversation. Said he's an old friend of yours from way back. Didn't sound that way to me. Just sounded like a nosy creep, not friendly"

"That is weird, Honey. Did he give you his name and number?"

"Yeah, it's all here on this sheet of paper. His name's Xavier spelled with an 'X.' His telephone's on there too. Wants you to call him."

Shaundra wobbled on her feet like she might fall. She caught herself by grabbing the edge of the sofa.

"What's the matter, Mom. You're acting funny. Are you okay? Who is that dude, anyway?"

"It's okay. Like he said, he's an old friend who I haven't seen or heard from in years. Lots of history. Lots of memories—some good, some bad. I'm going to go out in the kitchen and call him so I won't disturb you."

By then, Damey's curiosity was running amok. She never goes into another room to make a phone call. She always talks to all her friends in front of me. She never tries to hide anything from me—except when it comes to Ty. She's acted weird and uneasy. That makes me feel funny. What's going on?

When she came back into the living room, she said, "Call Grandpa and see if you can spend the night. Xavier's an old friend, and I'm going to meet him at the Outback in an hour. The place will be hammered and service slow, so I'll probably be late, very late. Besides, he and I have a lot of catching up to do."

She didn't act particularly happy or excited to meet up with this old friend. It looked to Damey more like one of those things people sometimes *have* to do.

"Mom, are you sure you're okay? "

"Everything's fine. The call took me by surprise, that's all. Now, call Grandpa."

"I don't need to call Grandpa. I can just go over there if you're trying to get rid of me."

"No, you know better than that. Call him and ask. Now, get your butt in gear and do what you're told without arguing for a change."

Without another word, Shaundra turned her back on him and headed to her bedroom to dress.

Why'd she snap at me? I didn't do nothing. Something 'bout that guy's got her all nerved up.

Damey called Grandpa. His going over and spending the night would be fine, just like he knew it would. Actually, he felt more comfortable doing it. He didn't want to be there if the dude came home with her after dinner for a drink or anything. Something didn't feel right.

Damey hollered up the steps and told his mom he was leaving and then ran across the street.

Grandpa listened to Damey's rant without commenting until the end. With all kinds of suspicions of his own, he tried to defuse the situation for Damey's sake. "Maybe he was trying to be friendly and didn't know how to do it. Not everyone knows how to deal with or talk to kids. Some adults have no kids in their lives and don't have a clue. Ever think of that?"

That's Damey's biological father, Bill thought. I know darned well it is What is he up to? What does he want? Why now? It has to be. Why else would he quiz Damey like he did? He damned near asked him everything except the size of his penis. Why do I think this is gonna be nothin' but bad news? Damey's suspicious, too. I'd better get him out of there for a while this afternoon and erase some of this from his mind for a spell.

"Damey, grab you coat. We're going over to the mall to get in a walk and then go to a restaurant for an early dinner. I don't feel like cooking. It's New Year's Eve. Then tonight we'll watch all the festivities on TV."

Grandpa walked the mall almost every day when it was too cold or rainy to ride his bike, so it seemed perfectly normal to Damey. He'd walked with him dozens of time.

Neither one said another word about the stranger on the phone, yet the tension lingered in the air. Damey didn't talk non-stop as usual. His answers were all short and to the point like he always spoke when he felt upset or nervous. Halfway through the mall, Grandpa nudged him. "Turn in there."

Both masseurs in the Chinese Massage parlor stood by the desk and greeted them. Grandpa normally got a massage every week. This would be Damey's first. Grandpa aimed him at the shorter of the two and said, "Gentle—relaxation—thirty minutes. *Very tense.*"

The masseur nodded and led Damey to a table. The boy had no idea what was going on. He just did what the man told him. He emptied his pockets into a basket, took off his shoes, and lay face down on the table with his nose buried in the slot provided and his arms down to his sides.

A half hour later when grandpa finished his massage, he looked over at the table where Damey lay motionless. "Asleep," said Chan, the masseur

"Good," Grandpa nodded. "When did he pass out?"

"Half way," Chan smiled as he bowed, "plenty relaxed."

As Bill dug out his credit card to pay, Chan said, "Only twenty minutes for boy. I stop early. Didn't want wake him,"

"He needed that," Bill told him. "He's all stressed out."

"I know. When start, very tense. Relax about ten minutes. Doze off fifteen and wake up. Doze off again, wake up. Doze off twenty minutes—don't wake up. I rub easy and stop after that. Snore soft and easy."

"Thanks," Bill said smiling. That's how he always knew when Damey was dead to the world. The kid purred like a kitten. "I guess I'd better wake him up so you can have your table back."

"Okay, not busy," he shrugged. " He can sleep."

Bill walked over to the sleeping boy and tapped his left shoulder with the back of his hand. "Hey, little buddy, time to wake up. We've got to finish our walk and then go eat."

Damey didn't stir. He continued to snooze. Bill placed a hand on each shoulder and gently shook him awake asking, "Hey, Damey, are you still alive?"

Damey jerked his head up with blurry half crossed eyes. "Huh? What? Is it morning already?"

With Grandpa and the two masseurs laughing at him, Damey's fog lifted, and he realized where he was and what had happened. Red faced, he tried to sit up and almost fell off the table. Chan caught him and helped him to his feet so he could get his belongings out of the basket and put on his shoes and coat.

When they left, they continued the second half of their walk sipping on the bottled water the masseur provided. "Grandpa, I'm sorry. I didn't mean to fall asleep. It just felt so good, I couldn't help it."

"Why are you sorry?"

"Because it wasted a bunch of your money. You told him to give me a gentle, relaxing massage. So,

178

what'd I do? I fell asleep. How could I enjoy it if I was sleeping? Didn't mean to."

Grandpa laughed out loud. "Listen to yourself. Are you making any sense? Yes, I told him gentle and relaxing. How much more relaxed could you get? I think I more than got my money's worth. Besides, he only charged me for twenty minutes because you were out cold as if someone had rapped you beside the head with a two-by-four."

"I guess it worked. I sure feel mellow, but it doesn't seem right."

Grandpa picked up the hiking speed for the last quarter of their walk so most of the chatting stopped until they reached the car with Grandpa puffing slightly.

"So, what do you want for dinner?" Bill asked.

"How about a double cheeseburger deluxe with extra greasy fries?" Damey answered with a straight face.

"I wonder if we could find a vegan restaurant around here so I could load you up with grains, veggies, and fruit?"

"I guess I could compromise by going for that baked salmon at the Outback," Damey said.

"Deal! Providing you don't fall asleep in the middle of dinner and let your face fall flat into your plate."

"*Grandpa!*"

CHAPTER 17

T he next morning started the New Year. Damey figured he'd go home and spend the day with his mom, since she didn't have to work. He looked out of Bill's window towards his house as he slipped on his coat and spotted a strange car in the driveway.

"Grandpa, I don't want to go home. Can I stay here?"

"Of course, but don't you want to meet the guy?"

"No," he said a little too quickly.

Bill stretched out in his Lazy Boy and put down the paper. He watched Damey fidget by the window. "Okay, no more one word responses out of you, young man. Talk to me. What's going on in that peaked little head of yours? I know you don't trust the guy, but why? What are you thinking? You've never even met him. He might be a great guy. Who knows if you don't give him a chance?"

Damey turned around with a pained expression on his face and plopped down on the sofa. He didn't put the leg rest up; he leaned forward with his hands grasping his knees. "I think he might be my father. I remember my mom talking to her mother one time on the phone, and she mentioned the name Xavier. When she got off the phone, I asked her who the guy was."

Bill put the legs down on his chair, stood up, went out to the kitchen, and poured another cup of coffee. Walking back to the living room, he watched Damey squirm. "So what did she say?"

"She got all nerved up, secretive, popped an attitude, and told me to mind my own business and quit listening in on her phone conversations, so I shut up. She stayed grouchy the whole day."

"Suppose it is? Wouldn't you like to meet your dad?" Bill said. "Seems like that would only be natural."

"No."

"Tell me why."

"He might be my father, but he'll never be my dad. If I had a dad, he'd be like you and Ty, and want to be a part of my life. He wouldn't have sneaked off like a wounded rat when he found out my mom was pregnant." Damey couldn't sit still and his eyes focused on the floor. "As far as I'm concerned, my so-called father is as bad as Mom's parents who wanted me aborted. I want nothing to do with any of them—never!"

"I hate to see you so bitter, little man."

"I've got a mom and a grandpa plus a bunch of adoptive aunts, uncles, and cousins. All I need, with maybe one exception." He looked at Bill with a sad longing expression on his face.

Grandpa nodded."Okay then, why don't you call Alex? We got about four inches of fresh snow last night, and Santa left both of you snowboards that you haven't used. I can hear the hills over at the park calling now, 'Aaaaalex, Daaaamey, where are you?'"

"Sounds like a good idea. You gonna take us?"

"Yep. I'll drive you over and then pick you up at bedtime."

"Grandpa, what about lunch and dinner?"

"Oh, I guess we'll have to figure something out, won't we. Give Alex a call and see if he wants to go."

• • •

Around three in the afternoon, Bill's phone rang. Caller ID said, 'Shaundra.' He'd expected to hear from her all day, and worried about how he'd answer all her questions. He didn't want to force Damey into something, but, on the other hand, Shaundra had the final say.

"Bill, where's Damey? I haven't seen him all day."

"I took him and Alex over to the park around nine this morning so they could go snowboarding on the hills," He said as he paced back and forth in front of the window looking across the street.

"About twelve-thirty, I picked them up, brought them home, and fed them some lunch. They needed to warm up and dry out. In the meantime, I'm sending you a bill. I think both of those brats are going through another growth spurt. They can inhale more groceries than a hog at Waller Creek.

"I know. His appetite is hard to keep up with. However, back to the reason I called. Is he planning on coming home sometime this afternoon? I'd like him to meet Xavier."

Bill decided to give it to Shaundra straight. She needed to know. If she hadn't told Damey the facts about Xavier, she needed to do it. If he and Damey were wrong in their suspicions, then it didn't make any difference.

"Shaundra, Damey doesn't want to meet him," he said.

Shaundra's voice sounded guarded. "Why? What's he saying?"

Hedging a little, Bill answered. "Ah, he's got it in his head that Xavier might be his father, and he doesn't want to have anything to do with him. I've tried to talk to him about the guy, but all he does is scowl and get angry. Shaundra, is Damey right about Xavier?"

Her voice softened, and she hesitated a second before answering. "Yes. But, how did he know?"

"Something to do with a phone conversation he overheard between you and your mother."

"That kid has the damndest memory for negative things I've ever seen. He can repeat verbatim discussions and incidents when I scolded or spanked him as a little boy, and then not remember what time I tell him to be home. I swear, he's going to drive me nuts."

"So, are you going to tell him about Xavier?"

"I don't want to be the one to do it. Will you?"

Bill knew Shaundra felt overwhelmed at times. She'd told him how she relished the fact he'd been able to step in and help her with Damey. Sometimes she relied on him too much. This time, however, she needed to step in and be the parent.

"No. You've got to do that, Shaundra. Are you open to a suggestion?"

"Yes, anything."

"Why don't you wait until about four o'clock, and then you and Xavier drive your car over to the park so he'll recognize it? Pick the boys up, drop Alex off at his house, and then go home so Damey can jump into the shower and warm up. After that, take him out to dinner someplace quiet and tell him what's going on."

Shaundra didn't say anything for a few seconds. Bill heard her take a deep breath before she answered. "How am I going to tell Damey that the father, who

184

I've always said ran away and abandoned him as a two-month fetus, has come back and wants to meet him?

"He's only going to be here for two days and then go back to Oklahoma. It's not like he plans to move in or anything. He wants to see what he produced. Is that too much to ask? Is it too much to expect Damey to be civil and not act like a little jerk as he does sometimes?

"If Damey does act up, is it too much to expect Xavier to stay civil? I swear, if they both cop an attitude, I'll walk out."

• • •

At four o'clock, Shaundra and Xavier drove over to the park using her car so, like Bill suggested. Damey would be sure to recognize it and come over. Soon she spotted what appeared to be the boys racing down the hill side by side. Two thirds of the way down, their boards collided causing an immediate explosion of boys, boards, and snow all flying out of control in different directions, landing and tumbling the rest of the way down the hill before everything stopped. Shaundra gasped. Xavier didn't react.

"Come on."Without waiting for Xavier, Shaundra jumped out of the car and ran in their direction.

When she got to them, both boys were laughing hysterically, which is sometimes the alternative to crying. At least they were standing and appeared to be okay except they looked more like snowmen than boys.

"Boys, are you okay? That looked terrible," Shaundra said.

Laughing as they brushed the snow off, Damey answered, "Yeah, that's not the first time it's happened. We race and then try to bump boards to knock the other one off balance to win. Sometimes it works, sometimes we end up in a pile at the bottom."

"Well, at least nobody's hurt. Boys, I want you to meet my friend, Xavier, from Oklahoma."

Xavier nodded and mumbled. "Dudes."

Damey and Alex both stuck out their hands to shake as Damey's grandpa had taught them. Both looked Xavier in the eye without smiling, and said, "Pleased to meet you."

With an audible sigh, Xavier pulled his hand out of his coat pocket and shook Alex's first and then Damey's.

• • •

Damey had talked to Alex about this anticipated and planned meeting all day. The biggest question he had in his mind was when, where, and how it would take place.

Damey stared hard into the man's eyes. His mind started working again. I'm a mini-version of this creep.

I look just like him. Will I grow up to be an evil, worthless piece of dirt like him? No way. Grandpa and Ty are my heros. I wanna be like them.

With a light smile, Shaundra said, "We're going to drop Alex off. Then I want you to take a shower and warm up and put on your good clothes. The three of us are going out to eat someplace to celebrate the New Year."

"Can Alex go?" Damey said.

"No. Not this time. I want it to be just the three of us so you and Xavier can get a chance to know each other. He's an old friend, and I think you'll like him. Tomorrow he has to drive back to Oklahoma. He's going to visit us during the first week of April, and then you'll really get a chance to learn all about each other."

The boys climbed into the back seat, buckled up, and squeezed their snowboards between them. On the way home, they laughed as they re-hashed their day and the fun they'd had. For the short ride back home, the adults sat silently in the front seat staring straight ahead.

When they walked into the house, Damey stalled. He sat down on the floor and pulled off his snow boots and lined them up on the little rug beside the door. Then he took off his coat and hung it over the back of a chair in the kitchen near a heat duct so it could dry instead of tossing everything in the closet like normal.

"Go take your shower, Honey, and get warmed up. You're wet, cold, and shivering. Then, remember, I want you to put on some nice clothes. Any idea where you might like to go for dinner?"

"Mom, why don't the two of you go? You can talk about old times without having me listening in. That'd be more fun for you, wouldn't it? I can grab something out of the fridge or talk Grandpa into feeding me."

"No, we want you to be with us. That's the only way you're going to get acquainted with Xavier."

Shrugging his shoulders and without another word, Damey headed to the shower. As he dug clean clothes out of the closet, he could hear Xavier snarling in the kitchen at Shaundra. He couldn't make out the words, but from the tone of his voice. Damey figured he and Xavier shared their hostile feelings about each other.

• • •

Xavier chose a corner table in the restaurant. Damey grabbed a seat where he could look out the window at a pond and waterfall which had been shut down for the winter. At least there were some birds to watch—even a duck. The waitress came and took their drink orders, and they settled in to look at the menu. Everyone pretended to be absorbed with dinner decisions. After their orders were finally taken, the silence continued to permeate the area.

Finally, Xavier broke the spell. "So, little man, tell me about yourself. What're your favorite classes in school? Do you play any sports? Got a girlfriend?"

The forced, frozen smile on Xavier's face looked so phony, apparently, even he realized it and erased the thing.

"You're nothing but my sperm donor. How many other kids you got spread around the country?" Damey's sarcastic tone cut through the tense mood at the table as he stared into Xavier's eyes with a tight, frowning expression on his face.

"What? What do you mean?" Xavier asked, looking away. He wasn't into playing 'stare-down.'

"I've taken sex ed classes in school. I know what happened. You got my mother pregnant and then ran away like a coward instead of facing up to your responsibilities because she wouldn't get an abortion?"

"I was just a kid myself, Damarian. The whole situation scared me. I couldn't face it," he said not meeting Damey's glare.

"You were eighteen. You were a man, at least you should have been."

"That's one of the reasons I'm back now—to face up to those responsibilities a little." Xavier sighed. "Maybe you and I can develop a decent relationship. Maybe I can be a helpful guide in your life." Xavier looked down unsmiling as he spoke.

"Not interested." Damey folded his arms and watched Xavier squirm.

"You're not willing to give me a chance?"

"Don't know. Don't think so." Damey clenched his jaws as he turned his head and looked out the window.

Shaundra said, "It really is a beautiful place here. All kinds of cool things to look at. I think we should try to enjoy ourselves."

Right then dinner arrived, but nobody ate much. Damey picked at his meal without touching more than a bite or two. Finally, Xavier asked for the check so they could go home.

They hadn't much more than walked in the house, when Damey said, "Mom, okay if I run over to Grandpa's for a while? It's still early. He won't kick me out for an hour or so."

"No, I want you to stay home tonight. Maybe you and Xavier can talk—civilly.

With a deep sigh, Damey picked up his iPad, opened up the Kindle app, and curled up in his chair. Any attempt at conversation by either Xavier or his mom, he responded to with one or two word replies.

After a while, they left him alone.

• • •

The next morning after breakfast, Xavier asked, "You and Alex planning on going over to the park this morning? I'd be glad to take you."

The pleasant tone of voice, the smile, and the offer took Damey by surprise. "Sure. That'd be great. Want Alex to come down here, or are we going to pick him up at his house."

"Either way. You two figure it out."

When they got to the park, Damey looked at Xavier and asked, "You ever try one of these?"

"No, no way. That big hill looks scary. I about crapped my pants when you two went into that crash 'n burn yesterday. I thought you'd killed yourselves for sure."

Laughing, Alex said, "There's a bunny hill over here on the side for beginners if you'd like to try."

"I think I'll pass. I'll come over around twelve-thirty or so to get you guys for lunch. Keep an eye out for me."

"Okay, thanks, Xavier. We appreciate the ride," Damey said actually smiling.

Xavier smiled too, but that didn't mean a truce had been signed.

• • •

That night after dinner, Damey turned on the TV to the History Chanel. Xavier walked in from the kitchen. "What's that crap you're watching? Don't you know the Big Bang Theory is on? Turn the channel quick so we don't miss the beginning."

191

"Here, do it yourself. I'm going over to Grandpa's." After tossing the remote to Xavier, Damey picked up his iPad, slipped on his coat, and walked out the door.

"Hey, how's my boy?" Grandpa asked when Damey walked in. "Come give me a hug. I haven't seen you all day. Things going any smoother over there?"

After their mutual hug, Damey sat down, put up the leg-rest on the sofa, and made himself comfortable. "Better, I think. At least we didn't snarl at each other all day. I even asked him if he'd like to try out my snowboard, but he chickened out. Alex showed him the bunny hill for beginners, but he laughed and said, 'No way.' I left just now because he came in and changed channels on me."

"Is there something on you wanted to see? You can watch it here if you like."

"No, it was just the object of the thing. I'll read my Kindle. I'm in the middle of a book, so that's fine."

"Ok, so you think you might grow to like this guy, or are you going to be a little jerk around him forever?"

"You want the kid-style version or the Grandpa-style?"

"You know."

"Okay, I'll probably be a little jerk forever."

"Well, good. At least you aren't telling me you're going to be the south end of a donkey's digestive track."

Damey's eyes and mouth gaped open simultaneously. Then he and Grandpa both laughed as

Damey walked over demanding another extended hug as they continued to laugh.

Damey enjoyed life at Grandpa's. He never knew what Grandpa would spring on him next.

Saturday morning Xavier packed up and headed west. He had to be back to work Monday morning. He and Shaundra parted with a sloppy kiss. Xavier and Damey shook hands, nodded, and grunting their goodbyes.

CHAPTER 18

The Day Xavier left, Damey relaxed. For the first time in a couple of days, he felt he could actually kick back and enjoy life again without constantly looking over his shoulder.

The next day Tyrone called. Damey listened to Shaundra's end of the conversation and tried to piece it together. Apparently, Ty had returned from his holiday visit to his parents in Chicago and wanted to come over.

Shaundra said, "So good to hear your voice again. Why don't you come over for lunch? There are some things we need to talk about."

When she got off the phone, she said, "Damey, you've either got to go to the park this afternoon after lunch or over to Grandpa's. You aren't staying here.

Ty's coming to have lunch with us, and then you're going to disappear until dinner. Got it?"

"I'll call Alex and we'll probably go to the park. Mom, you're not gonna dump Ty are you?"

"No, no. Not that, but I do need to talk to him. I'm going to tell him everything. Honey, I'm so confused right now, I don't know what to say. I care for Ty a great deal, but I've had this 'thing' for Xavier since I was fourteen. My brain's scrambled right now. I might not be the easiest person to live with for awhile, but I've got to get through this. Ok?"

"You know where I stand," Damey said. He had a slight frown on his face as he tried to read the situation. He wasn't quite sure where this all was going.

"Yeah, yes I do. Don't make this any harder on me than it already is."

• • •

After lunch, Ty and Shaundra took Damey and Alex to the park with their snowboards and dropped them off. When Damey started to get out of the car, he stopped, leaned over the front seat, and squeezed Ty around the shoulders. "Glad you're back." And then he jumped out of the car and raced Alex up the hill.

"So, what's going on?" Ty said.

"let's go back to the house. We have to talk." Shaundra said staring straight ahead, not looking at him.

As soon as they walked in the front door, Shaundra made coffee. She slipped a shot of Kahlua in hers. Tyrone declined. He wanted to find out what was going on.

She sipped her coffee for a couple of minutes and cleared her throat. "Xavier came to town over the holidays. I saw him for two days before he left."

"And?" It came out a little gruffer than he'd intended.

"He wants to reconnect our relationship," Shaundra said with her voice quavering. "He plans to take a vacation the first week of April and come back supposedly to visit his parents. Then he wants Damey and me to go out to Oklahoma for a couple of weeks right after school gets out. He can arrange another week's vacation then. I think he feels guilty about the past twelve years."

"What are you thinking?" His mind whirled at the scenario. Was she going to scuttle their relationship? Didn't it mean anything? What about Damey? God, he loved that little guy. He didn't want him hurt. He shouldn't have gone to Chicago. He had to. He has parents too. It was the holidays.

"I don't know. Like I told Damey, I'm so confused. Ty, I think I'm falling madly in love with you. But, I don't know how you feel for sure about me. I think I do, but we've never really expressed it. And then there's Xavier. I fell in love with him at fourteen. We had a baby together at sixteen, and I've fantasized about him for twelve years. I've never gotten over him after all this time." She stared at the bottle of Kahlua.

"What's Damey saying?" He noticed her staring at the bottle instead of making eye contact with him. He didn't like the vibrations.

"Damey's being a little turd. He despises him. He won't give him the time of day. Xavier called mid afternoon of New Year's Eve while I was in the shower and asked Damey a whole bunch of personal questions that he shouldn't have. That turned Damey off. The conversation made him suspicious, and he can't or won't let it go."

Ty watched as she squirmed on the barstool, shifting her feet back and forth from the leg rest on the chair to the one on the counter.

"I didn't tell Damey who he was at first. I wanted to see how our dinner date went before I said a word. Damey spent the night at Bill's, and when he woke up, he saw Xavier's car here. He automatically assumed he'd spent the night. Ty, he didn't. He came over early in the morning to spend the day and meet Damey. Damey's pissed about that because he doesn't believe me. I swear. Nothing happened."

Ty sat there trying to keep his face expressionless while he sipped his coffee. It didn't work. The news crushed his spirits. He'd been so happy to get back, and then this news felt like a right hook to the jaw.

Shaundra looked at his face and saw the pain. She continued with the story. "So what'd Damey do? Instead of checking in, he suckered Bill into taking him and Alex to the park. That afternoon I called to find out what was going on. Bill told me what had happened, and that Damey was still mad. He suggested Xavier and I pick up the boys, so we did. Damey recognized him immediately. He said it was like looking into a mirror twenty years down the road. They look so much alike, it's scary."

They sat without speaking for a moment or two as they sipped their coffee. Shaundra refilled their cups. Ty felt an empty lump in the pit of his stomach. He didn't know what to do or say. He considered getting up and walking out, but no, he wouldn't be a quitter. He'd fight for her one way or the other. She was right. They hadn't talked about their relationship. Maybe they should—now.

"Shaundra, what about us? I do care about you a great deal. I think I'm falling in love too. I really don't know what it feels like. I've never had a committed relationship. It's always been work, wrestling, school, going to Chicago to see my parents, name it. I've never taken the time for a personal life until you came along. I don't want to lose you. I don't want to lose Damey."

Shaundra sat quietly for a minute, looked at her cup, poured another shot, and sighed deeply. "I'd love to think we could carry on just as we have the past few months—like Xavier never happened. But I also know the reality of the situation. I can't be in love with two men at the same time. I love and respect you too much, Ty. I can't ask you to hang around in the wings while I make up my stupid assed mind. That's not fair to you. What do you want to do?"

"There are too many equations rolling around in my head right now. What's best for you? What's best for me? What's best for Damey? I could care less about Xavier. I'm not going to give up. I want both of you. But, maybe for the next few months, we should put our relationship more on a 'friends' basis instead of a 'courting' one."

Both sat there with their minds whirling. Both confused. Both speechless. Neither wanted to end the relationship, yet the other obstacle, Xavier, dangled in front of their consciousness.

Finally, Ty stood up. "Did you see the email I sent this morning? There's going to be a voluntary practice from three to five every day for the rest of the week. I'd like for Damey and Alex to be there. This is a great learning time since our season is right at the midway point. It starts in about an hour. Want me to pick them up or do you want to?"

"I'll go get them. No doubt. They'll be there."

Unlike Ty, when he stood up to go, he felt his body and shoulders slump. He rinsed out his cup, and put it into the dishwasher. Shaundra stood wobbly by the counter holding on to it with both hands. Ty slipped on his coat which had been draped behind the chair, and gave her a quick hug, no kiss.

"Talk to you soon." He took a deep breath, expanding his chest Then he marched to the door, with his head up, shoulders straight, and didn't look back.

• • •

At two-thirty Shaundra washed her face making sure no tear stains remained, dried it, blotted her eyes with a tissue, and headed to the park to pick up the boys. She did not want to discuss the situation with Damey, especially with Alex listening. She'd grab the boys and tell them they had practice between three and five and call it good.

"What's up, Mom? You're early."

"Tyrone sent an email this morning that I hadn't seen. You have practice every day from three to five. Do you need to pick up anything at home, or did you leave your stuff in your lockers over vacation?

"I left mine at school."

"Me too," said Alex.

"Oh, boy. I bet it all smells ripe. Both of you had better take your workout clothes home after practice tonight and get them washed. Why didn't you bring them home during break?"

"I dunno. Forgot, I guess," Damey said. "I was excited 'bout vacation. Stinky gym clothes was the last thing on my mind."

Shaundra let them both have it a little about how gross they would smell out on the mat, so they'd better work out with each other and avoid their teammates. That way, they could enjoy each other's stench.

After having Alex call his mom, she managed to keep up the nagging until she dropped them off promising to pick them up at five. The more she talked, the less chance they had to ask questions—the last thing she wanted right then.

The boys clenched their jaws and pursed their lips as tightly as possible to avoid laughing. They still managed mutual eye rolls.

• • •

Walking into the school and down the hall to the gym, Damey and Alex talked a little about his mom's and Ty's relationship and what might have happened that afternoon. Obviously, something had. The chatter about that topic ceased as soon as they got to the locker room. As they dressed for practice, Damey rehashed the car ride in his mind. Boy, she sure was grouchy. What happened? Did Ty break up with her? Will I see him outside of school again? How will he be at practice? Will he be nice to me? Will he be mean to me?

During the course of practice, neither Ty nor Damey mentioned the earlier meeting. It wasn't the time or the place even if there weren't too many kids there. He'd quiz his mother later. Ty demonstrated a move using Damey as his practice dummy. Then Damey had to repeat the move using Ty as his dummy. When he did, Damey managed to snuggle Ty a little with their cheeks together as he gave Ty a surreptitious hug.

When he completed the move to Ty's satisfaction, he gave Damey a pat on the seat and said, "Good job."

Damey smiled and relaxed a little. He knew Ty still liked him.

• • •

After practice, Shaundra picked the boys up, took Alex to his house, and then the two of them went home—saying nothing about Ty. Nothing, that is, until they walked into the house. "Ok, Mom. Let's have it. What's going on?"

"Not much. I told him all about Xavier coming and his return trip in April and our planned trip to

Oklahoma in June. We're going to stay friends to see how everything plays out."

"That's a bunch of bull, Mom, and you know it. You love Ty. How can you do such a thing to him?"

With eyes opened wide and bulging, Shaundra screamed at him. "Don't get in my face, young man. Keep it up and I'll take a belt to your ass right now. I told you earlier that this is hard enough on me without you butting in. I told you I'd probably be out of sorts until it all gets squared away. That's the way it is. Don't push your luck!" Then, with tears starting to leak out of her eyes, she put her hands on Damey's shoulders, looked him in the eye, and said, "Oh, Honey. I'm sorry. Please have patience with me."

Quickly wiping her face with the kitchen towel, she opened the refrigerator to figure out what she was going to make for dinner. It had to be fast and easy.

CHAPTER 19

Monday morning came, meaning it was time to go back to school. Week one after vacation would be used to learn new stuff. Week two would be review. And then, they crammed all the exams into four half days during week three.

On Monday of week two, Mr. Allen outlined the entire semester of pre-algebra on the board. "This is what you're responsible for on the final next week. Write it down. Then, I want you to break into groups of three or four people and review everything whether you think you know it or not. Go to the beginning and work your way through the outline. If no one in your group can figure something out, raise your hands, and I'll get to you as quickly as I can."

As class members started to team up, Damey and Alex were invited to join almost every group. Damey looked across the room and spotted Liam parked with his two buddies at a table looking completely lost. "Mind if I join your group?" he asked pulling up a chair and sitting down. Alex joined another struggling group.

Taken completely off guard, the three outcasts and former bullies welcomed him not knowing what to expect. Was he going to make fun of them? Would he laugh at them because they weren't as smart as he was? They didn't know what to expect.

"Ok, guys. Gots an idea how to do this. Let's start at the beginning like Mr. Allen said, and I'll teach ya all this crap, and you've gotta learn it. That's the best way for me to review everything for myself. We gots all week so we'll go as far as we can. Okay?"

The other three boys nodded, breaking a little sweat on their brows, not knowing exactly what to expect.

Watching progress like a hawk, Mr. Allen didn't stray too far away for the first day or so. By Wednesday he ignored them. At that point, Damey's group and Alex's group were the only ones who hadn't asked for help. The two group leaders played teacher, just like they did with Grandpa Tutor. Hopefully, something positive could be happening.

By Friday, they managed to get through half the outline. "Tell you what," Damey said. "I'll be at the city library from two to four in the afternoon Saturday and Sunday studying if anyone wants to join me."

Since Shaundra had flown out to Oklahoma for the weekend, Damey would be spending the next couple of days with Grandpa. Damey's putting his hand out to help the outcasts made Bill beam with pride. He promised to drive him to the library both days at two and pick him up at four. All four boys showed up both days. Alex had made the same deal with his group, and they all came as well. They occupied two corner tables in the library and learned math.

Finals came and went. Damey and Alex aced their finals and even Liam and his buddies passed math— much to the surprise of Mr. Allen.

• • •

Winter dragged on with tons of icy cold snow and frigid wind chills. The boys didn't get a whole lot of snowboarding time except on weekends because of after school wrestling practice and meets. Damey spent as much time with Grandpa as he could. He felt more comfortable there. The tension permeated the air at home.

Ty and his mom were still dating on Tuesday and Thursday nights—he thought. Nobody provided him with a whole lot of information. Grandpa claimed he didn't know anything either. Damey wasn't sure if he believed that or not.

The last week of March arrived along with the league tournament. Damey hoped he could win, but didn't know for sure. He'd wrestled all eight kids on his chart and beaten six of them. The JV tourney didn't generate as much pressure or excitement as the varsity one did, but he still wanted to win.

Even Shaundra managed to make it to this one. It was her first. She followed Grandpa around as he explained things the best he could. The only thing she understood for sure was when the final whistle blew, the referee raised the winner's hand.

As the day progressed, Damey won his first three matches. When finals started at seven, he'd be wrestling for the seventy-four pound JV championship.

"Honey, I'm so proud of you," Shaundra told him as the three of them snacked in the cafeteria. "I never realized the sport was so complicated."

"Yeah, there're all kinds of moves and different ways to score points. The best thing is to pin your opponent. That gives your team more points." He continued to talk—not eating a whole lot. Hungry as he was, Damey didn't dare eat too much. He'd never live it down if he puked on the mat.

Bill mostly listened, adding a tidbit or two as they gabbed. He wanted them to experience some quality time. There hadn't been a whole lot of it between them lately.

As they talked, Damey felt a surge of adrenalin kick in. His mom actually seemed interested and excited for him. He couldn't wait to get back out there to show her what he could do.

Shortly before he had to go and meet with the team, he felt a tap on the shoulder. "Can you slide over, little buddy? Thought I'd join you guys a few minutes before we have to get people warmed up for finals."

Damey moved over smiling as Tyrone slipped in between him and his mother. He looked over at Shaundra, "He's doing great, don't you think?"

"Yes. I am enjoying this. I just wish I'd been able to see his meets during the season."

"What do you think, Grandpa? The kid doing ok?"

"Yeah, but he should have pinned that Penfield boy in his second match. Looked like he had him for a second or two until the kid squirmed away. Oooh, the boy's shoulder was only an inch from the mat. One more chest-to-chest thump would have had him."

"I know. I felt like stomping my foot on the mat too, but since he won by six, I guess I won't complain too badly." Ty said as he nudged Damey in the ribs with his elbow.

They all laughed a bit at Damey's expense when another deep, male voice spoke behind them. "Mind if I join this little party?"

Ty stood up and stuck out his hand. "Hi, join the group. In fact, you can take my place at the table. I was just leaving. Got to get the boys ready for finals. My name's Tyrone, and you've got to be Xavier. You look just like my boy."

He looked over at the downcast Damey and smiled, "Take a couple of minutes and then head to the locker room. Don't want you to miss my classic pre-finals pep talk."

"I'll come now. Gots to go to the bathroom before we warm up." Without another word to anyone, Damey tossed his garbage and followed Ty to the gym.

That previous adrenalin surge hit the back of the urinal, and Damey walked to the sink feeling totally deflated. Washing his hands with cold water, he looked at himself in the mirror. He wanted to cry. He didn't dare.

A half hour later, the public address announcer called out Damey and his opponent's names and told them which mat to report to. Ty met him at the corner of the mat. He did something he'd never done before. He put his hands on both sides of Damey's face and lifted his head so they were eye-to-eye. "Do your best. Whatever happens, happens. You're still my favorite kid in the whole wide world. Which is good, because you know how I detest kids."

Feeling as rotten as he did, Damey couldn't help but laugh knowing Ty was just teasing him about hating kids. He'd do his best.

A minute and a half into the second period, the referee slapped the mat. Damey lay flat on his back pinned for the first time all season. He shook hands with his opponent as the referee raised the other boy's hand in victory. Damey trudged off to the side sweating and with tears flooding out of both eyes. He smelled like a well used wrestling mat, grungy and sweat stained.

Ty tossed him a towel and led him to the award's platform. Damey accepted his second place medal without a smile. The tears had stopped, but his nose hadn't. He wiped it with his arm again.

After the one minute ceremony, which consisted of handing out ribbons and congratulations to the first three place winners, Grandpa met Damey off to the side of the platform and walked him to the locker room again so he could shower and get dressed. Damey's day had been ruined, and he wanted to go home.

"I'll wait for you outside the door right here beside the bleachers," Bill said.

"Why? Why, Grandpa? Why'd he have to show up and spoil my whole day? He's not even due to be here until Monday. Why?" Without waiting for an answer, he turned on his heal, flung open the door, and stomped into the locker room wiping his eyes and nose again with his arm.

Grandpa looked around for Alex. No way would he be too far away. Alex had lost in the semis and had already showered and dressed. Bill spotted him and motioned with his arm for Alex to come. "Go stay with Damey. He needs his best buddy right now."

Bill went to find Shaundra and Xavier. The three of them had ridden together. "I think, if you'll agree, it might be better if I take Damey home while the two of you ride together in Xavier's car. I'll wait outside of the locker room until he comes out. It might be awhile. I sent Alex in to stay with him until he gets himself together."

"Okay. Maybe that's best," Shaundra said. "He's going to blame Xavier for losing, isn't he?"

"Yep. He already has," Bill said looking at both of them. "What if he doesn't want to go home? I can keep him 'til he's ready if you want."

"Okay, but he's not going to hide all week. He can stay tonight, but tomorrow he's got to come home. Boot him out the door in the morning if you have to, and bolt the thing behind him. He's got to come to grips with reality, whatever that turns out to be."

After they left, Bill went back to pacing back and forth in the area by the locker room.

Pablo walked up to join him. "Alex with Damey?"

"Yeah, I sent him in there to keep him company. They should be out any time."

"I'm ready to go home. Probably shouldn't do it, but I'm gonna open the door and yell for him." He did and Alex answered.

In less than a minute, both sullen boys walked out of the locker room—coats on, rancid smelling gym bags in hand, and ready to leave.

211

Damey looked around, apparently trying to spot Xavier and his mother. He looked up at Bill and said, "Let's go."

They did. The ride home provided for no conversation except for, "Your house or mine?"

"Yours," Damey snapped.

"Surprise! Surprise!"

When they walked into the house, Bill told Damey, "Throw your stuff in the dirty clothes basket, and then let's talk."

After Damey deposited all his gear, he came back to the living room to look out the window. Xavier's car sat in the driveway. "Can I stay here all week? I won't be any bother. I promise."

"No. Mom's orders. If you want to stay the rest of today and tonight, fine. She wants you home tomorrow morning at the latest—no sneaking off to the gym to shoot hoops with Alex and the gang. You have to make an appearance tomorrow morning."

Damey sat down in his favorite chair and curled his legs up underneath of him.

"But, Grandpa, it's his fault I lost. He blew my mind. I wanted to win so bad. I was all psyched up to do it too. Seeing him made me feel like a pricked balloon. All that excitement and energy just went poof."

He looked at the picture of the lone wolf hanging on the wall centering the sofa. That's the way he felt right then.

Grandpa said, "I saw you deflate on the spot when he walked up to our table, so I expected the results we got. I think Ty did too. What's done is done. You have to get over it and move on. And, you've got to get to know Xavier. You've got to ditch that attitude you're carrying around. You've got to give him a chance. He is your father. "

"He's not my father!" Damey growled under his breath still staring at the wolf. "He'll never be my father."

"Hey! Don't get mad at me." Bill said raising his voice just a tad. "I didn't cause all of this."

"I'm sorry, Grandpa. I'm not mad at you," Damey said, looking at Bill. "I'm mad at the rest of the world. It's not fair. I want Ty to be my dad, not some creep who wanted me aborted."

"Now, *you* be fair. He never said that. He just deserted the scene because he wasn't man enough at eighteen to do the right thing. Apparently he feels ready to do it now. You've got to give this whole situation time to play itself out. Xavier is only going to be here for a week—supposedly to see if the three of you can become a family of some kind.

"In June you're going out to Oklahoma for two weeks for a double-check. Ty can always stay your friend and mentor, but you've got to give Xavier a chance too. Think about something. If your mom's heart has ached for him for twelve years, he can't be all

213

bad, can he? You know, you could grow to really like and maybe even love the guy as your father and friend."

Damey sat in the chair staring straight ahead again. He pulled his knees up to his chest as he clutched them tightly with both hands, like he feared they'd get away. His mind shifted up into overdrive again. Mom has been in love with this guy since she was fourteen? That's a long time. Maybe I should give him an honest chance. It's always been Mom and me and then Grandpa. Maybe I'm just thinking of myself. I gotta think of Mom too. What does she want? I know she likes Ty really well, but does she really *love* this guy?

He decided that the next day he'd go home like nothing had happened and try not to be a total jerk. Grandpa was right. Maybe he should give him a chance. Maybe he could grow to actually like him. Maybe.

CHAPTER 20

Everyone wanted for Sunday to be a letdown day. Xavier needed to rest up from driving straight through from Oklahoma, and Damey wanted to unwind from the tournament. With wrestling season now finished, he wouldn't be seeing as much of Ty. He'd be with him every day in gym class, but it wouldn't be the one-on-one he had on the mat. Hopefully, when Xavier headed out, Ty and his mom would pick up where they had left off.

After lunch, Damey approached Xavier as he sprawled out on the sofa. "Want to play a game on the Wii with me?"

"Not today, I've got to catch up on my sleep. Why don't you play one of your games by yourself, but try not to be too noisy. Okay?"

"Okay, or maybe I'll go down to Alex's house. That way I won't disturb you."

"That'd be great. I'm just too tired to be much company today—much less start playing some silly damn game."

So Damey walked out, shutting the door a little harder than necessary. He went down to hang with Alex until he had to leave around three to go to his grandmother's. That left Damey on his own so he went to Grandpa's. Bill always smiled and made the kid feel more than welcome, whether he was or not. Damey never felt like he was a burden or unwanted there.

Damey never knocked; he walked in. "Grandpa, where you hiding?"

"Out in the kitchen. I'm trying a new recipe. Come out and give me a hand."

"What are you making?" Damey raised his eyebrows wondering 'What this time?' as he walked into the kitchen. Grandpa sprang more new recipes on him than he could count. Usually, they tasted great. Whatever Grandpa had made, it was already in the oven.

"It's a vegan pizza," Grandpa told him with a straight face.

Damey looked in the oven. Wrinkling up his nose, he muttered, "Oh, yuck. It looks like diarrhea on a crust."

"Close the door. Don't want to lose all the heat. It's on broil. Now, just to prove my point that you always yell before you're hit. Look at the box it came in and read it to me."

"One large pizza with pepperoni, ground beef, bacon, extra cheese, and mushrooms. Is that what it is really?"

"Yeah, but you probably won't want any since you think it looks like runny poop. I guess I'll have to eat the whole thing myself while you watch."

"Oh, not fair. Can't I at least have one piece?" By then Damey's olfactory senses had kicked in making his belly rumble. After all, he hadn't eaten anything for at least three hours.

"Okay, call your mom and tell her you're eating with me. If she hasn't started dinner yet, no sense for her to plan on you. At least try to act guilty that you're robbing me of half my dinner."

"You never eat more than half," Damey said. He knew Grandpa was teasing him this time.

"Call your mom, brat."

Damey rolled his eyes and called Shaundra. She told him it would be fine, and that she and Xavier would probably go out and get something on their own. She let him know to be home early and not to bother

Bill all night. He said he'd rather bug Grandpa, but promised he'd come home when he saw the car return.

Damey complained a bit about Xavier wanting to sleep all day and not play the Wii with him, but didn't push it too far. Actually, he acted a little more civil than he usually did when talking about him. Bill listened without passing any judgment. Time would tell how everything would work out.

• • •

On Monday, the first day of Spring Break, heavy rain pounded the area. Damey and Alex talked on the phone and decided they'd go over to the open gym at the middle school. Every day during vacation the school arranged to open the gym from one to five for anyone who wanted to come in and shoot hoops, play volleyball, or whatever. A custodian would be in charge, check out the balls, and keep an eye on things.

Alex's mom had a ladies church group she went to on Monday, so they decided to ask Xavier if he'd take them. If it wasn't raining, they'd have ridden their bikes. Shaundra had gone to work, so that left Damey and Xavier together.

"Could you run Alex and me over to the school? We're going stir crazy with this rain and want to get out for a while and play some hoops."

"Oh, jeeze, Damey. I'm right in the middle of a program. Can't you find someone else?"

Disappointed, Damey told Alex, "Let me get back to you. I'll call Grandpa."

Trying to keep his voice down so Xavier couldn't overhear his conversation, Damey called Bill. "Grandpa, is there any way you could take Alex and me to the school? I asked Xavier, but he's too busy sprawling out on the sofa watching TV and can't do it."

"Sure, I'll come over and get you now. Is Alex with you or do we have to pick him up?"

"Gots to pick him up."

"Okay, let him know. I'm on my way.

After he hung up, Damey scurried around, put on his gym shoes, found a jacket to help repel the rain, and waited for Grandpa.

"Nothing sarcastic about you, is there?" Xavier asked lifting his head off the pillow on the sofa.

"Why? What do you mean?" Damey said feeling uncomfortable. He didn't know Xavier had listened in and where this might lead.

"Whining to your grandpa about how I'm too busy watching TV is not exactly the best way to impress me with your smart mouth. Keep it up, and we just might have to do something about it."

The expression on Xavier's face sent chills through Damey. The guy was nasty and mean. Damey could feel it. Xavier hadn't really threatened him, yet Damey felt like he had. That's okay, he'd just avoid the dude as much as possible for the rest of the week.

And he did. Damey would get up in the morning and head out—either to Alex's or Grandpa's. Fortunately, the weather straightened up so the boys rode their bikes over to school every afternoon themselves. The rest of the Rainbow Gang started showing up after he and Alex made a few phone calls, so they played hoops for hours every day at one end of the gym.

Xavier planned to head for Oklahoma early Friday morning. It would be a two-day drive, and said he wanted to get home a day early so he could rest up and acclimate himself before going back to work. He slept in longer than usual giving Damey a chance to eat breakfast and disappear before he got up. That made Damey happy because he wouldn't have to say goodbye and be all phony pretending he'd miss him and all that crap.

He and Alex played on Alex's video games until after lunch when it was time to head for the gym. When they walked in, Damey stopped in his tracks. The gym monitor was Tyrone. As the boys grabbed a ball and headed to their hoop at the end of the court, Damey approached Ty. "Mr. Williams, would it be possible to talk to you in private?"

"Sure," he said as he tossed a ball to Alex. "Let's go to my office. I'll leave the door open in case of problems or someone needs something."

Damey could tell by the expression on Ty's face that he wondered what was up. He knew Xavier had been there all week and was probably curious about how things had gone. Since he and Shaundra hadn't had their Tuesday and Thursday night tryst, he wouldn't know if Damey and the guy had bonded during the time or not.

After they walked into the office, Damey edged away from the door as Ty followed. Out of sight, Damey grabbed him. "I gots to have a hug. Please, Ty. I miss you."

Tyrone held on to the sobbing boy and let him get it out of his system. He ignored the fact that the front of his shirt was getting wet.

After a few minutes, Damey quit gasping and got control of his emotions. He wiped his face with his shirt sleeve.

Ty tossed him a dirty towel that lay on the corner of his desk. "Isn't going through puberty fun?" Then he grabbed Damey in a headlock and gave him a light knuckle rub on top of his head. "Go into my private bathroom and wash your face and blow your nose while I take a look to make sure everything's running smoothly out there. Then you have to tell me what's going on."

Damey told him about his miserable Spring Break—how he'd tried to get to know the guy, but Xavier wanted nothing to do with him. He wouldn't even bring him over to school the day it rained so hard. He had to depend on Grandpa.

Ty let him talk and pour out his feelings. After Damey finally settled down, Ty told him, "I've got to go out and check up on things again. Stay as long as you need, but then get back to your game with your buds. Probably do you good to burn off some of that pent up energy and emotion."

Not too much later, Ty looked over at the Bows and saw Damey racing towards the basket with the ball. "Hey! You are supposed to dribble, you know."

Damey laughed. "Why? The pros don't."

"You're not a pro. Play the game right and play hard."

• • •

Over the course of the next two months, Shaundra and Tyrone continued their Tuesday and Thursday date nights after she finished her evening classes, and even occasionally dated on the weekends. One Sunday in May, Ty took Damey, Alex, and Grandpa to a Tiger game in Detroit. One of the players on the opponent's side had played ball with Ty in college, and they'd remained friends. He provided will-call tickets for them, and they had perfect seats—first base line, right behind the dugout.

Life felt good for Damey, except for that impending trip to Oklahoma for two weeks after school let out for the summer. He tried everything he could to convince his mom to let him stay home with Grandpa. It didn't work. She insisted.

School would be dismissed for the summer on the second Friday of June. Damey and his mom planned to leave Saturday morning. They packed enough clothes to last two weeks without having to spend a lot of time washing.

Shaundra said she didn't know if Xavier had a washer and dryer or not. Maybe she'd have to go to a laundry mat. If they packed enough, maybe she could avoid that hassle.

• • •

On the last day of school, Shaundra arranged for Damey to eat with Grandpa and spend the night. She and Tyrone needed to talk one last time before she and Damey left in the morning. Her frazzled nerves were accentuated by the fact she didn't know how she felt.

They went to the little, out-of-the-way local restaurant they usually went to after class. It stayed open until midnight so they had plenty of time. They occupied a corner booth which was somewhat secluded.

"It's okay, Shaundra," Tyrone said. "It's the only way you'll know for sure. If it's right, you'll have all kinds of decisions to make. You'll have to sell the house and move out there taking Damey away from me and his Grandpa."

Shaundra could feel him looking at her. She knew if she made eye contact, she'd cry so she stared at her cup of decaffeinated coffee as she held on to it with both hands.

" I'm not trying to put you on a guilt trip or anything," Ty said, "but it's not going to be an uncomplicated choice. It's not going to be easy for any of us. If it's not right after two weeks, I'll be here waiting for both of you when you return."

"I'm scared, Ty. I just don't know how I feel. I know this isn't right for you, but I have to do this."

When they parted that night, Shaundra held on to Ty for the longest time. She didn't want to let go. As they embraced, she asked herself, will this be the end of our relationship? Is this what I really want? If we leave in the morning and go out there, and it isn't the right thing, will Ty really still be here or is it all talk? I've loved Xavier for what feels like forever. Do I really love him more than Ty? I don't feel like I'm a strong enough person these days to make these decisions. Everything's depressing me. Why do I have to make this choice?

CHAPTER 21

Grandpa woke Damey about seven a.m. Saturday morning, fed him, and tried to shoo him out the door without any further meltdowns or drama.

"Grandpa, I don't wanna go. I wanna stay here with you. She can go see that creep by herself."

"Hey! It's going to be a fun adventure. It'll take you two days to get there, and you'll see all kinds of new and different things."

"No I won't. She never stops when I see things I wanna look at like you do. It'll be go, go, go from the time we pull out of the drive until we get there. Won't see or do nothing except sit in the car for hours and hours and stare at the highway."

"Yes you will, and there'll be all kinds of things to do and see when you get there. Have you Googled Lawton, Oklahoma?"

"No. Kept hoping I wouldn't have to go."

"It's a little smaller than Lansing but has a ton of parks. You'll see. Now give me a hug and get it in gear. Your mom's probably pacing the floor waiting for me to boot you out the door."

Damey grabbed his grandpa and didn't want to let go. He kept moving his face back and forth wiping his tears and drippy nose on Grandpa's shirt.

Bill shook his head, "You know, I'll have to change my shirt again after you leave. How much longer before you get through this? Will it ever end?"

Damey gave his face one last swipe on Grandpa's shirt before looking up with a red-eyed smile. Grandpa loved to tease him and he knew it.

"Here, put this in your pocket. Never know when you're going to need a pop or ice cream bar." Bill handed him three five dollar bills and five ones.

"Grandpa, I don't need this."

"Go. Your mom's starting to carry stuff out to the car. She could use some help."

After one more quick hug, Damey, scampered out the door, and ran across the street.

• • •

Bill watched as Shaundra and Damey loaded the car. Looked like she'd packed enough to last a month, not two weeks. Eventually the car backed out and headed down the street. Bill sighed as he waved to Damey as they drove by. He would never wish bad luck on anyone, but he sure hoped the experiment didn't work out the way she hoped. He wanted his Damey back. He plopped down in his soft, cushioned leather chair, and stared out the window.

• • •

As they waved goodbye to Grandpa and drove down the street, Shaundra handed Damey a folded laminated map. "You're in charge of getting us there. I know how to get onto I-69 and to Indianapolis, but from there on, you're in charge of directions. I've marked out the route so keep me informed on turnoffs and highway switches, and we'd better not end up in Florida."

With that, she tapped him on the shoulder with a balled up fist and smiled at him.

"Too bad Grandpa didn't offer to let us borrow his car for two weeks," Damey said. "His OnStar Navigation System would take us right to the door without any wrong turns or guesses."

"That's why I've got you. You're gonna be my GPS system. You might as well open it up and start figuring things out."

"You know, Mom. It'd be a lot more interesting if we took the back roads instead of all Interstates. I hate the big highways. They're so boring." Damey looked at the map with a deep sigh knowing that all he'd see for the next two days would be cars, trucks, and pavement. Shaundra didn't even bother to answer.

He pored over the map along with the written directions. It shouldn't be any big deal. She even had printed step-by-step instructions once they hit Lawton that directed them right to Xavier's house.

• • •

Shaudra settled back in her seat as her car edged up the ramp onto I-69. She double checked her makeup in the mirror, smugly nodded to herself, and they were on their way. Around Indianapolis they'd have to get on I-70 and that's where she needed Damey because of all the little switches from one business route to another to get on the right road. Would the little imp look at this as a challenge, or would he pull something unexpected behind her back? She'd been serious about not ending up in Florida. That might be a slight exaggeration, but she wouldn't put anything past him. He *so* didn't want to go.

About an hour after they headed south, Damey started squirming. Shaundra watched and waited. He was too old for, 'Are we there yet?' but he'd have his own version—mostly complaining about how boring the ride was. "Honey, there's a bag of apples and some bananas in the back seat if you want a snack. We'll stop for lunch after we get past Indianapolis and are on I-70. That's the main road heading west."

"This printout says 16 hours," Damey said with a pained tone to his voice. "Does that mean actual driving time, or does that include taking time out for lunch and dinner?"

I think that's straight driving time. Why don't you look out the window at the sights? You might spot something different."

"Why? You wouldn't stop if I did? You'd say we didn't have time."

"Damarian, is this going to be a peaceful trip, or are you going to be a pain in the butt the whole way?"

"I'll be good. How much further to Indianapolis?"

"About three hours."

"Aargh! I'll read my iPad."

• • •

They'd been driving since early morning stopping only for lunch and quick breaks. Bored out of his mind, Damey fell asleep. About four o'clock Sunday afternoon, Shaundra woke him up when she called Xavier. "I'm guessing we're a couple of hours out. Should we stop on the road for something to eat, or do you want us to wait until we get there?"

Damey stirred in his seat and listened to her end of the conversation as she repeated things knowing he was listening.

"Okay, we'll drive straight through and the three of us will go someplace. We can't wait to see you, too."

Damey rolled his eyes thinking, I like the way she says, we can't wait to see him. Ha!

He looked at her and smiled. He guessed he was glad he'd decided to behave himself during the trip, she looked excited and ready to have the long drive over, and he didn't want to spoil things for her. Oh, sixteen hours of driving made your butt and body weary. He needed to get out of that car.

When they pulled into the drive, Xavier came out to greet them. The house was a small, two-story bungalow with an unattached garage. He had Shaundra pull over onto the grass beside the drive because there was only room for one car in there. If she parked in the drive, he couldn't get his car out. Then he helped them unload their suitcases.

As they walked into the house, Xavier said, "Damey, I've fixed you up the sofa bed down in the basement. That'll be your room. There's a TV and dresser by the sofa. You'll find a toilet and a shower over in the corner so you should be all set. I also have wireless so when you're ready to hook up your iPad, let me know, and I'll give you the password."

Damey took his suitcase downstairs and looked around. Xavier had made the sofa bed up, so that was good. Wow! It even had a pillow. Looked a little bumpy though. He guessed the dresser was a Salvation Army reject, and the TV appeared older than Grandpa. He couldn't help but wonder if it even worked? He knew one thing for sure; the darned thing definitely wouldn't be high-definition. Didn't matter. He didn't plan to be there all that long.

He had to pee so he checked out the stool and shower in the corner. How classy, he thought to himself. Both were completely exposed without even a shower curtain. He looked up the steps to the basement door as he stood in front of the toilet. It was a straight visual shot from there to the doorway. If anyone like Xavier sneaked the thing open, he could stand right there and watch him using the john or taking a shower. He wondered if his privacy was as safe there as it was at home or at Grandpa's. He didn't trust the man, period.

Right then his mom cracked open the door and called down to him. Fortunately, he'd already zipped up and flushed. "Come on, Damey. We're going out to dinner."

Finally, Damey thought. He felt mortally starved. He washed his hands in the dirty sink and looked for a towel. Not finding one, he wiped them on his pants. He would check into towels later when he took his shower. He'd like to have taken one then, but it could wait. He thought it would wake him up a bit or something. Doing nothing for two days besides sitting in the car and watching for road signs had taken its toll.

"Where we goin' to eat?" he asked when he got upstairs. He thought he'd at least try to be friendly. They'd only be there for two weeks, if that.

"One of the local watering holes," Xavier told him. "Jump in the car and buckle up."

Oh, good. Damey thought to himself. He knew that 'watering hole' was a slang term for a bar so that's where they were going. He wondered if they'd even let him in the place. He also knew that Xavier had been drinking before they got there. He could smell it on him when they walked into the house.

Xavier seemed to drink a lot when he visited them in April. Damey didn't know how much, because most of the time he'd avoided the guy. However, he did know of at least two cases he polished off there at their house in only a week's time.

Dinner went okay. Xavier did most of the talking telling about the place being a hangout for him and the guys he worked with. Shaundra made small-talk and replied to his banter, but Damey essentially kept his mouth shut—obviously so.

Damey spent most of his time looking around. The place was dirty and smelled like a combination of booze and burned meat. The grill sat right behind the bar and the smoke and fumes permeated the place. Even the waitress looked grubby. She had on a dirty white apron of some kind with all kinds of old and new stains. Probably spilled drinks or slopped over food when she tried to carry too many empty plates at the same time.

Several of Xavier's friends stopped by the table to say hi and check out Shaundra. Damey watched the looks in their eyes and expressions, and wished they'd all go away. He didn't like the way they looked at his mom. Eventually, the strangers all disappeared. Damey noticed with every fresh beer, Xavier's volume inched another decibel louder. Was he celebrating their arrival, or is this the way he acted all the time?

"You're awfully quiet, little dude. That chopped steak taste good? It should've. Probably the first decent sit down meal you've had in a couple of days. I bet those garlic fries really hit the spot. They're known for them here."

"Yeah, it's good. I've just been listening. You've got a lot of friends. You come here a lot?" Damey said pretending to be interested. He bet Grandpa would gag at those greasy fries. They made his own stomach feel queasy. He wiped the oily residue off his mouth.

"Pretty much. Eat dinner here almost every night. Being all by myself gets pretty lonely. That's why I'm so glad you and your mom came to visit."

"Hopefully, it'll be fun," Damey responded sneaking a glance at his mom. She didn't approve of drinking and had nagged and warned Damey about it for as long as he could remember. The fake smile pasted on her face gave her thoughts away to Damey. He knew she wasn't happy. Xavier remained oblivious. He ordered another beer.

The ride home scared Damey. Xavier kept going over the center line and then would auto-correct to the right side of the road. Once he bounced off the curb causing Damey to yelp.

Xavier glared at him in the rearview mirror but didn't say anything. He didn't have to. The two of them made eye contact, and Damey got the message—don't say a word. Shaundra talked nervously. Damey could tell by the way she squirmed that she was wishing they'd hurry up and get back to the house.

When they walked into the place, Xavier turned to Damey. "I think it's time you got your butt to bed, boy. It's late, and your mom and I have a lot of catching up to do."

"Two things," Damey said. "Where are the towels? I want to take a shower. Also, what's your wireless password? I'll probably look at my iPad for a while before I go to sleep."

"Towels are in the bathroom closet. Take enough down there to last you. Just toss them on top of the dresser. The used ones you can throw on the floor in front of the washing machine. You don't shower every day do you?"

"Normally, I do every night before I go to bed."

"I may have to teach you how to use the washing machine then. I don't have that many towels."

"Don't worry, Xavier. I'll take care of the laundry while we're here and make sure everything stays washed up and put away. Damey, run on down now and get settled in for the night."

"Password?"

"It's easy, and no hacker would ever figure it out." He spelled it out as Damey wrote it down. "It's X-a-v-i-e-r-n-o-1. Stands for, Zavier's number one. Pretty cool, uh?"

"Ah, yeah. Nobody'd *ever* guess that one. Thanks."

Damey went into the bathroom and grabbed a couple of bath towels and hand towels, and headed down the steps to the basement. He wiped off the dusty dresser with a wash cloth before setting the towels down.

He tried the wireless password on his iPad before he did anything else. It worked--amazing. Then he stripped down and jumped into the shower. It wasn't a relaxing, pleasant event because he kept his eye on the door at the top of the steps. He'd left the towel on the toilet seat where he could grab it quickly if anyone opened the door. No one did.

Sleep sneaked up on him pretty quickly when he crawled into bed. It'd been a long, long day, and he felt exhausted. Thanks to Grandpa, he normally found himself in bed by nine whether he was tired or not. He didn't remember the last time he'd stayed up until

11:30, but that's what the clock said when he turned out the light.

Damey woke up early but didn't stir until he heard footsteps above him. He dressed in clean clothes and went up stairs. An empty bowl and cereal box waited for him on the counter. They told him to go ahead and help himself.

He noticed Xavier had a beer in his hand, and saw a slight frown on his mom's face. "You drink beer for breakfast?" Damey blurted out without thinking.

"Damey!" his mom said in her scolding voice.

"Why? You got a problem with that, boy?" Xavier sneered.

"I'm sorry. I've never seen anyone drinking their breakfast. It surprised me."

"There'll probably be a number of things happen around here that you aren't familiar with. Get used to it. You're in a man's world in this place."

Damey ate his breakfast in silence, thinking that certainly wasn't the way to get the day started off on the right foot. Maybe he'd try to make amends. After he finished, he rinsed out his bowl and put it in the dishwasher. He walked into the living room where Xavier and his mom sat talking.

Damey looked at the scene, and it felt some tension in the air. "Xavier, you want to go out and throw a football around for a while?"

"Nah, I'm too old for kid's games. When I'm not working, I like to just hang out in front of the TV and relax with a brew."

"So, are we gonna do anything today?"

"Nothing special. Your mom needs a day to get her breath back. There's a lot of stress caused by driving two straight days. Heavy traffic and unfamiliar roads get to you after a while. She needs to let down a little. You know what? I've got a bike out in the garage if you'd like to go check out the neighborhood. You'll probably have to pump up the tires, but there's a hand pump out there someplace. Why don't you go look to see if you can find it?"

"Ah, do you by any chance happen to have a map of the city? I don't really want to get lost out here in the middle of nowhere."

"Yeah, I do. If you stay nearby and pay attention, you shouldn't have any problems, but I do have a small, laminated, folded city map you can use. Let me see if I can find it."

Xavier started rifling through drawers in the living room with no luck. He moved to the kitchen and checked another drawer. He found it. He lay it out on the counter while Damey watched and put an X on their street and wrote the house number and his cell phone number on top. "If you get really lost, find someone with a phone and have them call me. I'll either come and get you or tell you how to get back."

"Thanks. I'll go check the tires and see what I can find interesting around here."

Then he went in to say goodbye to his mom who had curled up in a chair while she stared at the television. "You be careful out there and check in every once in a while. If you find something to occupy yourself, call one of us so we know you're okay."

As he walked out the door headed for the garage, Damey thought back. When's the last time I saw Mom sitting in a chair watching television in the morning? Ever?

CHAPTER 22

D amey walked out to the garage and looked around. Xavier had left his car in the drive so he had full access to the place. It looked like one of those Oklahoma tornados he'd heard about had blown through it. Tools, empty boxes, junk, crushed beer cans, and who knows what else littered the floor, shelves, and walls. It smelled dusty. He managed to avoid stepping in an oil puddle where the car normally sat. He figured that's all he needed would be to track black, greasy oil into the house.

What a bunch of junk. What's this? He wondered. Thrown on top of the workbench he found a rope measuring about eight feet long and maybe three-quarters of an inch in diameter. Why would anyone save something like that? Couldn't even use it as a tow rope. Too short.

After looking around the most logical places, Damey finally found the bike hanging on a peg on the back wall. He took it down and felt the tires. Both were soft. Now to find the air pump, he thought to himself. Surprisingly, he found it hanging a foot from the bike. After pumping up the tires, he looked around some more. No sign of a helmet anywhere. He could hear Grandpa screeching at him from there, "No way are you riding without a helmet, young man." Damey smiled.

He looked around a little at some of the other junk, shook his head, and wheeled the bike out of the garage. The seat was too high so he had to let it down. The handlebars would be okay.

Riding down the street, he looked around making sure to keep his bearings. He wondered if he could find his way back without using the map. He bet he could. Every turn he made, he logged into his head along with the name of the street. Eventually he rode into a more commercial part of town. He spotted a little restaurant, *Ella's Place*, tucked in between a couple of other stores.

He parked the bike on the sidewalk hoping nobody would steal it. He didn't have a lock. He walked in and saw a little sign propped on the counter, "Seat Yourself." There were some small, two-person booths against the wall so he grabbed one of them. He didn't see another soul in the place. He looked at the clock on the wall, and it said ten o'clock. Too early for lunch.

That's okay. He didn't want lunch yet anyway. All he wanted was something cold and wet in his mouth. He'd been riding for a couple of hours and felt hot and sweaty. Luckily for him, Grandpa had given him some money. Nobody else had.

Right then, the most gorgeous girl he'd ever seen in his life walked up to him. Guessing fourteen, wavy blond hair, not too short, not too long—beautiful blue eyes, clear complexioned, and sporting a big smile. "Hi, cutie. You need a menu?"

"No, all I want is a cola of some kind. Whatever you got. Not fussy."

"You don't want a straw with that do you?" she asked with her lips turned downwards into a semi-frown.

"No, I guess not. Why? What's the deal about straws?"

"Real men don't drink out of straws. There's something about watching a guy slurping on a soda using a straw that totally grosses me out. Makes them look like sissified little girls."

When she delivered his drink, she served it with a straw, but he left if lying on the table top unwrapped. She slipped down into the seat across from him. "Mind if I join you a minute. You're the only one in here, and I'm bored out of my mind. There's nobody else here but the cook, and he's getting stuff ready for the lunch crowd."

"No, that's great. I don't know anyone around here so at least I'll have someone to talk to my age for a change." He noticed her name tag, Ella. "You own this place?"

"No, Mom and Dad bought it when I was a baby and named it after me. Kinda dorky, if you ask me."

"Nah, that's cool. You work here every day?"

"Just about. Since my mom and dad own the place, I get to be their source of cheap labor. During the summer, I'm here every day from when we open at six for breakfast through the lunch rush. Then I go home and take a nap, at least that's what I tell them." She sprouted that big smile again and said, "Truthfully, that's when I go hang out with my friends. I can sleep when I'm old."

Damey laughed. He liked her personality as well as her looks. He'd never paid that much attention to the girls in his class other than being classmates and friends. He wondered if older women attracted him. This girl made his insides feel funny as he squirmed in his seat.

"Tell me about yourself," she said. "I've never seen you around here before. To start with, what's your name? As you've already figured out, I'm Ella."

"My name's Damey, and I'm only supposed to be here two weeks. Mom doesn't know what she wants so we came out here to visit her old boyfriend for a couple of weeks just to see if it would all work out for them. I hope not. I don't like him."

"Why? What's he like? Where's he work? How come you don't like him?"

"He works in the oil fields, so I guess he makes a lot of money. Big deal. He's not very nice to me. I feel like I'm in the way all the time. He won't do anything with me. I've tried to get him to play computer games, pass the football around, and stuff like that, and he always has an excuse. I also get this creepy feeling around him, like he's watching me."

She looked Damey straight in the eye. "Has he ever touched you in a bad way? Has he ever hit you?"

"No, neither one. It's probably all my imagination, but he makes my skin crawl. I don't like him, and he don't like me. Simple as that."

He took a drink of his cola and waited a few seconds. She didn't say anything.

"Do have a question for you though, Ella. When we leave, I want to get my mom to go back to Michigan using the back roads. For instance, is it possible to get to Tulsa without taking the main highway. I hate those things. They're so boring."

"Sure. We go that way all the time. My grandparents live in Tulsa. You actually start by going right down this road we're on straight to the east for a long time. The highway is just a couple of miles away, but instead of getting on the turnpike, you keep going.

Tell you what, I'll make you a map so if you come in tomorrow, I can show you the route."

"Cool."

When Damey left the restaurant, he rode to the east until he hit the city limit. Looked pretty desolate and lonely out there. Finally, he turned his bike around and rode back past the restaurant. He didn't stop because it had filled up, so Ella would be busy. He found his way back to Xavier's. Pretty simple. It was time for lunch.

"You're late. Where you been?" Xavier snapped at him when he walked in the door. "We already ate. There's some tuna salad and milk in the fridge. Make yourself a sandwich. Chips are in the pantry. How come you didn't check in? Your mom was worried about you."

"Been riding around looking at stuff, and time got away. Cruised by a couple of parks. Didn't realize how late it was. What time is it?"

"It's one o'clock and we eat at noon."

"Nobody told me that," Damey said with a little edge in his voice. He knew darned well his Mom probably had worried a little, but that dude sure hadn't.

"*Mouth!*" Xavier snarled.

There he goes trying to pick a fight again, and Mom sits there not saying a word. Is he my boss now? Damey bit his lip to keep from saying anything else. Didn't want to piss him off. Didn't know what he'd do.

After lunch, Damey looked around, and it appeared pretty obvious that nothing was happening there. He'd go for another ride if they'd let him. "Okay if I take the bike and go look around some more? I'll be back whenever you tell me."

"We eat at six. You'd better have your butt back here by then, washed up, and at the table or there'll be more trouble for you than you'll know what to do with. Understand?"

"Sure, but I don't have a watch or anything. I'll try to keep track of the time."

"Shaundra, why don't you let him put your cell phone in his pocket. That way he can check the time, and we can get a hold of him if we want him for some reason."

"Okay, but you'd better not lose it."

"I won't. Promise."

• • •

After cleaning up his mess from lunch, Damey took note of the time, 1:30. He knew exactly what he planned to do. When he rode by the restaurant, he almost stopped, but Ella would be gone so he didn't. He wanted to check out the road out of town. When he made it to the outskirts, he stopped and checked the time again. It had taken him an hour to get there. He could ride straight for another hour and get his bearings. Then he'd have to turn around and head back.

While he rode out of town, the traffic headed for the interchange seemed a little heavy. There were no sidewalks out that far so he had to ride in the road. Seemed like a couple of cars passed kind of close. Once he got beyond the on-ramp, he hardly saw another car. Riding east of the interchange for an hour and then back, not more than a dozen vehicles passed him. Perfect. That's what he wanted, a quiet, untraveled route out of town. Hot, smelly, dripping with sweat, and parched, Damey pulled into the driveway at 5:30. He had time for a quick shower and a long, cold drink of water before six.

During dinner, Damey watched the interaction between his mom and Xavier. She waited on him while Damey was on his own. They passed him the fried chicken, canned corn, and potatoes, but didn't say much to him. He felt like an outsider, almost invisible. Not used to that. At home and at Grandpa's everybody talked continuously. That's what made meals so much fun.

After dinner, King Xavier, lord and master of the empire, told Damey that he had to stay home. "You can watch television with us or downstairs, either way. I don't care. The main thing is, you don't need to be out wandering around on your own in the evening. If you want to go out on the patio and read or play games, that'll be fine too. Just make sure that when it starts to get dark, you get your butt in the house."

"Okay, I'll go out and sit on the patio. Maybe I'll dribble my basketball around in the driveway too."

As soon as he got out there, he settled himself into a patio chair. No clouds in the sky and a refreshing breeze. Really pleasant. He dug Shaundra's phone out of his pocket and called Grandpa. He was pretty sure he'd have a private conversation, because Xavier and his mom weren't about to come out and join him.

Bill flipped open the phone on his end on the second ring without even looking to see who had called. "Hello," he mumbled under his breath.

Damey laughed. That was the tone Grandpa used when solicitors called wanting to provide him with mortgage or credit card relief—which was ridiculous because Grandpa paid off his credit cards every month and didn't have a mortgage. "Hey, Grandpa. What's going on?"

"Hi, little man. I'm sitting here watching the Tigers smoke the Twins. They're ahead eight to zip. Good thing they're playing in Minnesota, 'cause it's raining here. So, what are you doing?"

"Sitting on the patio wishing I was watching the game with you. Only been gone three days, and I'm already bored out of my gourd."

"Everybody using today as a rest up day?"

"That's what they said. I've been riding around all day on Xavier's bike. Met a cute girl too. She works at a restaurant. I went in to buy a pop, and we talked for quite a while. Got a question for you."

247

"Shoot," Grandpa said.

Damey could hear the lilt had returned to Grandpa's voice. At least somebody was happy to talk to him. "I've never noticed, but do you use straws when you drink pop or water out of a glass at a restaurant?"

"Ah, normally not. Almost never unless it's something like a milkshake with whipping cream on top. Then it's either use a straw or get your nose smeared. Why?"

"Ella told me that real men don't use straws, just sissy types. Never heard that before."

"I don't think that's necessarily true. I think maybe Ella's biases are showing."

"Whatever. I didn't use a straw today."

Grandpa laughed. They chatted for probably fifteen minutes.

When they hung up, Damey thought about what was said and what wasn't said. He knew Grandpa wanted him to have a good trip, but not like it too well. He didn't say as much, but Damey knew he didn't want him to suddenly start pushing his mom to move out there. Damey knew that would never happen, but Grandpa didn't. Grandpa even told him that Xavier might be a really decent guy. Yeah, right. He shook his head, staring out into space. Couldn't put his finger on it, but for some reason or the other, he didn't trust him. Really didn't think Grandpa did either. Just something about him.

• • •

The next day looked to be a repeat of the previous. Right after breakfast, Xavier and Shaundra had to go to the grocery store, but didn't have any big plans. Nothing they told him about, anyway. Damey watched as they pulled out of the driveway as Xavier held a beer in his right hand and tried to back out of the drive steering with his left. He couldn't believe his mom didn't have a hissy fit over it. How many times had they talked about some of the tragedies that happened around home where alcohol was suspected to be a factor? He knew the intent of these discussions was to keep him from drinking illegally at a young age, and that was okay. She cared about him and didn't want him to get hurt.

Damey wasted no time. He jumped on Xavier's bike and headed for the restaurant. He wanted to make it so he'd get there about the same time he'd done the day previously. When he walked in, an elderly couple sat at the booth he occupied last time, so he grabbed another one across the room—as far away from them as he could.

"Hi, Damey. Got something for you," Ella said as she handed him a cola and slipped into the booth across from him. "Did some research yesterday afternoon. All my friends were tied up doing one thing or another, so I was on my own. Instead of sitting around staring out the window and doing absolutely nothing, I got on Google Maps and figured out a route you and your mom could take from here to Lansing where you'd never get on a major highway. Look it over while I collect from this other couple. They're ready to go."

As his jaw slowly dropped, he stared at the pack of sheets Ella had handed to him. He couldn't believe his eyes. She'd mapped out the entire trip for him. It sure wasn't a straight line, but who cared? First they'd ride north, than east, dip south for a while, back east and on and on it went. It bypassed every major city on the way and never connected to a major highway. Perfect.

After chatting with Ella for an hour, he hustled back to Xavier's hoping they wouldn't be back from the store yet. They weren't. He dug into the trunk of Shaundra's car and pulled out his backpack where he'd carefully stashed it before they left Lansing. He didn't know at the time why he did, he just had. He put the papers into it, carried it down to his room in the basement, and stashed the thing under his bed. He'd pour over them at night when he turned in, and try to memorize the route.

When Xavier and Shandra came back, they found Damey in the driveway dribbling his basketball that he'd brought along. Xavier didn't have a hoop, but Damey could dribble left and right handed and through his legs. He showed off a little when they got out of the car.

"Put that away and help us carry in groceries. You might as well do something useful to earn your keep," Xavier said. He didn't smile when he said it. He frowned like always. Yet, when they'd pulled into the driveway, Damey'd noticed they were both laughing.

Carrying the bag to the kitchen, Damey couldn't help but think. It had to be him. The two of them obviously got along fine when he wasn't around. If they didn't, he knew his mom would load up the car, and they'd head for home.

His mind wandered. They were a couple, and he was the lone wolf just like in Grandpa's picture. He thought about it. He had a bike, a backpack full of maps, and maybe he should make it happen. Would his mom would be happier and better off if he did? Did she think now she should have aborted him way back when? No, she wouldn't want that, but she might like to have him out of her life. He'd talk to her when Xavier passed out that night.

Damey knew he shouldn't try to over-think the situation. He knew in his heart his mom loved him and would never feel that way, but he felt miserable and didn't know what to do about it.

CHAPTER 23

That night when Xavier fell asleep on the sofa, Damey motioned to his mom to follow him to the kitchen. They sat down at the table and faced each other. "Mom, are you happy?"

"What do you mean, Honey? What are you getting at?"

"When it's just the two of you, you're both laughing, smiling, and looking like you're having fun. If I walk into the room, the mood changes. You go quiet and Xavier gets ornery."

"Oh, I think that's just your imagination. We have had some fun, but we've also had some discussions. I don't like his drinking so much, but that doesn't seem to matter to him. That's an issue. He's so used to being on his own, he's finding some things hard to change. He'll be fine. I'm sure."

Damey picked at a thumbnail as he stared at his hands in his lap. Unable to look at his mom, he said, "Okay, then I've got another question. How about if you put me on a bus or train and send me back to live with Grandpa until you two get it all figured out? I know I'm not wanted here. I'm in the way. If you really love the guy, I don't want to come between you. I don't want to hold you back from having a perfect life."

"Damey, don't be silly. No way. You haven't even given him a chance yet. You two will be fine. After all, he is your father. He's trying to act like one."

"He's not my father. He was the sperm donor. That's it." He spit out the words with an angry snarl.

"*Attitude*, young man." She pushed her chair back and stood up slouching slightly. "It's going on nine. Why don't you take your shower and get a good night's sleep tonight. Think about it while you're down there. You aren't being very rational. You know I love you and would never give you up. The two of you will just have to bond. You can do it. Look how easy it was for you and Grandpa and you and Ty."

Without another word, Damey hopped out of his seat, walked to the basement door, and slowly walked down the steps. He took a long, hot shower as he fantasized about Ella. After he finished, he lay on the bottom sheet in nothing but his underwear without covering up. It took a few minutes for his body temperature to cool off. Then he rolled over, stuck his head over the side and under the bed, and pulled out his backpack. He wanted to look at the maps.

• • •

Thursday morning Damey walked into the restaurant and saw Ella leaning on the counter red faced, unkempt, and with tears leaking out of her eyes.

He walked over to her. "What's the matter? Looks like something terrible happened."

"It did. Go sit down and I'll come over and tell you. I've got to talk to someone, and my parents don't want to discuss it."

She poured his drink and made her way over to the table. She handed it to him as she skooched over on the booth's seat to face Damey. As usual, they were the only ones there. "My best friend committed suicide yesterday morning. I found out about it last night."

"What? Why? Tell me about it."

She sat there for a minute, head down, with tears puddling on the table. Then she slowly lifted her head, looked at Damey, and spoke. "Her stepdad raped her. When she told her mom about it, her mom blamed her. Said she'd been coming on to the guy. She hadn't. They didn't get along. She couldn't stand him.

"Amy told the counselor at school, and he called the police. They arrested him. He's in jail without bond. Her mother yelled at her accusing her of breaking up their happy home. Everything was her fault.

"So, she crawled into the bathtub and slit her wrists using his razor. She bled to death in the bathtub of her own home because her mom chose her rapist husband over her daughter."

"That's terrible. Why didn't she talk to someone?" Damey said.

"Who? The counselor at school? Some guy in a mental health clinic? Her mom wouldn't go along with that. She told her to get over it."

"Wow! That's bad. What's gonna happen?"

"He'll probably get off. They're denying anything happened saying she made it up out of spite. No victim. No witnesses. No crime."

"That's not right. Not fair to her or her memory. That's scary."

"I know," Ella said. "They blasted it all over the news last night. I hate to say it, but when he gets out, I hope someone takes care of him."

Damey and Ella talked until the lunch crowd started arriving. She thanked Damey for listening as he slipped out the door. He left her a larger tip than normal. She needed something to brighten her day.

• • •

Damey's mind whirled as he pedaled back to Xavier's house. Are kids that big a burden when their moms are trying to start a new life? If Xavier did something really bad to me, would Mom stick up for Xavier's or me? Would she blame me for anything that happened? I don't think so, but who knows? Nobody, until something happens.

That night at dinner, Damey looked around. Nothing had changed. He sat there trying to be invisible, his mom said very little, and Xavier put on his macho, tough dude act, drinking one beer after another.

When dinner was almost over, his mom looked over at Xavier. "You going to tell him now or later? Thought we decided you'd mention it during dinner."

"Oh, yeah. That's right. Your mom and I are going to Oklahoma City tomorrow to see some old friends of mine. You can ride along if you want, but you'll be bored out of your mind. It's going to be a long day. We won't be getting back until late—probably way past your normal bedtime.

"Or, you can stay here and cruise on the bike all day exploring as you like to do. Your choice. If you want to stay here, I'll give you some money so you can buy lunch and dinner out at one of the fast food joints if you want. What do you think?"

It couldn't be more obvious to Damey that they didn't want him to go if he'd come right out and said so. "I'd rather stay here. It'll give you two a chance to have some fun without having to bother about me. You've got to go back to work on Monday, so other than the weekend, it's your last chance."

He'd hang around the restaurant and have lunch with Ella. He might even go back to the same place for dinner. It'd give him a lot of time to explore the route out of town.

"That's what we figured you'd want to do. Here, here's twenty bucks. That should get lunch and dinner easily if you don't get carried away." Xavier actually smiled at Damey.

Damey knew that's exactly what they wanted. They wanted him out of the picture.

The three of them spent the evening like every other one. Xavier drank himself to oblivion as one inane television show after another crawled across the screen.

It was raining, so Damey stayed inside and blocked it all out of his mind as he sat on the loveseat with his iPad thinking about Ella's friend Amy. How sad. He wondered if Amy's mother even cared, or was she only pissed because her husband ended in trouble. Maybe she was sorry now? He couldn't get it off his mind. Too many similarities.

The next morning everyone crawled out of bed early. His mom and Xavier wanted to get on the road early and would be home late. Good, Damey thought. Glad to get them out of his hair.

Damey continued eating his cereal while his mom and Xavier backed out of the garage and driveway. Peeling a banana, he heard the front door open as Xavier walked back in. He'd left the car running in the driveway with Shaundra sitting in the front seat waiting.

With a mouthful of banana, Damey stood up to look to see who had walked in. Xavier stomped into the kitchen and without a word, blasted Damey across his left cheek with the flat of his right hand slamming Damey's head into the cupboard before he landed in a dazed heap on the floor.

Then Xavier screeched, "Listen, you little asshole. You've got exactly one day, twenty-four hours to figure it out. You're going to lose the attitude, or I'll beat your ass to a bloody pulp. Believe me. I'll do it every day if I have to. You're just damned lucky I'm not whipping on you right now instead of talking. One more thing. I told your mother I wanted to come in and double check to make sure you hadn't changed your mind and decided to go. You gonna remember that story, or should I jerk my belt off right now and give you a little taste of what's coming if you don't shape up?"

"I'll remember," Damey said still half dazed as he lay on the floor with his head screaming, 'Don't cry. Don't cry.' He didn't. He sat there leaning against the cupboard door completely in shock until he heard the door slam and then the car drive away.

Leaving his unfinished bowl of cereal on the counter and the remainder of the banana on the floor where it landed, Red and puffy faced Damey stood up, dusted himself off, and said out loud, "I'm outta here."

It probably took him five minutes to grab his back pack, fill it with the last four bottles of mountain-spring water from the refrigerator, a couple cans of baked beans, the last two bananas, one apple, and a roll of toilet paper—he wouldn't make that mistake again. He'd have a great head start. They wouldn't be back until late that night. He'd be long gone on his way to Michigan.

After sliding into the backpack and attaching the straps, he ran out to the garage to get the bike. He stopped and looked at the work bench. That rope—he grabbed it and stuffed it into his backpack. He really didn't know why, he just did. Maybe it had something to do with Ella's friend. Not sure. He just knew he was all upset and not thinking clearly. He didn't have time to worry about it. He jumped onto the bike and pedaled out of the garage, looked for oncoming traffic, and aimed for *Ella's Place.*

When he walked into the restaurant, he didn't even sit down. Ella grabbed him by the shoulders, "Your face. What happened? Did somebody hit you?"

"Mom's boyfriend." Then he quickly explained what had happened. "I'm headed for Michigan. I've got the maps you printed off for me, and I'm leaving. Promise me, Ella. If anyone happens to come by asking about me, you've never seen me."

"Damey, there's no way you can ride a bike from here to there. Do you have any money?"

"I've got about thirty bucks. Would you make me a couple of sandwiches to go? I'll be okay."

Ella poured him his cola and told him to sit down and rest, he'd need it. She'd pack him a lunch. Five minutes later she returned with the bag, told Damey to turn around, and she put it in his backpack.

"Damey, you can't do it. Not possible. You don't have enough money for food much less a place to sleep at night. Why don't we call the police and they will protect you until your mom decides to go home."

"No. They won't be back until late tonight. If I pedal hard and don't stop too often, I'll be a long ways down the road before they ever discover I'm gone. I gotta go. How much do I owe you?"

"Nothing. This one's on me. I'm the only one here but the cook so nobody will know. Please be careful. If you change your mind, come back here. I'll make sure you're okay."

Both looked at each other wistfully knowing they'd never see each other again. They'd bonded in the short time they'd had, even with the two years difference in ages. They'd shared their stories, emotions, and fears. She grabbed him in a quick mutual hug, kissed him on his sore cheek, and then he raced out the door before she saw the flush on his face.

He jumped on the bike, looked over his shoulder and waved at Ella who stood in the door waving back, and pedaled down the road to the east.

He loved this route. If half a dozen cars passed him, after he passed the interchange, he'd be surprised. About eleven, he had to urinate. He spotted a lane headed off the side of the road and pulled in, parked his bike, and slipped behind a tree so he'd be out of sight of any passing traffic. Zipping up, he laughed thinking of his poison ivy fiasco. He was sure glad he'd slipped that roll of toilet paper in the bottom of his backpack.

He decided to look in the bag Ella'd packed—two sandwiches, a bag of chips, a can of pop, and a bunch of Wet-Ones. Good thinking, he thought to himself as he pulled one out and washed his hands. He threw the used wet-one on the ground, climbed back on his bike, and headed back down the road.

Two hours later, his butt hurt from the bike seat, and his legs were tired. Time for lunch, he said to himself. He found another place to pull off, walked around a little to stretch, and found a tree stump to use as a table. Looking in the bag, he smiled. Decisions, decisions—did he eat both sandwiches then or save one for later? He ate one, drank his pop, peed on another tree, and got on the road again. He wondered what time it was. He had intentionally left his mom's phone sitting on the counter. Didn't need it anymore. Didn't want them calling him. Nobody could track him.

The sun began to fade in the west around eight o'clock, so he figured he'd better find a place for the night. He'd consumed the second sandwich hours ago. Starved, he kept riding until he spotted an old gas station out in the middle of nowhere. Looked like it'd been closed for years. The windows were broken out, a door on the side swung open, and it smelled of gasoline and oil. He sneaked a look. Completely empty. He pulled his bike inside and sat down on the workbench.

He peeled off his backpack and rested a minute. He still had an apple and banana. That would be dinner. He looked at the cans of baked beans and realized he didn't have a can opener. He put those back, made a quick trip out behind the station a few yards with his roll, checked for three leafed plants, and did his duty.

After eating his gourmet dinner, he curled up on the work bench using his backpack for a pillow, and fell instantly asleep. He woke up a couple of times during the night shivering from the coolness of the evening, but fell back asleep.

When the sun peeked through the windows waking him, he went out behind the station and relieved himself, double checked his maps, gingerly climbed back on the bike, and pedaled down the road.

His body wasn't used to riding that long at a time. His legs ached and were stiff so he pedaled slowly at first until he limbered up. He wished he'd bought a towel or pillow of some kind for his bike seat. It felt like things were getting raw and blistered back there.

Damey & Grandpa Tutor   Larry Webb

CHAPTER 24

Shaundra and Xavier returned home close to midnight. "What's going on with this?" Shaundra asked when she saw the bowl on the counter and banana on the floor. "That's not like Damey to leave a mess."

"Just being spiteful. I didn't tell you, but when I came in and asked to see if he didn't want to go after all, he copped an attitude again. I grabbed him by the shirt and shook him to get his attention. That's when he dropped the banana. Guess he's still pissed. Leave it there. We'll make him clean up his mess in the morning. He's got to learn that kind of behavior is unacceptable."

An evil smile crossed Xavier's face. Oh, how he would show him how unacceptable it was. He'd warned him, now he was going to get it. He'd beat his ass until he begged for mercy.

Neither one thought to check downstairs. They assumed he'd gone to bed hours ago. The next morning proved to be different. After Xavier and Shaundra got up and wandered around the house for a while Shaundra said, "He doesn't normally sleep in this long. Wonder if he's okay."

She went over to the basement door and called to him. No answer. She walked down the steps and looked. All she saw was a made up, empty bed and no Damey.

"Xavier," Shaundra yelled with a panicked edge to her voice. "Come here, now! Damey's gone. That bed hasn't been slept in. Either something's happened to him, or he's run away."

"Oh, don't jump to any conclusions. Maybe he feels guilty and got up early and went for a walk or something. He couldn't get the bike out because I locked the garage last night. Been doing that lately 'cause there's been some break-ins in the neighborhood."

"Go look, will you? I've gotta know where he is."

Reluctantly, and fearing the worse, Xavier grabbed his keys and headed to the garage. Shaundra followed. He unlocked the door and slid it up on its rails. Gone. The bike was nowhere in sight. Damn, thought Xavier to himself. So help me, I'll break his scrawny little neck when I find him. Where could he be? I gave him a map of the town. I bet he slept in a park someplace.

"Come on, Shaundra. Get in the car. There are three or four parks relatively close by. I'll bet he camped out on a park bench some place. Let's take a look."

Shaundra started shaking. She tripped over the entryway to the car and fell face first onto the seat. Embarrassed, she straightened herself out and sat down. Xavier had to snap her seat belt for her. Her hands shook so badly, she couldn't hit the slot.

They drove around for two hours searching every park in the area. As they passed a little restaurant on the main drag, Xavier said, "Let's stop in here for coffee and decide what we're going to do."

"I know what I'm going to do. I'm calling the police. Are you sure all you did was shake him?"

"Oh, I yelled at him. That's no big deal. Then I joked with him a little and told him if he didn't behave, I'd turn him over my knee and spank him like a two year old. He knew I didn't mean it."

"I hope so. Spanking doesn't work with Damey. I've found there are better ways to punish him when he needs it."

. . .

The waitress couldn't help but overhear the conversation as she delivered their coffee. She took one look at Xavier and knew exactly who they were and what had happened. Yeah, right. She said to herself. That's not what you did, and that's not how you threatened him. You're lying and trying to look innocent and all that crap.

Shaundra flagged her down. "Have you seen a little twelve year-old black child riding a bike around here?"

"There are a lot of kids who ride by here every day on bikes, ma'am. Haven't noticed anyone in particular," Ella told her with a completely blank, unexpressive face.

Damn, I'm good, she thought. Maybe I should take up acting. No way would I rat out Damey. I don't like that guy's looks either. Funny, looks just like Damey, but mean as can be. How can two people who look so much alike be so different?

. . .

As soon as they arrived home, Shaundra searched the house again for any sign of Damey or any hint of where he might have gone. Nothing. She called the police against Xavier's wishes. The police officer taking the report suggested he might be lost and afraid to ask for help.

Regardless, under the circumstances, they classified him as a runaway. The television stations posted his picture and asked anyone with any knowledge of his whereabouts to please call the police. The one and only person who saw the posting and could have helped, smiled and kept her mouth shut.

Nobody seemed to take the situation too seriously except for Shaundra. She knew his temperament. She also understood where the authorities came from. Typically, a child runaway cooled off and returned home when he or she got hungry enough. Bullheaded Damey wouldn't do that. Only problem was, she didn't know what he would do or where he'd go. If she did, she'd go find him.

"I'm going to call Bill. Damey trusts him more than anyone else in the world. Maybe he's heard something."

"Oh, God, Shaundra. He'll come back. Don't bother the old man. He'll worry himself to death, and there's nothing he can do anyway."

"I don't care. I'm gonna call him."

"Go ahead and call him then. I'll go clean up the kitchen. I don't want to hear your conversation with Bill and all the drama anyway. Fortunately, I get to go back to work Monday and avoid most of it until he gets back. I'm still telling you, Shaundra, what that little brat really needs is a good old fashioned belt to butt whooping."

"I'm calling Bill, and you aren't touching Damey. Got it?"

"Going to be real pleasant around here 'til he gets back here, isn't it?" Xavier said. Then he went out to the kitchen and snagged another beer out of the refrigerator, cleaned out Damey's bowl, rinsed it, and put it in the dishwasher. After that, he picked up the banana, threw it away, and wiped up the floor.

The phone rang twice before Bill answered. He saw Shaundra's name on the caller id and figured it was Damey. "Well, hello. How're things out there in Oklahoma?"

"Bill, this is Shaundra. Damey's run away. Have you heard anything from him?"

"No, not a word since he called earlier in the week. When'd he leave?"

"Not sure, but guessing yesterday morning some time. Xavier and I spent the day in Oklahoma City, and those two had words before we left. I was in the car so I'm not one-hundred percent sure what happened. Don't know if Xavier's told me the whole story or not."

"So, what do you know for sure?"

"He's missing. He's got Xavier's bike, and he took some bottled water with him. What else, we don't know."

"Have you talked to Ty?"

"No. Would you please call him? Damey might try to contact him too. I figured if he called anyone, it would be you."

"I think so too, but I'll call Ty. Keep me posted, will you, Shaundra?"

"I will, and you do the same if you hear anything. Bye."

• • •

Bill paced back and forth a minute or two wondering what the kid had done and why. He especially wanted to know the why. It didn't take a Rhodes Scholar to feel the vibes between Xavier and Damey. If there was ever anything like a human electrical short-circuit, they were a perfect example.

Then he called Tyrone. Naturally, Ty wanted all the details. After Bill told him what he knew, the two of them spent another half hour speculating. None of it good. Damey might do most anything.

CHAPTER 25

Saturday night Damey hunkered down in a little grass clearing he found in a woodlot on the side of the road. He hadn't eaten anything all day. All he'd had was one bottle of water, which hadn't quite satisfied his needs. He sat leaning against a tree thinking he hadn't peed but once all day. Maybe his body was drying out?

He wondered about his mom. Would she be glad he was gone? Would this make life easier for her? When he got back to Michigan and called her, would she agree that he could live with Grandpa if she wanted to stay there with that loser? Damey couldn't feel any positive vibes, and he didn't try. He felt and looked dirty, smelly, tired, and hungry. His legs ached, and his butt hurt. His whole body hurt. Maybe Ella had been right. Maybe he couldn't ride that far. He'd starve to death first. He hadn't even seen a restaurant on any of the roads he'd been on. Didn't matter. He wouldn't go back.

He pulled the cans of baked beans out of his backpack. He tried banging them against a rock. He dented the cans, but couldn't spring as much as a leak in either. He couldn't figure anyway to open them. He had no can opener, tools, or anything that might work. Discouraged, he threw both cans as far into the woods as he could. He pulled out the rope, looked at it, and wondered. He thought about Ella's friend.

He shinnied up the tree and sat at the base of a large limb. Leaning against the trunk of the tree for balance, he tied the rope around the branch and then pulled on it to check if his knot would slip. It didn't. He looped the other end around his neck and sat there. Then he thought of all the people in the world he loved and were important to him—his mom, Grandpa, Ty, Alex and the Bows, his favorite cousin, Sean, and all uncles, aunts, and other cousins on Grandpa's side of the family. He couldn't hurt them the way Ella's friend had hurt her. He guessed he'd never make it as that lone wolf in the picture on Grandpa's wall. He liked his family and friends too well to do something that stupid. He undid the rope from around his neck and climbed back down the tree. He lay down in the grass. Shivering, he curled himself up into a ball, and fell asleep. The next morning when he walked his bike to the side of the road, he left the rope hanging in the tree. He wouldn't need it—one less thing to carry.

About four o'clock the next afternoon, he saw a road sign—Okmulgee. He laughed. A town? I'm actually coming into a town? He felt excited. Maybe he could get something to eat. The first commercial building he spotted was a gas station. Gas stations sometimes had food. He parked his bike in front of the door and walked in. Pop in the vending machine was $1.50. He needed change. He went to the cashier and changed one of his dollars into quarters. He bought a pop and a bag of chips.

Chewing on a handful of chips and washing them down with a drink, an idea popped into his head. He walked over to the clerk. "Could I use your cell phone, please? I forgot mine and need to check in."

"Yeah, but put your can and chips down. I don't want you klutzing up and dropping my phone. It cost a lot of money."

Bill looked at the caller id on the phone. "What!"

"Grandpa, it's me, Damey. Wanted to let you know I'm okay in case Mom's called you."

"Damey, thank God. Sorry I snarled into the phone. Thought it was another robo-call. I've been waiting to hear from you. Where are you?"

"I just wheeled into a little town called Okmulgee, Oklahoma. I'm at a gas station. I asked the guy to let me use his phone, and he did."

273

Damey & Grandpa Tutor   Larry Webb

"How do you spell it?" Grandpa asked as he raced down to his office and pulled up Google Maps on his computer.

Damey spelled it out as Grandpa typed it in. "You're almost 200 miles from Lawton. How'd you get there?"

"Been riding a bike."

"Listen to me, and listen carefully. I want you to ask the attendant if there is a mom and pop type motel around there close. Ask him now."

Damey'd never heard of that term for a motel and felt foolish, but asked him anyway. The guy said he'd find *Mary's Motel* about two blocks further down the road on the right.

"Your mom called me and said that you and Xavier had some kind of a falling out. She's suspicious that maybe he didn't tell her the whole story. What happened?"

"He slapped me across the face hard enough to knock me off my feet and into the cupboards. I got a goose-egg on my head. He told me if I didn't straighten up, he'd beat my ass to a bloody pulp. Those are his exact words, Grandpa, not mine. When they left for the day, I took off. I'd been kind of planning on it, and then when he did that, I left."

"Go down to that motel and ask the desk clerk to call me. Understand? No more running. I'm going to come and get you."

"Are you gonna call Mom?"

274

"No, not until I have you and know you're safe. Go to that motel right now. I'm going to hang on to this phone until you call me back. Now, get moving."

Damey handed the phone back to the clerk, thanked him, and then wolfed down the rest of his pop and chips. He climbed back on the bike, shifted around until he could find a place to sit that wasn't sore, and rode down the street. He spotted the place easily. It didn't look too big and fancy like most motels. In fact, he didn't see any cars parked in front of rooms. He walked into the lobby.

The man at the desk looked at him a little suspiciously.

Damey had looked at himself in the mirror at the gas station and could almost read the man's mind. He figured the guy was thinking, what does this grubby looking kid want? Is he asking for a handout? He came to the wrong place, if he is. I'm about to go carry a, 'Will work for food' sign myself.

"What cha need, bud?" he said peering down at Damey.

"I just talked to my grandpa from that station a couple blocks down the road. He told me to come here and ask you to call him. He's in Michigan."

"Why?"

"I think he wants me to stay here. He's gonna come and get me and take me home. Will you call him?"

"Why not? It's been a slow, boring day. What's his number?"

Unlike Bill's usual slow motion way of checking the caller ID before saying anything, he answered on the first ring. "Are you the motel clerk?"

"Yes. My wife and I own the place. How can I help you?"

"I would like to give you my credit card number and have you put the boy up until I can get there. I'll be leaving Michigan within the hour. I'll drive as long as I can tonight. I should arrive tomorrow afternoon sometime. I'll probably stay tomorrow night and leave the following morning. All I can tell you that there is a serious domestic issue going on, and he may be in danger. He needs to stay out of sight until I get there. How bad does he look?"

"Not real good. He and his clothes are grungy, sweaty, and dirty. He also has what looks like a huge welt on the left side of his face that appears new and ugly."

"Ask him when's the last time he ate."

"What's his name?"

"Damey, actually, it's Damarian Martin."

"Ok, hold on. Damey, when's the last time you ate?"

"I had a couple of sandwiches two days ago, and just now I had a pop and bag of chips at the gas station."

Grandpa heard him over the phone and groaned. "Would you be willing to use my credit card information and feed him until I get there? I'm throwing clothes in a suitcase as we speak."

"Ok, we're not busy, so it won't be any problem. One thing I want to make clear, though," he said turning so Damey couldn't pick up on his conversation, "when you get here, if I don't feel comfortable with the situation, I will call the police."

"That's fine. Now, will you give me your exact address for my navigation system?"

After Bill ended the call, he punched in Ty's number. "What're you doing?" he asked as soon as Ty answered. "Want to go for a little ride?"

"Where you going? I just returned from the gym after working out, and shouldn't go or do anything until I shower and change clothes."

"Some place called Okmulgee, Oklahoma. Sound familiar?"

"You found him?"

"Yep. I've got him all squared away in a motel. I've got to fill up the gas tank, and then I'm pulling out. I'm throwing some of my and Damey's clothes in a suitcase right now. Then I'm headed that way."

"I'm going with you. Let me grab that quick shower. We taking your car or my SUV?"

"Mine. I get twice the mileage that you do."

"Mine's got more leg room, but you've got better tires. Pick me up after you gas up. I'll be ready. I'm stripping right now."

"Okay, I'll tell you everything I know when we're on our way."

CHAPTER 26

W hen the motel owner hung up the phone, he looked over at Damey who stood in front of the window rubbing his butt.

"Did the guy who slapped your face smack the other end as well?"

Damey blushed. "No, I've been riding a bike for three days. It's just sore from that hard seat."

"Okay," he said. Then he opened the door behind the desk, "Mary, could you step out here for a minute?"

She walked out from the kitchen wiping her hands on her apron. She looked at Damey, raised her eyebrows, and glanced at her husband.

"We're babysitting a waif until sometime tomorrow. He essentially hasn't taken care of any of the essentials for the past three days. He rode a bike here from Lawton. His grandpa will be leaving Michigan within the hour and is going to come and get him. Some kind a domestic problem. Do you think you could find him something clean to wear in that pile of stuff people have left? If I'm figuring right, he needs to shower, change clothes, eat, and go to bed in that order. Any suggestions?"

"What's your name, son?" Mary asked.

"Damey. That is, most of the time. My real name is Damarian, but I only get called that when someone is yelling at me. The rest of the time I'm Damey."

Mary smiled. "Come with me and let's find you some clean clothes. We've got a bunch here that people have left and never bothered to come back or send for."

She took Damey into the storage room. It was filled with clothing, cell phones, old iPads, and other assorted things people had left behind. She told him that about once a year, she'd gather everything up and take it all to the Salvation Army. Looked like she was about due to make another trip.

"Do you know what size you wear?" she asked.

"No. Mom and Grandpa buy all my clothes. I never pay any attention to that."

"Okay, turn around. I'm going to peel back your shirt collar and the waist band on your shorts and take a look."

"But, but—"

"Hold on and relax. I'm not taking your clothes off, I'm just checking for sizes. I'm not going to hurt you. Stand still."

After determining his shirt and pants size, she fished through the pile of boy's clothes. She'd separated the kid and adult outfits so it went relatively quickly. Within minutes she found shorts, a short-sleeved shirt, socks, and underwear.

"You like spaghetti?" she asked as she stacked the piles of clothes back the way they were.

"Love it."

"Okay, go with Tom and he'll open up your room. Get into the shower right away and soak that grime off of you. You're not only filthy, but you stink," she said as she flipped the end of his nose down with her finger and smiled at him. "Then, put on the clean clothes and come back to the office. Bring your dirty clothes with you. Here's a plastic grocery bag. Throw your dirty stuff in it, and I'll wash it all tonight. I have the motel laundry to do, so I'll just throw yours in along with the sheets. I plan on dinner in about a half hour."

"You gonna feed me?" Damey asked rubbing his stomach with both hands. Those hunger pains had returned just thinking about food.

"Yes. You heard what Tom said. We're watching out for you until your grandpa gets here. Now, scat and go get cleaned up."

Tom took him to the unit closest to the office, room one. He showed him how to open the door with a plastic device that looked like a credit card. "Keep the curtains pulled and the card in your pocket so you don't lock yourself out. The door automatically locks itself when it's closed.

"When you're in for the night, pull this little latch on the door over like this. That way nobody can get in, even with a key. After you use the shower, throw your towel on the floor in front of the tub—same with wash cloths and hand towels. When Mary cleans your room tomorrow, she'll know which ones are used and which aren't. Any questions?"

"Nope. Oh, yeah. What about soap?"

Tom showed him the wrapped bars of soap and the shampoo. He also showed him the pamphlet with all the television channels before he left.

Damey pulled the curtains most of the way shut, pulled over the extra lock on the door, and headed for the shower. He emptied his pockets on the counter and tossed his filthy clothes in a pile. He turned on the water, adjusted the heat, and climbed in. He let the water pour over his body for several minutes before he bothered with either the soap or shampoo.

He could feel his aching, tense body relax. Suddenly he jerked back to alertness. He'd almost fallen asleep standing under the hot water. That's when he peeled off the wrapper on the soap, tossed it out of the shower, and started washing.

Completely scrubbed and wearing clean clothes, Damey wrapped his dirty stuff up in his tee shirt, stuffed it all into the bag she'd given him, and headed to the office—after first checking to make sure he had his key card securely in his pocket.

"Oh, you look better," Tom said smiling at Damey when he entered the office. Some man with a lady sitting in the car was registering at the counter. Tom opened the door into their living quarters and motioned for Damey to head back there.

Feeling somewhat foolish, he looked around as Mary had her back to him as she stirred a pot on the stove. The smells coming from the stove top and oven almost doubled him over with cramps. He groaned getting her attention.

"Hi, squirt. You bring your dirty clothes with you?" Mary asked without even looking at him. "Throw them in that hamper inside the little bathroom over there." Without taking her eyes off the kettle in front of her, she thumbed in the general direction.

Damey did as she told him and then looked around a little more. Three places were set at the table. They still planned on feeding him. Thank, God.

"Dinner's just about ready. As soon as he gets that customer out there squared away, we'll eat." Then she pulled a pie out of the oven along with the warm garlic toast. "You like blueberry pie with ice cream? If I'd known we were going to have company, I'd made apple. Everybody likes that."

The combined odors of the spaghetti, blueberries, and garlic gave Damey another cramp. Trying not to double over in pain, he managed to squeak out, "Blueberry's my favorite.

After dinner, Damey went back to his room to watch TV. They told him if he needed anything, he could get a hold of them by pushing zero on the phone or just walk over to the office. If they didn't see him between then and morning, breakfast would be at eight.

• • •

"Oh, boy," Tom said after Damey'd left and was safely tucked into his room. He'd kept an eye on him until he saw the door close. "How'd you like to feed that one on a regular basis? We'd go bankrupt."

"If you remember, Thomas my dear, our boys were no slouches at the dinner table, and they never went two days without eating. That poor kid was starved, literally. I saw him double over a couple of times because his tummy hurt so bad before we actually sat down and started to eat."

Tom made his rounds about eight o'clock. "I did a no-no," he grinned when he walked in the door.

"What's that?" Mary asked.

"Damey didn't pull the drapes completely shut. I noticed it this afternoon when he first got into his room, but didn't say anything. Figured he do it when he settled in for the night. He didn't. The room appeared dark when I walked by so I peeked through the opening in the drapes. Looks like he threw the covers back, flopped down on the bed, and fell sound asleep on the bottom sheet wearing nothing but underpants. Anyone walking to or from the office could look in and see him.

"I half considered trying to sneak the door open and close them tight, but figured he'd hooked the security latch. All I'd accomplish would be to wake him up. He needs his sleep worse than his privacy."

During the course of the evening, the motel filled to the point where at eleven, Tom lit up the 'No Vacancy' sign. Then he did his last tour for the night.

When he got back, Mary had just finished taking the last load out of the washer. All of yesterday's towels and sheets, as well as Damey's clothes, were washed, dried, folded, and ready for another day.

"I hope he ain't dead," Tom said smiling. "That kid hasn't stirred since I checked in on him earlier. He'll get cold during the night."

"If he does, he'll cover up," Mary laughed. Her mind filtered back to when their kids were that age. She only wished she could sleep as soundly as they did.

• • •

Bill raced over to the gas station, filled up the car, and headed for Tyrone's. The car hadn't even stopped when Ty came out the door with his overnight bag. Bill popped the trunk. Ty tossed it in, slammed it shut, ran around the car, and jumped into the passenger side.

All scrunched up with his knees resting on the dash, he grumbled. "Good grief! Who's been riding in this seat? He fumbled for the buttons as he adjusted the thing.

"Who do you think?"

"Who else, Damey Wayne himself," Ty laughed. "So tell me everything."

Bill unloaded the details as he knew them. Ty listened without interrupting except for once.

"Slow down, Bill. We don't need to get stopped for an hour while some cop writes you up for 55 in a 35 zone."

"Oops. Wasn't paying attention to that. Just trying to get to the highway." That's when he pulled the address out of his pocket and handed it to Ty. "Ready? You can talk to Tilly at OnStar."

Bill reached up and pushed the little blue button to get navigational directions.

Setting the cruise-control at seventy-three, Bill settled back in his seat and got himself as comfortable as possible. Ty spent a little more time adjusting the seat, but finally was satisfied.

After turning onto I-70 at Indianapolis, they pulled off the highway to fill up with gas, get a snack, and switch drivers. Every four hours or so, they repeated the process. About one o'clock in the morning, they pulled into a rest stop.

"I think we should crash for a couple of hours," Ty said as they got out of the car to use the restrooms."

"Works for me. You want the front seat or the back?"

"You're shorter than I am, Bill. You take the back and curl up the best you can. Maybe you can actually get a couple hours of sleep. I'll lower the seat back as far as it will go and stretch out. I just need to quit staring at the road for a while."

Exhausted, both men fell asleep. About six-thirty a truck horn blasted and the squealing of brakes could be heard before the crash. Someone had pulled out in front of a semi in the parking lot and got broadsided. Bill and Ty both sat up bleary eyed and not really ready to wake up.

They watched as the two drivers got out of their vehicles and yelled at each other. "Potty time," Ty smiled as he looked back at Bill.

Fifteen minutes later, they pulled out onto the road again headed west juggling large coffees and some kind of scrambled egg sandwich combination mixed in with hash browns and bacon.

• • •

At seven, Tom did his normal inspection of the premises. Everything looked quiet and peaceful, and it didn't appear like any cars had been broken into over night. He'd be ready for the morning rush of checkouts.

"I guess he's alive," Tom told Mary when he walked back into the office. "At least he covered himself up with a sheet sometime during the night. He's still out cold."

"I'll get breakfast around in about a half hour. In the meantime, look what I found. I think this swimming suit will fit him perfectly."

"Good move. He can play in the pool all day and stay out of sight. I hope he likes the water."

About seven-thirty, Mary dialed Damey's room number. It rang four or five times before he finally answered. "Wha, hello, ah," he stammered into the phone.

"Good morning, Damey. This is Mary at the office. Time for breakfast," grinning from ear-to-ear enhanced the lilt in her voice. Poor kid. She probably should have let him sleep, she thought. No, this was more fun. She could visualize him stumbling around grabbing for the phone still half asleep.

"Uh, okay. Gotta get dressed."

"Take your time. Get in a shower if you want, just don't forget to brush your teeth." She couldn't resist that last little dig. The day before when she'd given him the toothbrush along with the paste sampler, he'd joked about, 'No floss and mouth wash?' Then he told her how Grandpa nagged him if he didn't 'floss, brush, and rinse,' morning and night. She remembered that when he told her, he had a wistful, faraway look in his eyes. She knew he missed his grandpa.

She stopped and paused for a second. She wondered if he missed his mother as much. He hadn't really mentioned her all that often.

A little after eight, he bounced into the office freshly showered and brushed. He looked so much better than he had when he'd stumbled through the door the day before.

Interrupted by three checkouts, they still managed to get in their breakfast. While they ate, Mary asked, "You like to swim?"

"I'm not real good at it, but I do like to play in a pool—especially like to cannonball off the diving board."

"We didn't tell you yesterday because you were so tired and needed to clean up, eat, and get some sleep, but we have a twenty by forty foot swimming pool out back. There's a wall around it so it's perfectly private. You can play out there today with the other guests while you wait if you'd like."

"I'd love to, but I don't have a suit. Uh, and I don't skinny-dip in public either."

"I hope not. Besides, I've got a suit for you. After breakfast you can try it on."

After they finished eating, she told him to go try on the suit, and bring back a towel with him and not to forget his door opening card. When he came back, the sidewalk had already heated up from the sun and the bottoms of his feet had no covering. He skipped, hopped, and jumped to the office door.

Mary showed him the entrance to the pool. A couple of other people were splashing around in the water keeping cool. The temperature had already climbed to the mid-eighties, and it was only nine am. "Okay, listen up a minute. You know that you're supposed to wait an hour after a meal before you try to swim. You can play in the shallow end, but stay out of the deep end until ten o'clock. There's a clock right there," she said pointing at the wall behind them. "Remember, there is no life guard on duty, so you have to be careful and watch out for yourself."

He thanked her again, and she went back to work leaving him to his own devices. He jumped into the pool. The water was only three feet deep at the shallow end so he squatted down so only his head bobbed above water. It felt so good.

He explored that end of the pool and found one of the water jets. He stooped down again so the stream of water hit him mid-back just below the shoulders. It felt so good—reminded him of the massage parlor Grandpa used to take him to. Thinking of it made him tear up.

He pushed away from the wall and swam across the width of the pool keeping his face in the water.

CHAPTER 27

At twelve-thirty, Mary called Damey in for lunch. Wrapped up in his towel, he went into the kitchen. She told him there was no reason for him to get dressed just to eat and go back to the pool. He ate his grilled cheese sandwiches and tomato soup and shivered. They'd turned on the air conditioner, and he was cold. He couldn't wait to get back in the water.

"Before you go back to the pool, we've got to get you covered with sunscreen. Should have done that this morning. You're gonna burn to a crisp."

She left the room for a minute and then returned with a large tube. "Come here and stand right in front of me so I can get your face and back. You've got goose bumps all over you. Are you that cold?"

"I'm freezing."

"This will only take a minute and then you can go back to the pool. Stand still and quit squirming. The faster we get this done, the sooner you can get outdoors where it's warm." She slathered the goo all over his face, neck, the top of his shortly cropped head, and his back. "Okay, you do your chest, belly, arms and legs— and feet. Don't miss between your toes either. Hard to wear shoes when your feet are blistered."

Finally, he passed inspection and ran down the hall to the pool area as she shouted in the background, "Forty-five more minutes before you go to the deep end."

Damey watched the clock carefully. When time expired, he dashed to the diving board to continue experimenting on a variety of cannonballs. During lunch, he'd thought of a couple new twists he'd like to try.

• • •

About three o'clock, Bill and Ty pulled into the little overhang in front of the office door. Both climbed out, stretched, and yawned. This last stretch took five hours. The closer they got, the less willing either one was to stop. After getting rid of all the kinks, they slowly walked to the door checking the place out without saying anything. Tom watched, knowing exactly who they were. He stuck his head into the living area and asked Mary to join them. They looked at each other with raised eyebrows. Damey hadn't said that his grandpa was white. Both wondered who the black man was. '

Bill walked straight to the desk, opened his wallet, and pulled out his driver's license. "Hi. I'm William Berkley, Damey's grandpa, and this is Tyrone, a special friend of the family. Where's my boy?"

Tom looked at Mary with a smile and expression that said, "I think we're okay."

"He's in the pool," Mary said. "Follow us."

They walked down the hallway and opened the outside door. Several people splashed and played around in the water, and they didn't spot Damey at first.

"There he is, getting on the diving board," Ty said.

They watched as he ran to the end of the board and bounded as high as he could into the air. Then he grabbed both knees as he pulled them close to his chest, and hit the surface on his backside with a swoosh as water flew straight upwards and out to all sides.

He swam to the side of the pool, and pushed himself out of the water, swinging his butt around and sitting down on the edge in one easy motion. He didn't bother with the ladder five feet away. He stood up and started for the board again.

Bill and Ty both clapped. "Bravo!" yelled Bill.

Damey stopped in his tracks, turned around, looked, and then screamed at the top of his lungs. "Grandpa! Ty!"

He ran down the pool deck towards them as fast as he could move completely ignoring the *Do not Run* sign hanging on the side of the wall. Ty could tell what was about to happen by the expression on Damey's face. At the last second, he shifted slightly in front of Bill and braced himself. Damey leaped from about four feet out and into their arms, with Ty taking the brunt of the assault. They squeezed Damey to their bodies with Damey's feet dangling in the air. He soaked both men with pool water—not an issue. Damey held on to their necks for dear life and buried his head between theirs and on their shoulders.

Tom and Mary watched as Damey sobbed convulsively. Tears rolled down Bill and Ty's cheeks as all three of them talked at once. Nobody could understand a word Damey blubbered, and it didn't matter.

"Now, I know we're okay," Tom said as he smiled at Mary. She nodded in agreement as she wiped the tears out of her eyes.

A lot of the activity around the pool had stopped when Damey screamed, but by then everyone ignored them and had gone on about their own business. They recognized a happy reunion when they saw one.

Holding seventy pounds in the air gets heavy after a while, and Ty had to set him down. When he did,

Damey grabbed Bill and buried his face in his chest wiping snot, tears, and spit all over his grandpa's shirt. At Mary's suggestion, they led him back to the office where he finally composed himself.

Tom gave Bill the extra key to the room and commented. "There are two double beds in there. Do two of you want to share a bed, or should I bring in a roll away?"

"He's not sleeping with me," Bill said with his eyebrows raised. "He sounds like a snowplow scraping through six feet of that beautiful white stuff when he snores."

"I do not," Damey said with a tear-streaked grin. "You've always said that I sound like a purring kitten when I sleep. Besides, I can spend the night on the floor if you give me a blanket or something to lie on."

"Snowplow, cat, whatever. You're still not sleeping with me," Bill said as he rubbed his knuckles into Damey's scalp making sure to avoid the bump.

"A roll away would be great if you have an extra," Ty said. "I'll take that"

"No you won't," Damey said trying to sound all business. "You came all this way to get me; you're sleeping on one of the regular beds. I sure don't need anything that big anyway. I can doze off on anything."

Tom went down to the storage room and rolled back the small bed along with sheets, a pillow, and blanket. After everything seemed to be in place, he said, "What

about the bike? Are you taking that with you? I've got
it in the storage shed right now so it'll be out of sight."

"Would you mind leaving it there for a little while?
We'll make sure the owner knows where he can find it.
I would assume he'll come and get it, probably next
weekend," Bill said.

"No problem. I'm going back to the office. The
three of you need some time together. If you want
anything, let me know."

"Thank you," Ty said. "You have no idea how
much we appreciate your watching over this little man.
He's very special to us."

"I noticed," Tom said with a grin. He left and went
back to the registration desk as Mary checked a new
couple in and gave them their keys. After they left, he
filled her in on everything.

About an hour later, Damey walked in fully dressed
carrying his iPad. "Thought I'd go out on the deck and
read my book for awhile so I don't disturb them.
They've both crashed. I've got strict orders to wake
them up at five so we can eat an early dinner and then
come back. They want to get started for home as soon
as possible in the morning."

"Damey, I love your smile. You are so cute when
you grin this way. It's the first time I've seen you
weren't frowning, looking serious, or crying," Mary
said.

His lips curled up with a mouth full of teeth showing. Damey blushed. "You gots no idea how happy I am right now."

"I think I do." She paused for a minute smiling at him. "It shows all over your face. However, don't you think you've had enough sun for today? I don't want you to burn. The temperature's in the nineties. Why don't you stretch out on that lounge chair in the corner and read. You won't bother a soul, and nobody'll bother you."

At five o'clock, Mary went over and gently shook Damey's shoulder. "Wha, what? What time is it? Did I fall asleep?"

"I don't think you read more than five minutes before your eyes sagged. Then you went out like someone rapped you with a baseball bat beside the head. You better go wake up Grandpa and Ty so you don't get into trouble."

Damey stood up, yawning, stretching, and sporting that big toothy grin of his. He spread his eyes wide open trying to wake up as he headed for his room. Time for dinner, he thought. It'd been a long time since lunch.

When Tom made his rounds at nine, all was quiet and dark in room one. Even the drapes were securely drawn. He smiled. Life was good in their little worlds.

After settling his bill in the morning, Grandpa left a hundred dollar tip as he listened to the arguments from Tom and Mary. They'd been more than happy to help out with Damey and were thrilled seeing him so happy. They didn't want anything extra. Bill and Ty shook hands with both thanking them profusely for their services. Damey wanted hugs.

Between the motel and Tulsa, they pulled into a restaurant for a quickie breakfast and then it was back on the road. By ten they crossed the border into Missouri—time to make the call. "When she answers, Damey, you talk to her first and let her know you're okay."

Using the Bluetooth touch-screen device on Bill's dashboard, he went to the contact list and dragged it down to 'Shaundra.' He looked in the mirror at Damey who sat forward up in his seat straining against the seatbelt. "Ready?"

Damey nodded and mumbled something about Xavier answering and not giving his mom her phone. For the first time since their reunion, fear and anxiety showed on his face.

"You said he was supposed to go back to work this week, so he shouldn't even be there," Ty said.

Bill tapped the name on the screen and waited. The phone rang twice, and after Shaundra checked caller id, she answered. "Bill, have you heard anything? I'm having a nervous breakdown. I've driven all over town all weekend looking for any possible hiding place. The police have been here a couple of times. I'm popping Xanax like it was candy."

"Mom, mom, stop. It's me, Damey. I'm okay. I'm safe. I'm with Grandpa and Ty and their taking me home."

The scream that came through the phone bounced all three of them back in their seats. Then, nothing but silence.

"Shaundra, you still there? Are you okay?" Bill asked.

Then came a softer response as she choked back the sobs, "My baby, my baby. You're okay? Really? Tell me again. You're safe."

"Yes, Mom. I really am. When you come home, I'll be there."

"I'll be on the road in less than an hour. Your suitcase is already in the car. Mine is packed except for what I'm wearing. I've been waiting for someone to find you so we could head back."

"What about Xavier?" Damey asked with a hint of concern in his voice.

"Xavier is past tense. We talked it over on Saturday as we drove around looking for you. It's not going to work with us. He's not the same man I knew twelve years ago. That night I moved into your room in the basement. Now, Damey, plug your ears a minute.

She paused for a few seconds before she cut loose, "Bill and Ty, I'm pissed. Oh, how I'm pissed. How long have you known Damey's whereabouts and kept it a secret?" Her tone of voice had changed from loving to extremely angry in a heartbeat.

"Damey called me Sunday afternoon from a town called Okmulgee, about 180-200 miles from Lawton depending how you go." Bill said. "I didn't call you on purpose for Damey's safety. I wanted to wait until we had him out of Oklahoma. As soon as we crossed the border just a few minutes ago, we called."

"That's kidnapping, Bill. I should have you both arrested. The police are looking for him now."

"Shaundra, quit yelling and listen a minute," Ty broke in for the first time. "If we'd have called you, you would have gone and picked him up, right?"

"You're damned right I would've."

"That's the problem. If you had, Damey might not be safe. I don't know what Xavier told you, but remember the day you went to Oklahoma City, and he left you sitting in the driveway? When he went back into the house, he slapped Damey hard enough he bounced his head off the cupboards before he landed in a dazed heap on the floor. Then Xavier told him very matter of factly that he had twenty-four hours to lose his attitude. If he didn't, he'd beat his ass to a bloody pulp every day until he did. Those are Xavier's words, Shaundra, not mine or Damey's."

"Over my dead body. Nobody'd better ever abuse my baby that way. If they do, they'll go to sleep some night and not wake up. Is Damey okay now?"

"The bump on the back of his head has gone down, but you can still feel it if you rub your fingers over it. Damey doesn't like it when you do because it's still

301

tender. His face still shows the outline of a hand print," Ty said.

Bill jumped back into the conversation. "When Tom, the motel owner, called, Damey looked like he'd been dragged down a dirt road by a truck—filthy, sweaty, sporting a huge welt on the side of his face, and half starved to death. They cared for him until we got there. Gave him a room, clean clothes, and fed him. His wife, Mary, said he ate like he thought food was going out of style. They laughed about his appetite. Couldn't understand where he put it all."

"Ty and Bill, I'm sorry. I know that neither one of you would ever do something that wasn't in the best interest of my boy. I promise, I'll make it up to both of you. I was just so scared."

"Do you want us to hole up some place in a motel and wait for you to catch up to us?"Bill asked.

"No, keep going. I'm probably six hours behind you by the time I finish packing, notify the police, and get out of here. The sooner you get Damey home, the better I'll feel. That's where he belongs. I do want to stop at the motel and thank them for what they did. Would you give me the name and address of the place?"

"Mom, would you also stop at that little restaurant on the main drag out of town called *Ella's Place*? There's a girl who works there named Ella. Her parents named the restaurant after her. Will you tell her I'm safe and okay? And thank her again for the sack lunch she packed for me. I would've starved to death without it."

"Yes, honey, I know exactly where and who you're talking about. Xavier and I stopped in there Saturday when we were looking for you. I asked if she'd seen you, and she played dumb. She never told on you. I'll stop in and tell her you're okay and thank her."

"You might want to pay her. She wouldn't take my money," Damey said.

They talked for a while longer before hanging up. While talking, she put her makeup and other things in her suitcase and zipped it. The three in the car could hear the wheels bump as she tugged it up the basement steps.

Out of breath when she reached the top of the stairs, she paused and then spoke. "Ty, this whole thing was a horrible mistake. I'd been carrying feelings for over twelve years, but I was wrong. Like I said earlier, Xavier is not the person I thought he was. I don't know if you can find it in your heart to forgive me or not, and I understand if you can't. Before we hang up, I want you to know I love you. Damey and Bill, you are my life. There's no way I can explain what all of you mean to me." She sniffed a couple of times unable to go on. She ended the call.

Nobody in the car said a word for at least an hour. Finally, Damey broke the silence. "I'm hungry. When are we gonna stop for lunch? Besides, I gotta pee."

CHAPTER 28

S haundra sat down at the kitchen table with pen in hand and paper in front of her. She thought for a few minutes, and then wrote the note.

Xavier,
Damey's been found and is safe. He's on his way back to Michigan. I've already notified the police.
We agreed Saturday that whatever it was we thought we had, was a mistake. Please do not ever contact us again, even if you visit your parents in Lansing. I am going to try very, very hard to rekindle my relationship with Tyrone.

I've already apologized to him, now I have to prove myself, if he'll let me.

I know what you did to Damey that day you left me in the driveway to check up on him before we left for Oklahoma City. The handprint still shows on his cheek. I also know about the threat you made about beating him. As I said, do not—ever—contact us again.

Shaundra

Shaundra pulled out of the driveway and never looked back. Her first stop was 'Ella's Place.' Walking in, she spotted the girl behind the counter so she walked up to her. "Hi, Ella. You probably don't remember me, but I was in here Saturday asking about my son, Damey."

"Uh, yeah. I remember you. He was missing. Ever find him?"

"Yes, he asked me to stop in and let you know he's safe and on his way back to Michigan. He's with his grandpa and the man I'm going to try very hard to turn into his stepfather."

"Ty?" she asked as her face slowly turned into a smile for the first time.

"Yes, Ty. They're all together and I'm chasing after them now."

"How far'd he get?

"Okmulgee, outside of Tulsa."

"Amazing. But, he's a tough little nut and about the sweetest thing going. Funny, he and I kind of clicked even if he is two years younger than me. Lucky for him he's not going to live here. He'd be mine." She laughed at her own joke. "If I give you my email, would you have him shoot me a message when he's all settled back at home, happy, and feels safe and secure again?"

"Sure. Just write it down."

As Ella wrote it on a napkin, Shaundra asked her how much she owed her for the sack lunch she'd fixed for Damey.

Ella smiled again and told her, "You're the second person who's tried to pay for that lunch, Damey and now you. Tell you what. If that ornery looking character you were with on Saturday comes in and tries to pay, I'll take his money. I'll know him too, 'cause he looks like an older version of Damey. Weird, isn't it? Like, there are two people who look so much alike, yet one looks mean as he possibly could, and the other is the complete opposite. I don't think Damey would swat a fly, much less hurt someone. You should see his face. Nasty."

Shaundra had Ella pour her a large coffee to go. She wanted out of that town—the sooner the better. If one more person mentioned that welt on Damey's face, she'd scream. Next stop Okmulgee. Before she raced out the door, Ella mapped out the route Damey would have taken. She followed it.

Three hours later, she pulled under the canopy at the office door of *Mary's Motel*, stopped, and went inside not knowing exactly what she planned to say. She rang the little bell on the counter, and a man stepped out wiping his mouth.

"Sorry, we were having a," he looked at his watch, "very, late lunch—early dinner, whatever. You need a room for tonight?"

"No, I'm looking for Tom and Mary."

"Well, I'm Tom. Just a second," he stuck his head in the door and waved with his hand for Mary to join him. "Mary, this lady is looking for us."

"My name is Shaundra Martin. I understand the two of you took exceptional care of my son, Damey, for a couple of days until his grandpa could get here to pick him up. I wanted to stop on my way back to Michigan just to thank you and let you know how much I appreciate what you did for him. I don't know what they told you, but there was a domestic situation going on. It's resolved now, and I'm heading back."

"Oh, yes," Mary exclaimed. "I'd keep him in a minute. He's the sweetest little guy going."

"I don't know where Ty fits in," Tom said, "but when the reunion happened, it was the most touching three-way tear filled hug fest you ever saw. I don't know who was the happiest, Damey or the two men."

"I think it probably was a three-way tie. Hopefully, when I get back it will be a four-way tearful hug fest.

Quick question before I go. How bad did Damey's face look by the time he left?"

Mary answered. "I could still feel a hint of the bump on his head, but the bruise on his face has started to fade. Hopefully, by the time all of you get home it will be unnoticeable unless you look for it. I think he's worried about his best friend seeing it. A pride thing, you know?"

With parting hugs all around, Shaundra headed for her car. Mary followed her and handed her their business card. "When everything settles, and all the domestic crap has erased itself from the universe, would you have Damey drop us an email letting us know that he's still happy, he's still wearing that beautiful smile, and that life is good for him?"

"I guarantee that will happen," Shaundra said as she started the car, waved, and pulled out of the drive heading for I-44 East. She was going home.

Shaundra drove for as long as she could and finally stopped in some motel out in the middle of nowhere. She didn't even look at the name of the town, much less the motel. A bite to eat, a hot shower, and bed. That's all she wanted.

• • •

After they pulled off of I-69 and headed up the road on Saginaw Street, Ty looked over at Bill. "What say we drop Damey off at your house and then swing back to the mall and get a massage? I am so stiff and sore from riding. What about it?"

"Sounds good to me."

"Wha, wha, what about me?" Damey stuttered as he scooted up in the seat again straining against the seat belt. "I'm stiff and achy too."

"Yeah, right," Ty said trying to keep a straight face. "You're just gonna go to sleep anyway. You might as well go lie down on your bed. It'd be a lot cheaper."

"I won't fall asleep this time. Promise. I've only done that a couple of times."

"What?" Bill piped up. "You fall asleep at the twenty minute mark every time."

"Tell you what," Ty said. "I'll spring for your massage, but you'd better stay awake.

They parked outside the mall and climbed out of the car and stretched. They'd been riding four straight hours. They took the direct route to the men's room before hitting the Chinese Massage.

Ty looked over at the masseur. "Keep track of him. If he doesn't last at least twenty minutes, it's coming out of his piggy bank."

"I don't gots a piggy bank," Damey sputtered.

There they go again, Damey thought to himself, as he crawled up on the table, settled himself comfortably, and put his nose through the provided crack, hiding his grin. They're messing with my head again. I don't know who likes to tease me more, Ty or Grandpa. The only problem is, I always bite when they do and take them serious. Then they laugh at me and make me feel foolish. Damn, it's good to be home. If only Mom were here.

When Bill and Ty finished their massages, they found Damey sound asleep as usual. After they woke him up to the point where they could pick on him, Ty asked. "Okay, how long'd he last this time?"

"Oh, twenty minutes. Yes. Twenty minutes."

When Ty looked at his credit card bill, he'd been charged for one thirty minute massage and one fifteen. He showed it to Damey pretending to look stern. Damey raised his eyebrows and looked away trying to keep from laughing out loud.

Chan bowed as they walked out the door. "Yep, twenty minutes. Maybe twenty-one."

"Good grief!" Ty laughed. "Even the masseur sticks up for you. Go figure."

• • •

The next morning Shaundra pulled out of the motel right about eight o'clock. She figured she had roughly eight hours more to go. She timed it perfectly. At four o'clock, she pulled into Bill's driveway. Damey ran out of the house and almost tackled her beside the car. They held on to each other for the longest, most emotional time. Finally, she broke his grasp, held his head in both hands and looked at his cheek. Then she felt for the bump on the back of his head. It caused a huge lump to form in her throat.

"If I ever get my hands on him, I'll—"

That's when Ty and Bill stepped in and joined the circle.

That night at dinner, she made Damey repeat the story of his three-day sojourn down the back roads of Oklahoma. He told her about everything except the rope. Forgotten? No, but he never mentioned it, not even to Alex.

• • •

A couple of weeks later, Damey had just finished mowing Bill's grass. He sat down on the patio with a glass of ice cold lemonade, looked at Bill, and said, "Not sure, Grandpa, but it almost looks like Ty's moved in. That's why I'm not spending Tuesday and Thursday nights with you right now. Ty's there keeping tabs on me. Most of his clothes are there, and with school being out, he's been doing the laundry, cleaning, and cooking except when we go out."

"You okay with that?" Bill said.

"Yeah, sure. You know how much I like him. Know what else I think is weird? Every time they go someplace, they automatically take me. They don't even ask, they just tell me where we're going, and then say, 'Get in the car.' They include me in their conversations, and act like they actually like having me with them.

"The only time they don't take me is Friday. That's their 'date night.' That's why I come over here to eat and sleep. They won't leave me home alone. They don't think I'm old enough. I am, but I don't complain—as if it would do me any good if I did. Besides, I like spending time with you."

"I hope so. I've been missing you. But, it's a good miss. I know you're happy and safe, and that Ty's looking out for you, which is very important to me."

"Me too."

By the end of July, they'd blended into a family— Shaundra, Ty, and Damey. They even spent one weekend together in Chicago visiting Ty's parents.

After they'd been home from Chicago for about a week, it happened.

"Damey, we need to talk." Shaundra said as she and Ty walked into the living room. Ty pushed the off button on the remote to the TV. That was okay with Damey. It was the history channel, and he'd seen the program before.

"What's up?" he asked, thinking they looked awfully serious. What had he done this time?

He put the legs down on the chair and leaned forward so his chin rested on his folded up fists with his elbows balanced on his knees. If they were going to yell at him, he might as well get ready. Only problem was, he couldn't think of a thing he might be guilty of. He *thought* he'd been pretty good lately.

"Are you ready to pay attention and listen?" Ty asked keeping his straight face while sounding stern.

That didn't sound good. If they were going to yell at him, usually Mom started it. In fact, Ty had only chewed him out a couple of times and only punished him once when he sent him to his room to "Think about things." Not fair. Grandpa, Mom, and Ty always ganged up on him and compared notes. They all knew he hated it when they sent him to his room. Not his fault that when they did, he actually thought about what he'd done and blamed himself. He'd a lot rather be mad at one of them than at himself.

"What'd I do?"

Not being able to suppress his smile any longer, he told Damey to sit up and look at them. "It's not what you did, it's what I did. I asked you mom to marry me, and she said yes. I hope you're okay with that. I know it's always been just the two of you, but I think we make a pretty good family."

"You're kidding—really? You're not lying to me? Yahoo!" Damey screamed at the top of his lungs as he jumped out of his chair. "You know that's what I want. What took you so long?"

"Now, quit yelling!" Ty laughed. "Don't make me have to start acting like a parent tonight so I have to scold you to settle you down." He reached over and grabbed Damey in a headlock around the neck and kissed the top of his head.

"We wanted to make sure it was right for us, for you, and what we all wanted with no questions regarding Xavier or anyone or anything else. No way could we take this step and have any lingering issues. It has to last forever."

"When are you going to do it? This ain't gonna be one of those long engagements is it? Like, you gonna do it right away?"

"Yes. Neither one of us want a big fancy wedding. Just us, Grandpa Bill, my parents, and a few friends like the Veras family and Sean and his family. We both want to invite a couple of our own close friends from work. That's it. We want to do it the second Saturday of August. Think Grandpa would be willing to babysit the brat while we sneak off for a week by ourselves?"

Damey rolled his eyes and shook his head at the 'babysitting' and 'brat' comments. Ty got that from Grandpa as well. With his mouth wide open showing practically every tooth rooted in his jaw bones, he said, "I'm gonna finally feel whole,"

Damey stood there staring off into space as a soft, closed mouth smile gradually replaced the wide open grin. Then he looked at Ty and spoke almost inaudibly. "I've always had a mom. Then I got a grandpa along with a whole slew of uncles, aunts, and cousins. I never had a dad. I always wanted a dad. I want *you* to be my dad—the sooner the better. Will you adopt me?"

"Do you want me to?"

"Yes, please do. Please. I wanna be yours legal and forever."

"It might take awhile because I'm sure Xavier will probably have to sign off, don't know if it'll work for sure, but I promise, I will if I can. Damey, I don't just love your mom. I love you too. Understand?"

Damey couldn't answer. The tears flowed too hard. He gasped, choked on his saliva, tried to speak, but could only cry as he grabbed Ty and his mom in an extended family hug.

Still holding the boy tightly, Ty continued. "One thing you have to understand, if I do, your name changes from Damarian Wayne Martin to Damarian Wayne Williams. You okay with that?"

Nodding furiously, he wiped his tears off on Ty's shirt and Shaundra's blouse as he nuzzled between them. Damey sniffed. "Yeah, yes, please."

"We'll start checking into it right away."

Damey blurted out between sobs. "When can I start calling you Dad? Do I have to wait until you're married or I'm adopted or what?"

"Why wait? Why not now?"

"Dad."

"Son."

• • •

• • •

"Mr. Williams, are you okay?" asked Mr. Lambert as he slid the box of tissues towards me.

"Oh, yeah. I'm fine," I said. "I guess my mind wandered back a few years. I've been thinking about that first year with Grandpa, my adoptive family, friends, and then Dad. In fact, I think, maybe, I just relived the whole thing. That's the year my life changed forever. So much happened."

As I sat there, my mind drifting again. Then I caught myself. "I'm sorry. What were you about to say?"

"I'd just said that I wanted to continue with the section that pertains to you, as the only non-blood-related heir. When I'm done going over your part, you're free to leave."

"Okay, again, let me apologize again for losing focus. I'm embarrassed."

My uncles laughed at me and told me to forget it. Since I'd been reminiscing instead of reading, I had a surprise coming. Boy, did I ever.

When Lambert started to read, I got the shock of my life. "I bequeath to Damarian Wayne Williams the significant sum of money indicated below with the following stipulations—"

"No! Stop! I can't take that. Grandpa's money belongs to his biological sons. Grandpa and I informally adopted each other, and being the great family they are, they went along with it, but his money belongs to them."

My three uncles laughed. Uncle John said, "You haven't heard the stipulations yet, Damey. You know you aren't going to get a free ride on this."

"I bet I know at least two of them," Uncle Bob said with a huge grin.

I laughed. "I'm pretty sure I know what two you're talking about."

"Shall I continue?" asked the lawyer smiling. He obviously enjoyed the interchange between us. I think he may have been concerned about someone contesting the will. "The first stipulation is that you pay off your college loans. That master's degree in Robotics Engineering did not come cheaply. The second and third stipulations are a package deal. If there is any money left after you pay off your college debt, ten-percent goes into your retirement fund and ten-percent goes into savings."

All four of us laughed that time. We knew those last two stipulations were coming from past experience. Over the years, he'd started two savings accounts for each of us. Twenty-percent of everything we made, including our allowances, went into those two accounts.

After the brief interruption, the attorney continued to read. "If there is any money left, you may spend it as you see fit. I know a couple of things I would enjoy seeing you do, but it is strictly up to you. I would love to think you and your beautiful bride, Zandra, would make a down payment on a home and get out of that apartment. I'd hate to let you forget how to mow a lawn and shovel snow. I would also like to see a PhD attached to your name. However, those are not stipulations. That's the old man dreaming. However, don't forget. I'm watching."